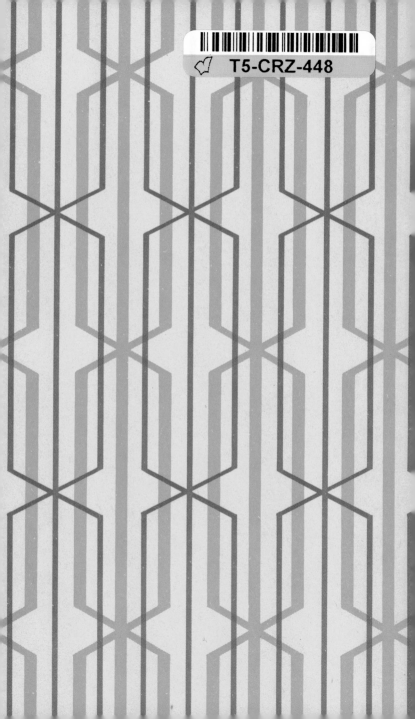

MEN OF EARTH

MEN OF EARTH

BY
BERNICE BROWN

Short Story Index Reprint Series

BOOKS FOR LIBRARIES PRESS
FREEPORT, NEW YORK

First Published 1924

Reprinted 1970

STANDARD BOOK NUMBER:

8369-3525-X

LIBRARY OF CONGRESS CATALOG CARD NUMBER:

70-122692

PRINTED IN THE UNITED STATES OF AMERICA

CONTENTS

MEN OF EARTH

MIRACLE

MIRACLE

I

JOHNNIE DEAUTREMONT sat on the step in front of Bondi Ruml's shack, his big hands between his knees, his head bent forward, his little eyes vacant with the stare that is turned inward. He had sat there so long that the veins in his hands were swollen. It was beginning to grow cold, too, for April in northern Minnesota has a bitter dampness, and the fog settles down evenings as in September.

He hunched the collar of his mackinaw closer about his neck, but he did not move. There was something terrible in the man's stolidity, something ominous in the control he possessed over his great body. It seemed that he scarcely breathed, and the focus of his tiny eyes never altered. Even in repose his physical power carried a challenge. He was forty-one, and his muscles had lost their first suppleness, perhaps, but they had gained in endurance. His face had the hard, dissipated look that

3

often belongs to men who have undergone great physical hardships.

Johnnie Deautremont was the boss logger of northern Minnesota. Winters he was foreman for the North Star Lumber Company, and all the men in the outfitting village of Belle Fleur worked for him. Every year, after the first snow, he left the miserable huddle of shacks built around the saloon and the company store to lead his crew up into the long white silence of the forest. Belle Fleur was not much of a town to regret, squatted down at the edge of the timber, with its rotted corduroy-road, its sidewalks torn into shreds by the spiked boots of the loggers, and the floors of its shacks ground into sawdust.

But in Belle Fleur, at least, one escaped from the forest, from the cold that brings a long agony in bleeding chilblains, from the sound, day and night, of the wind in the branches, from the buried light under the pines, where it seems as though one were imprisoned beneath a sea of jade.

In the summer Johnnie Deautremont was a cruiser. Then, all alone, he went up into the forest, his pack on his back, to blaze the tract that would be logged the next winter. In the parlance of the North he had a nose for timber. Johnnie Deautremont knew trees as a stone merchant knows jewels. He could estimate with uncanny accuracy into how many feet of lumber a tract would fell and cut.

In his own world nobody disputed Johnnie Deautremont and nobody liked him. Even last spring, when he had risked his life in a vain attempt to save Bondi Ruml, no man's heart had skipped a beat in admiration. It had happened up on the Lumber River, a tricky stream with a vicious current down which the tree-trunks were floated to the mill at Black Fork.

Like a narrow black carpet, the logs stretched along the water as smooth as the aisle of a church. On the shore tramped the loggers, with their long pike-poles shoving the stray logs away from the shallow water at the edge out into the current. It was tame business most of the time, like herding a flock of sheep into a fold at sundown; but the faces of the log-drivers never relaxed. Over the slow-moving carpet their eyes kept swimming, alert and suspicious; for they were getting into the white water, where the rapids began. The river was high that spring, for the snowfall of the winter before had been heavy.

Then, suddenly, something happened. In place of the smoothness was a grinding mass of logs, rubbing against one another, hurtling lengthwise, piling up in grotesque, hideous playfulness—the logjam, for all the world like a giant's game of jackstraws.

Johnnie Deautremont was ahead with Fritz Terschak and Jacques. This was Bondi Ruml's moment. He must act at once, for behind him would come driving on the rest of the timber. Over the slippery rocks and on to the tangle of logs he scrambled. It is ticklish work finding the king log that is the key to the jam, and Bondi Ruml worked in a fury of haste. With a heavy, double-bitted ax he drove a way into the tangle; the king log was reached. Then comes the moment when the man must flee for his life; for with the king log dislodged, the mass disintegrates as quickly as it has formed. Bondi Ruml leaped from log to log, balancing himself, lunging, falling, saving himself again.

On the shore Johnnie Deautremont, Fritz Terschak, and Jacques waited. They saw Bondi stand for one second erect; he was all but safe. Then he disappeared into the broiling rapids. An instant Johnnie Deautremont looked. Without a word he slipped off his heavy jacket and plunged into the icy water. It was courting death, and he knew it, and so did every man who was watching; but out of the mess of timber he brought Bondi Ruml ashore. But Bondi was dead, crushed by the logs.

Johnnie Deautremont looked at the tall Bohemian on the ground beside him.

"Bury him," he ordered.

Nobody said anything. They dug a shallow grave where the water had thawed the frost out of the earth and left him there.

Nobody knew, either, that he went on sending back to the daughter of Bondi Ruml the dead man's pay envelope. Johnnie Deautremont possessed a grim sort of justice that had neither compassion nor understanding. It would be a terrible thing if Johnnie Deautremont fell in love.

On the opposite side of the road Willa Terschak, when she went out for an armful of wood, saw Johnnie waiting on the Ruml doorstep.

"Holy Mary!" she said, "the devil has come back again!" Could old Johnnie be waiting for Thea? Willa Terschak's heart stood still. Then she shrugged her shoulders. Thea was seventeen. It was time she should marry some one, especially since her father's death had left her alone in the world. Thea, just because her mother had come from Prague and could read and write, had no reason to be uppish. After her mother's death the child had been sent to the convent at St. Pierre. She was a little different from the other girls in the village, Willa conceded, but she had no right to *feel* different. Anyway, Willa had troubles enough of her own.

Johnnie Deautremont, as he sat there, was thinking about the first day he had ever seen Thea. She was fifteen then, long-legged and slender and shy. She was playing before the shack with a big white goose on whose right wing lay three long black feathers, as though some one had stroked it with sooty fingers. Johnnie noticed that the goose held its wing slightly distended and downward, so that the edge skimmed the dust as it walked.

"What a fool you are," he had said, "to want such an ugly thing for a pet!" He had kicked at the bird as he passed.

In two years Thea had become a woman. Unlike most Bohemian girls, she gave an impression of fragility. Her hands and her feet were small, and her head was exquisitely modeled. Her hair, which was smooth and black, waved away from her low forehead. Her eyes had the purple blue of iris, and her skin, though healthy, was curiously white.

Thea Ruml's face was lovely, but it was her

body that possessed her charm. There was grace in the long line of her thigh, in the delicate contour of her young breasts. There was something wistful about her, and exquisite and disarmingly young.

She did not see him that evening until she turned in at the thinly cindered path leading to the shack. Then she stopped.

"You!" Her face was strangely white against the twilight.

He rose slowly from the doorstep.

"Yes, me." He hesitated a moment. "There is business I must talk over with you."

"I—I'm sorry I kept you waiting." She had the humility of a child that fears punishment for an unknown fault. "I stopped in to play with the Djursen children. Little Rudi is fourteen now and almost as big as I am. You should see the statue of St. Joseph he carved out of wood. It is as swell as the one in the church, only little, like a doll." She lighted the lamp on the oil-cloth-covered table, and she hoped he had not seen how her fingers trembled. She must not let him know she was afraid. "Trudel thought it was a doll." She giggled nervously. "She dressed it up in a shawl. Oh, Rudi was mad, like a hornet." Again she laughed, this time hysterically.

Would he never say anything? What had he come for? She bustled around the kitchen.

"I shall make you a dish of tea, eh?" All the time she had never quite caught his eyes. She smiled gaily now, but she looked just over his shoulder to the chromo of Mount Vesuvius, given free with a cough medicine, that hung on the unceiled wall of the shack. "Old Mother Petri is sick again. She prays every day in the church, cold like a barn, and that makes her rheumatism worse. Then she curses the saints for not making her well. Father Fonda sent her home to bed for a week as a penance."

Thea built up the fire in the stove, filled the copper kettle from a pail of water in the corner, and laid out the heavy cups and saucers. To make it seem like a party, she put on the table the cruet-stand with the empty pink glass bottles she had bought from an Italian peddler. "Swell, eh?" she said as she held it up for the man's admiration.

She was sorry at once she had done it. She knew he was not looking at the cheap thing in her hand, but at her, at her slenderness, her softness. Thea felt with a panic the grace that her body held. She did not want to torment him, to lure him.

"You talk all the time," he said, "like a mud-hen. Never quiet."

She dabbled an inquiring finger into the tea-kettle.

"Not even warm yet," she said. "This stove too damn' slow. In winter I stay here all day and poke wood, wood, wood into his mouth. He is like a bad child that is always hungry."

"Thea——"

With a gasp of fear she started back against the wall, her lips parted, and her eyes for the first time on his face. He had not come back to the village, then, to hear her chatter about the Djursen children; he had not sent her the wages her father had ceased to earn out of simple friendliness. Still, he was her benefactor; he had been kind to her. Through a terrible justice she felt she belonged to him if he wanted her.

He was standing close to her now, and her eyes finally struggled to his.

"Thea——" Still he had not touched her. He was like something suffocating. She had no strength left against him. He was like the east wind that twists the wild geese out of their course, crippling their wings with invisible fingers.

With a half-sob she covered her face with her

hands and waited. It was useless to struggle, for the thing that was in his eyes was neither lust nor passion. He loved her, and love has a terrible power.

He put his arms around her, and when she trembled, he held her with a desperate tightness. His lips touched her hair, and she could feel his breath upon her forehead. She believed she would die if he kissed her mouth.

"To-day," he said, "I buy the McCurdy house. Next week, when we are married, you move in there. You will be glad to leave this dump, eh?" He smiled down at her, sheepishly. It was a candid appeal for approbation as ludicrous as it was sincere. He made her think of an awkward dog that fairly overturns one in his zeal to bring attention to the muddy stick he has retrieved.

Thea struggled to smile.

"It is a swell house," she said, "too good for me."

The man looked at her curiously.

"And in Duluth last week I buy you a dress for the wedding," he went on. "It is white, and as soft as the breast of a wild duck." He puzzled a moment. "So soft I could not feel it; it was as if I touched nothing." He spoke as though finding words were a thing of physical struggle. "I go now to see Father Fonda, and then back to camp before daybreak." He waited a moment. "In a week I come back, and on Sunday we marry." He waited for her to say something, but she made no answer. "Well, I go now." He stood by the door, but he made no motion to open it.

She knew he expected her to make some sign, to come to him. She felt even a strange compulsion to put her hand on his sleeve, perhaps, to try to be grateful. Even though the veins in her throat still throbbed with terror she was sorry for him. It seemed to her, suddenly, that this moment had always existed and would endure forever, as though the two of them had always stood opposite each other in the low-ceilinged, half-lighted kitchen, smelling of wood-smoke and kerosene and the damp wool of clothing. Thea wondered if perhaps the Virgin might not wrap around her a mantle of invisibility and carry her up to heaven. Something must happen to save her.

Then came a curious pecking against the wooden panel of the door.

"Toni!" she gasped, and flew by him to open it.

Out of the darkness came in the creature, more grotesque even than Johnnie Deautremont had re-

membered him, cackling, waddling, excited, the
great wing dragging like a broken sail.

Johnnie made a move toward Thea, but the bird
intercepted him, turning in clumsy half-circles,
cackling still, and stretching out its wings in a hideous sort of playfulness.

"Devil!" said the man, and kicked at it resent-
fully.

"Oh!" Thea gathered the great bird in her arms
and held it against her.

Johnnie Deautremont looked away suddenly from
the fear he saw in her eyes.

"You are a silly child to keep such an ugly goose,"
he said. He was ashamed of his anger and fearful
lest he should betray his chagrin. From the open
doorway he looked back. She still held the creature
in her arms, and her small dark head looked
strangely fragile above the bird's bulky whiteness.

A curious anger swept through him that he could
neither analyze nor conquer. With a great spurt
of will he slammed the thin door behind him, and ran
down the path to the road before he should have
time to change his mind.

Overhead gleamed the first stars of the cold
April twilight, and above the hill, behind the
scraggly silhouette of forest, rose the moon, large

and very white and cold. Johnnie Deautremont thought suddenly of the forest. It had done something terrible to him. It had put into his soul its own blackness, its own sullen loneliness. It was not like a bridegroom, gay with the blustering assurance of happiness, that Johnnie Deautremont stamped up the shallow steps before the cottage of Father Fonda.

II

In the days that followed Thea went about like a person in a trance. She scrubbed the splintery floor of the tiny shack, she polished the copper pans, hanging over the stove, that had come all the way from Bohemia, she washed and ironed the calico frocks with the stiff little frill of Bohemian lace around the neck and wrists. During the day she could live, in some way, with only the surface of her mind; the rest lay drugged in a sort of stupor. But at night the potion wore off, and into her dreams came the terror she could beat down during the daylight. She grew afraid to sleep; so she lay at night long hours, looking out between the slits of turkey-red curtains at the window up into the starlight.

She was afraid as is a child that has been frightened by a story it has only partly understood. She became even slenderer, and her face grew whiter, and under her eyes lay shadows of unhappiness. She was afraid of the wind when it lashed the thin sprays of woodbine against the window, afraid to blow out the lamp at night, afraid of to-morrow. She did not play any more with the Djursen children. She did not want to see any one, and she was afraid to stay alone.

On Saturday Johnnie Deautremont came down from Duluth, and he brought a great white box to Thea. She untied the extravagant yards of string, took off the cover, and there, under the fragile sheets of tissue-paper, lay the dress so soft that Johnnie Deautremont could not feel it with his fingers. Gingerly, Thea lifted it out and held it against her.

"Pretty, eh?" he asked.

She looked away suddenly from the pleading in his eyes.

"It is too good for me." There was a long moment of silence. "It was nice of you to buy it, you bet." She knew she had hurt him. "I—I thank you."

"Put it on," he commanded. "I come back in

an hour." He waited another moment. "It was the best one they had in the store. It cost thirty dollars."

Thea shook her head gravely.

"It is too good for me," she repeated.

After he had gone she still stood in the middle of the room where he had left her. Perhaps she remained there five minutes; then a wave of terror gulfed over her. "He will be coming back now. I must hurry." She unbuttoned the dark-blue calico, which dropped in a ring around her feet, and put on the new dress frantically.

She could not hurry now, there were so many hooks. It was difficult to match hook and eye together, especially when one's hands had become strangely rebellious. Then she looked down at her feet in their coarse leather shoes. For a second she hesitated. Then she sat down on the cot, unlaced them, and tossed them into the corner. It was better now, even in her bare feet; the old shoes had become so ugly.

There were footsteps on the cinder path and at the door. Thea hesitated a moment. She must not keep him waiting even long enough to put on the boots again. As soundless as a timber fox she flew to the door and opened it. Then she stood there, motionless, her hand on her throat, where it seemed the veins would burst with throbbing.

After a moment the young man before her drew off his cap.

"I—I'm sorry." His eyes never left her face as he spoke. "They told me at the company office I'd find Johnnie Deautremont here. It—was rather important."

Thea took a step backward.

"No, he is not here."

For another long moment neither moved. There seemed nothing to do but to stand there and look. There was no room, no village of Belle Fleur, no existence in the world anywhere but the two of them, the man with the sun in his hair and the girl in her white-satin dress, barefooted, and with eyes the color of lake water before a storm.

"Perhaps I shall meet him on the road," he said.

"Perhaps."

Still he did not go. His eyes were blue, too, but light like the sky of June at noonday. His hair, too, was light, and the close-cropped ringlets fitted tight to his head. He had probably been miserable because his hair curled. His mouth was large and turned up a shade at the corners, and his teeth were very white.

After a moment Thea echoed:

"You might meet him, perhaps, on the road."

"Yes," he said. "It was about the survey I was to see him. I'm from headquarters." Neither one of them cared what it was he was saying; neither one of them listened.

Johnnie Deautremont, who had come down the river road, stopped stock-still in front of the shack. He saw the young man bow and in some way get down the steps and on to the path. When he met Daniel Pherson at the corner, there was a look in the boy's eyes as of one who had come from a long way off. It was an instant before the young man could speak with any concentration about the surveying prospect the company had sent him out from headquarters to accomplish.

III

On Sunday Thea and Johnnie Deautremont were married. Johnnie had sent Toni Benedo clear to Duluth for the stockings and white-satin slippers. Toni carried with him a pair of old shoes, copper-toed and heavy-soled, and he brought back the cheap white slippers that to Belle Fleur represented the magnificence of an empress. When she finished dressing, Thea confronted herself in the small, speckled mirror that hung, below the chromo of the Virgin, over the table. It was little enough she could see of her splendor in the tiny, bedimmed reflection, but she wished suddenly that she were old and ugly and crippled like Mother Petri. Then she thought of the young man with the straight shoulders and the sun in his hair, and she wondered curiously why the vision of her own loveliness had conjured up his face.

It was a day of watery sunshine, alternating moments of summer warmth and the reminiscent bleakness of March. The day before, Johnnie had carted over to the new house all the things he had selected at Thea's. "Not worth the skin of a summer otter," he had said after he had completed the task. Sunday Johnnie Deautremont came for her.

All the village watched them on their way to the church. Most of the village attended the ceremony. They were all impressed by Thea's splendor and by Johnnie's munificence, but it could not be said to be a day of festival. Father Fonda's eyes were grave when he blessed them. Willa Terschak's remarks afterward possessed all the unpleasant candor of peasant frankness. Daniel Pherson did not go to the church. Instead, he tramped up the river, fishing, but it did not seem that the sport held for him the zest that it once had.

After the ceremony Johnnie Deautremont took his bride home. It was the best house in town to which he brought her. Jim McCurdy, who had built it, had been the boss of the saw-mill before the company moved it down the river to Black Fork, and he had taken seriously his position in the community. The house was a square frame box of two stories, painted a cold, pale blue. It was plastered inside, and the only house in the village that had a parlor. Johnnie Deautremont was proud of it. Saturday he had arranged Thea's furniture, but he was not satisfied with the result, and he determined to write for the splendid golden-oak cabinet and easel he had seen in the mail-order catalogue. Then the house would look as magnificent as any house in Minnesota.

Still strange in her wedding-dress, Thea sat on the one chair in the parlor. It was cold in the room, and she shivered.

"Wait," he said, and he brought his mackinaw. As he put it around her shoulders his hand touched her neck. He stopped suddenly, and Thea sat motionless as he stroked her cheek with his finger. "It is like the dress," he said solemnly, baffled at his discovery—"too soft to feel."

When her husband went out to split up the wood for the kitchen stove, Thea took off her wedding finery and put on her old blue calico and the copper-toed shoes. An instant she stood alone in the parlor, then she silently opened the front door, closed it behind her, and ran down the road. In ten minutes she was home again, breathless, frightened at her own temerity, irresolute. She did not go in at the front door; it was no longer home inside. At last she sat down on the step, her hands gripping each other fiercely between her knees, and her eyes stared at nothing. Suddenly there was a sound in the dead leaves banked up for winter protection against the base of the shack.

"Toni!"

In an instant she had seized the great bird and held him fiercely in her arms. In grotesque playfulness he pecked at her with a brave show of anger.

"Hush up, big idiot!" she said. "I have come back for you."

Daniel Pherson, returning empty-handed from his journey, saw her across the road. A long moment he stood and looked. Then he went on again slowly. She had not noticed him. Well, perhaps, it was better so. Suddenly he hated the pitiful huddle of shacks that made up the village of Belle Fleur. What strange creatures men were to dump in the midst of these forests the squalor and wretchedness of their own lives! Belle Fleur indeed! He laughed unpleasantly.

Johnnie Deautremont, coming down the road, did not notice him, either. Tell Haley, from the Winnipeg office, was with him, and Tell was explaining something. In front of the saloon they stopped, and Tell went on talking. Finally, he took some maps out of his pocket. They went into the saloon, and Tell spread the maps on the wooden counter, scarred with initials and sticky with spilled brandy. With a stubby blue pencil he marked off a tract. It was the Calumet tract above Dudley, ten thousand acres of timber, as black as cypress and as precious as Lebanon cedar.

"You go up to Duluth to-morrow," Tell finished, "and start out from there. Next winter you round up your crew early. Nothing left this year but Bohunks and Ginnies; Northwest folks bulled the market. Pie every day." He spat viciously. "What they need is beans and enough red-eye to kill 'em when it's over."

Johnnie Deautremont made no answer, and even

Tell Haley was cautious enough not to press him.

"You'll be solid with the company if you put it over, and it'll run you a thousand. A thousand." His voice was husky with emphasis. Then he ordered two drinks, and then two more. "How about it? You go up to-morrow?"

"To-morrow." He did not look at any one when he left, and the shack trembled as the door slammed to behind him. Tell Haley ordered a third drink. He was lucky to get Johnnie Deautremont, and a thousand dollars was cheap, dirt cheap. If somebody didn't kill him, Johnnie would get the job done before snowfall. You could bet on it. Then Tell Haley chuckled, and ordered a fourth.

It was dusk when Johnnie Deautremont came at last upon Thea. She was still sitting on the step of the shack, and the great bird waddled and strutted before her. Johnnie was very sure now that he hated that creature.

"Come!"

With eyes black with fright she stared up at him, then rose and followed him down the road to the new house, the great bird close behind her. It was a fantastic procession they made through the twilight, past the company office, past the church, past the saloon.

Without speaking she followed him into the mansion that had been built by Jim McCurdy, and he bolted the door behind her. With a thousand dollars he could give her everything. He could make this the most beautiful house in the world. She should have two golden-oak cabinets and a picture of Niagara Falls and a hat-rack.

He lighted the lamp that stood on the oil-cloth-covered table in the kitchen, and started the fire in the stove. The room looked less bleak in the half-light, and the wood snapped and hissed with a jolly noise. This was his kitchen, where the lamp glowed so agreeably. It was his stove, which he had set up himself, that would soon make the whole house as warm as an evening in August.

"Thea——"

She had not moved from the spot where she had stood when she entered. Her hands hung quiet at her side, and her face never changed expression. He liked her better, he thought now, than in her wedding-dress. Anyway, just as well. But she should have a dozen dresses as fine as the white one when he came back from the Calumet.

He wished she would smile. She was cold, perhaps. He got a chair and brought it up to the stove.

"Here," he said. As she came forward slowly, he brushed against her. "Thea——"

She closed her eyes, and it seemed as though she had ceased to breathe. He put out his arm to steady her as though she were a child.

"Thea," he repeated. At once his arms were around her, and he held her against him with all the fierceness of a love that had never had expression. He was not thinking of her now or even of himself. He was in the grip of something more powerful than he. He had ceased to exist as a person. He seemed to be nothing but a blind desire, a tormented, baffled longing. He was as powerless now as she was, and as desperate. Suddenly he forced her face up to his, and he kissed her again and again with a terrible, awkward fierceness. It was the first time he had ever kissed a woman when it mattered. Then he noticed that her skin was cold.

For the first time he thought about her. A second he stood there motionless, his arms still straining her to him. She was sobbing. At first he could scarcely hear her. It was like something one has dreamed of. At last it seemed to him he had heard that sound all his life, as though he should always hear it. It became at once the only thing in his universe. His arms dropped away from her. He did not look at her as he moved over to the stove and sat down in the chair he had drawn up for her, his head bent forward, his great hands listless between his knees.

IV

Next morning Thea found on the kitchen table two grimy greenbacks of ten dollars each. Twenty dollars! He had gone, then. The heavy mackinaw was no longer hanging over the hinge of the kitchen door. He had taken the roll of bedding, too, on which he had slept in the corner of the kitchen. It was strange she had not heard him. Perhaps, after all, he had not left.

She moved around the house, at first on tiptoe, fearful of the sound of her own footsteps, fearful even to move. The sun streamed in at the kitchen window. Finally she opened the back door and stepped out into the square of clearing that stood between Belle Fleur and the forest. The McCurdy house was the last one in the village. It seemed almost as though it had been built up against the wall of blackness, as shops, in the Old World, are cuddled up against the great wall of a cathedral.

There were high white clouds in the sky, and the wind held the languor of June. Thea lifted her face and closed her eyes against the blaze of the sun.

Gradually warmth came back to her. He had gone clear away, to the Calumet. Perhaps she had only dreamed what had happened. Anyway, she was free now, and the sun was warm upon her eyeballs. It was good to be alive.

Next day she went to the company store and bought coffee and tea and sugar and flour. She hung the pictures that had made gay the rough walls of old Bondi Ruml's shack. One by one the women of the village came to call and sit in the only house in town that had a parlor. No one asked her about her husband, and she never mentioned his name. It seemed almost as though he had ceased to exist.

May passed by, and June and July. Twice the office in Winnipeg had sent Thea money. She had spent only a little. The rest she had put away between the leaves of her prayer-book, which lay, beneath the rosary, on the little shelf above her bed.

In June Daniel Pherson came back from a long survey to the North. It had been a hard trek, and he looked thin and older. The skin across his cheekbones was drawn, and there were new lines around his eyes. Thea saw him first on the village street. She did not know whether they had spoken. She only knew it was difficult afterward to listen to Jacques Pierre at the butcher shop when he told her about the deer he had shot last week in defiance of the tyranny of game-laws.

"Soon we have no rights at all," he had blustered. "There will be right away a law a man cannot beat his wife!" He shrugged his shoulders with elaborate affectation and sighed. *"Eh bièn, la vie c'est la vie."*

Next day was Sunday, and Thea sat on the step that looked up against the forest. She was not lonely, only waiting. It was as black as a stormy twilight ten feet away from the patch of clearing. Partridge and grouse sallied out from the thicket of underbrush as impenetrable as a wire entanglement. Always in the pines was the sound of the wind, like the distant flowing of water. Those trees had always been there, like a barricade to surround her. Somewhere on the other side of that wall was the man she had married. She shivered and suddenly bent forward, her forehead pressed against her knees, her thin brown hands clasped together about her legs. She looked like a

Naiad of Rodin, exquisitely young, exquisitely for-lorn.

Then she looked up, startled, into the eyes of Daniel Pherson. An instant she stared, and they both laughed. Under his arm was the great goose, its head to one side, its tiny eyes blinking mali-ciously.

"It was clear up the road that I met him," Danny Pherson explained. "I argued with him a little about changing his direction. Then I picked him up, and here he is." He put the bird down and pushed him away playfully. "A fine fellow you are, to be sure." He laughed.

Thea laughed, too. A long moment they stood there. They could not have said why they were happy. Perhaps it was a little ridiculous to laugh at nothing, especially if one's father had been Scotch. Danny Pherson made a half-motion to leave.

"Well, I'm glad I could find him for you. I s'pose you set considerable store by him, somehow."

The laughter was all gone from Thea's face now. She made a little gesture toward him, but she did not speak. Then she again sat down on the step.

"Next Sunday," he said, "I shall bring you a

trout from the pool—this long." He made a boasting gesture. Then, after a moment, "Shall I?"

"Yes," she said.

He was glad she was not looking at him. It was difficult enough to leave without her eyes upon him.

Until next Sunday stretched for Thea an eon of time. All day it was in her thoughts not as anything definite, but as a beautiful, elusive pleasantness that transformed the rest of existence. Sunday she put on her second-best dress, but she changed it before he arrived to the dark-blue calico. She would even try not to look glad when he should come, but pretend he was only a person who was bringing her a speckled trout for her dinner. This deception was not so much a sop to morality as a defense against disappointment. Suppose he should not get back from the surveying job? Suppose he should not go fishing Sunday? Suppose he should forget to come? With all these eventualities Thea tormented herself not because she believed them, but for discipline. Unlike most of her countrymen, she had no lucky talent for enjoying the world recklessly. Neither, indeed, did Daniel Pherson, with his long line of Scotch Presbyterian forbears. But Danny's mother had been Irish. It was from her that he received the blue eyes and the mouth that turned up at the corners. Danny had both the Celtic responsiveness and the Anglo-Saxon capacity for relentless, unswerving emotion.

All week the Irish in Danny Pherson triumphed, but on Sunday he was Scotch. During the six days he was not to see her she had a way of intruding her small, serious head between his eye and the copper transit, and instead of observing certain trigonometrical imbecilities of interest to the North Star Lumber Company, he saw only her white brow, her eyes the color of iris, and the smooth black hair that he wanted to stroke with his fingers.

Sunday, with a curious Puritanical defiance, he came down the village street to the house of Johnnie Deautremont's bride instead of compromising on the forest road where he would be unobserved. Again Thea sat on the steps in the sunshine, the great white goose on the ground at her feet.

She stood up suddenly, and a slow color mounted under her pale skin.

"Oh, you are early, eh?" It was a naïve admission that she had not allowed herself to hope for him so soon.

Danny Pherson smiled.

"Too early?" He held out toward her the silver-scaled fish, flashing and iridescent in the sunlight. "See what I have brought you."

Thea waited a moment.

"I, too, have a present for you." She disappeared, and returned from the kitchen with something in her hands. Suddenly ashamed, she held it out toward him. After all, it had been a childish trick, the little basket of woven grasses, lined with birch-leaves and filled with wild raspberries. "Now you think I am silly," she said, "that I am no older than the Djursen kids." Her eyes pleaded for reassurance.

Awkward because he would be gentle, Danny lifted the fragile basket by the woven-grass handle. An instant he held it before him.

"It is like beads of coral in a velvet jewel-case." He blushed, suddenly ashamed of his simile. "My mother had a string of coral once she kept in a green box. It made me think of that." Then something happened. The slippery grass of the handle became loosened from the basket, and the little mound of raspberries went leaping and rolling over the rough wood of the steps.

"Oh!" It was suspiciously close to a sob. She was standing on the step above him, her face looking down into his.

"Thea—" In a blundering agony of apology he caught both her hands; scarcely realizing what he was doing, he pressed them against his lips. She bent her head over his until her cheek touched his hair.

In an instant his arms were around her, and her hands held his head against her breast. They did not move or speak. It was something neither one had expected, neither one could have avoided. It was as natural, as inevitable as the response of the willows to the first warm day in April.

"Thea!" he whispered. "Thea! Thea!"

Her hand stroked the tousled head beneath her lips.

"Little one! *Draga!*" It was a word she had heard her mother use. She did not know what it meant any more.

Unheeded the great goose snapped up the scattered berries until every pink fleck of color had disappeared. Thea saw him and smiled. Except for him, perhaps, she might never have known.

Finally Danny released her, and they stood for a long moment silent, their eyes never faltering.

"Thea——"

"I love you." Her voice was as quiet and as

grave as a woman's. "You love me. It has happened that way. There is nothing to do for it.
No."

It seemed an agony of time before he answered.

"Yes, I can go away." His face had become old
suddenly, and his voice sounded strange and distant.

Her face was old, too, with the terrible knowledge
of youth, and it seemed, when she tried to speak,
as though no sound would come.

"Yes," she repeated finally, "you can go away."

She did not move when he left her. He stumbled
along like a school-boy. He was almost running,
and his breath came in terrible, choking gasps. He
was afraid to stay and afraid to go. Well, he had
made a decision.

He was leaving. To-morrow he would finish his
report to the company, drive his Ford over the trail
to St. Denis, stay all night at the company shack
in the timber, and catch a train next day for the
North. From Quebec he would be off West. There
was a job he could have up in British Columbia.
Anyway, what did it matter? He must get away,
that was all. He supposed after a while he would
get over seeing her face and the haunted look
in her eyes that were like lake water before a
storm.

V

Monday noon he pushed back his chair from the rough deal table and folded up the paper on which stood his calculations, copied in ink and arduously neat. He hated the office, with its splintered floor and great brown splotches of tobacco stain. It occurred to him that men were unnecessarily bestial. He hated Tell Haley, who sat opposite him, with his square yellow teeth and heavy nostrils.

"That Calumet country's goin' big," Tell confided. "Johnnie Deautremont's no fool when it comes to timber." Tell Haley spat in the general direction of the company cuspidor. "He's due back here this afternoon, down the river. Got a letter from the Winnipeg folks." He got up and slouched over to the window, where he squinted up at the sky, across which hurtled dirty storm-clouds. "Hell-damnblast!" he said. "We don't generally get a blow like this so early."

Danny Pherson did not move. The windows, loosely set into the casements, rattled with noisy, maddening persistence. In the winter the wind drove the snow in until the floor was white, the way a storm-lashed ocean drives the salt fog inland. Life on the lumber border was a ruthless one. It

was no wonder men drank and gambled and car-
oused to escape even for the moment from the
heartbreak of reality.

Tell Haley slouched out of the office across the
road to the saloon. He had flung out an invitation
to Danny, but Danny, it appeared, had not heard it.

Johnnie Deautremont was coming back. It had
seemed in some way as though Johnnie Deautremont had ceased to exist, as though, perhaps, he
had never really existed. Danny remembered him
suddenly, with his heavy, stooped shoulders, his
small eyes far apart, and his shock of black hair.
He remembered Thea, too, in her dress of white
satin and her bare feet and the terror in her eyes.

Suddenly the door to the office opened.

"Thea!" He got up, but he did not go to her.
She stood with her body against the door, her
hands behind her holding the knob until the knuckles
grew white. Her lips were open, but she did not
speak. He could not endure her eyes on his face.
They were like the eyes of a child in torture.

"He——"

Danny Pherson nodded, but he did not look at
her.

"I know."

There was a long moment of silence, and neither

one stirred. At last her hands fell at her sides, and the tension went out of her body. Something curious, too, had happened to her face. All the terror was gone. In its place was a beaten, listless resignation.

"I—I don't know why I came. I just found myself running and running." She stopped a moment. "It seemed I must look at you, only look at you. I don't know. Like some folks run and kneel to the Virgin when there is a storm." Again she stopped. Finally, she drew the back of her hand across her eyes and she shook her head like a bewildered child. "I think I shall not be able to see your face again—even in my mind. It is hard so, is it not?"

"Thea—" In an instant his arms were around her, and his hands stroked her hair and her shoulders in a fumbling agony of tenderness. They clung to each other like children desperate in the face of danger. "Thea!" he repeated. It seemed that his language was shorn of all but her name.

"I—love you."

At once there appeared just one thing for him to do. One does not dispute the ethics of what is inevitable. Danny Pherson had no time to convert his Scotch Presbyterian God to the thing he had made up his mind to do. Perhaps he could never convert Him. Well, then he would have to discover a new God, or get along without any.

Thea knew the thing that had happened in Danny's soul.

"I shall be ready." She met his eyes with grave candor. "There is nothing for me to take with me —only Toni. I am frightened to leave him, great stupid."

Where the village road, like a trail that disappears over a mountain, was lost in the somber shadow of the forest Thea waited. The wind bound her skirts about her, twisting and wrapping and unwrapping them. It rushed past her ears like the startled flight of a covey of partridges. It lashed the forest into a frantic, tortured protest.

VI

Tell Haley, coming out of the saloon, saw Dan Pherson crank the car and scramble in over the door. He saw him stop again at the edge of the forest and a woman in blue with something white under her arm get in beside him. Tell Haley was reasonably drunk, but he understood what had happened. It was he who, an hour later, broke the news to Johnnie Deautremont as he came up the path from the river. Tell Haley had no particular intention of courting his own destruction or of bringing torment to another. Liquor always made him garrulous.

"Your little Bohunk girl's flew the coop," he said. "Flew the coop with Danny Pherson. Damn shame you didn't float down the river a coupla hours sooner." He beamed expansively.

Johnnie Deautremont stood stork-still. For a moment it seemed as though he did not understand English. After a man has been four months alone in the timber it is difficult to fit back into the intercourse of people. He is like a child who by some mistake has been put at school in a grade too advanced for him. With a single gesture Johnnie pushed Tell Haley off the path into the briery thicket of hazel and stamped on. Tell Haley was only drunk.

But Johnnie Deautremont did not go home. First he stopped at the office, but it was empty and the door locked. Then he strolled down the road, the wind twisting eddies of dust into his face and eyes. The people he met he greeted sourly, but his eyes searched their faces with a frantic hope. Surely their faces must reveal to him something if what

Tell Haley had said was true. He even met Father
Fonda. The priest nodded and stopped him. Had
his journey been successful? The priest evidently
knew nothing. No, it could not be true.

But before he went home Johnnie Deautremont
stopped at the saloon. He had no intention of getting drunk, but one drink or two would make him
easier in his mind. Besides, it had been a long time
since he had drunk anything. He deserved a bit
of spree, a man who had been four months stark
alone in the timber. It wasn't right to be alone
like that; it did things to a person.

At last Johnnie Deautremont turned home. The
wind was behind him now, and it was easier walking, but he did not hurry. Like a lagging school-
boy he pushed open the gate and walked up the path
to the house. The windows were closed, and the
door. Well, she was probably in the kitchen. Of
course. She wouldn't be sitting alone in the parlor.
How silly! He laughed out loud, and the sound of
his voice startled him. Yes, the forest had done that
for him.

So he went around to the back and pushed open
the door into the kitchen. The place had a curious
silence and the cold smell of a house long deserted.
On the shelf the cheap clock from the company store

was still ticking, and the room was just as he remembered it.

"Thea." It was only a whisper. After a while he would call to her. "Thea! Thea! Thea!" He was shouting now like a man who must make himself heard above a storm at sea. He stamped through the house, his great shoes scarring deep into the pine of the floors. There was no one here, no one.

Finally, he rushed out doors and to the road that led into the forest. Tell Haley was right. Clear in the soft sand lay the marks of the tires. They would stay to-night at the shack above Lumber River.

They had almost two hours' start upon him. He began to run forward. Then he stopped again. This was madness, madness. They were only a few miles from him as the crow flies, for the road, an old Indian trail, following the creek, was a tortuous one, fairly doubling back on itself in its way across the hills. He could almost shout to them, but he could never reach them, not for months, maybe for years. Danny Pherson was no common logger. Danny Pherson could outwit him, could escape him.

An instant Johnnie Deautremont stood there, the

wind crashing the trees above him. The branches knocked against one another and strained and snapped as though they labored to loose themselves and to go hurtling off into space. The wind was due east, and it would stiffen with the sunset. Already it was blowing a gale. A long moment Johnnie Deautremont listened. Then a thought came to him. This time he knew he was mad, but he did not care. He could get even with all of them, the slender girl whose eyes were the color of iris, with Danny Pherson, with the forest.

Near as they were to him in miles, he could not overtake them. He knew that, *but the wind could.*

Kneeling beside the underbrush at the side of the road, he struck a match to the dry leaves of hazel and blueberry. He had seen fires start before, seen them race along the slippery floor of pine-needles, dry now as tinder. The flames were many at first, and little and very blue. They were like thousands of blue lupin that the children gather in the spring. Then the wind would find the fire and suck it upward, wind it and twist it and torment it until it reached the branches of the pines. Then the flames would shout back to the wind, screaming and spitting and sending on great gulfing waves of smoke before them.

Johnnie Deautremont laughed. This was splendid, his fire. Already it had gone forward toward them. It could travel faster than a man on horseback. If they turned back or tried to push on, they could not escape. Johnnie Deautremont knew that trail well, how it snaked in and out and seemed never to make any progress. No, they had better stay in the shack and say their prayers. They could never escape the messenger he had sent on to say that he was coming, to say he was coming though they would never see his face.

VII

For two days he neither slept nor ate. He was like a person who has already ceased to exist. The villagers did not notice him; but if they had, they would have said Johnnie Deautremont was just as usual. There was nothing new in his face, and his actions betrayed neither emotion nor excitement.

But the calm of his manner was not peace. It meant only that all his sensations had been suspended. His mind was like a deserted telegraph office, equipped and in order, but with no one there to record the incoming vibrations. Before the first rescue party was rounded up in the village Johnnie

Deautremont had set out. He carried neither compass nor luggage. He trekked that country as the ancients navigated the great sea, by instinct, by starshine, by the will to arrive.

The ground he walked on was as soft as dust, and his feet sank into it like wet sand. The heavy leather of his boots became scorched with the heat, his eyes smarted from the smoke that still hung, like poison gas, in the hollows. Often it seemed he could not breathe, but he went on, blackened and foot-sore. Against the noonday sun stood the charred tree-trunks, like the towers of a ruined city. By sunset it was ghastly country, a mad man's nightmare. At dusk he swam across the boiling Lumber River. The wooden bridge was gone, of course, and swimming would have been no tame adventure even for a man who had eaten and slept; but Johnnie Deautremont crossed over.

Down the gully a mile and to the left would be the spot where the company shack had stood. It had a wild choke-cherry-tree beside the door that always flowered early. It was like a slim girl in her wedding-dress against the dull green of the pines. Another mile, and the creek would bend. Then he would clamber up out of the gully, and he would have reached his destination. They had had a short moment of·paradise, those two, before his messenger had reached them. Well, he, too, had had a short moment.

It was almost dark now, and the gully was choked with shadow. Head down, like an animal, he was plodding. He had become almost without sensation. He could keep walking forever, even though he were dead. Suddenly he came to a halt, and for the first time the breath caught in his throat. Something was moving. There was some other living thing beside himself in this hideous wilderness.

For a long moment his eyes strained into the twilight, and he waited. Then he saw something white coming down the gully to meet him. It zigzagged in a crazy fashion and it moved with blundering caution. Johnnie Deautremont stared at it as though he were bewitched. Then the great white goose passed him slowly, hesitated an instant, and slid down into the black water of the river.

Johnnie Deautremont rubbed his blackened hand across his eyes. He must be dreaming. It could not have happened. In a panic of haste he ran along the gully and clambered up over the ridge. It seemed that his lungs would bleed with the pain of breathlessness, and he stumbled along with his eyes shut. Suddenly he stopped. The land felt different to his

feet now. It was cushioned smooth. He dropped
down, and his hands groped over the land. Grass!
It was cool to touch, and he stretched down on it,
his face pressed against its dewy softness.

Finally he lifted up on his elbow and opened his
eyes. There before him stood the shack, squat and
black against the starlight. There was a light in the
window, and through the open door a stream of
radiance fell upon the wild choke-cherry-tree, heavy
now with crimson fruit. Like an animal he crept
nearer. He was calmer. Cautiously, he felt his way
up along the house beneath the window. At last he
stood up beside it, and his eyes looked into the room.
He had seen that room often, the rough bunks with
the coarse, brown blankets; the iron stove in the
middle with its boarded-up parking of sawdust; the
rough deal table, and the wooden bench beside it.

Danny Pherson stood in the doorway, facing the
twilight, and Thea was putting some things on the
table. Johnnie Deautremont could smell the fragrance of bacon and coffee, and there were pancakes.
Her face was pink with the heat, and she moved
like the flicker of aspen-leaves.

"You can turn around now," she said, and she
waited, her back to the table, her eyes eager with
the anticipation of his presence. "He is a very good

dinner to-night, like you'd pay fifty cents for in the swellest hotel in Duluth."

Danny Pherson turned back to the room, and in his hands were some branches of cherry. "I sent clear to St. Paul for your roses," he said.

He handed the branches to her, and bowed with mock gravity. For an instant they stood there; then he knelt down on the bench before her, his arms strained her to him, and she drew his head against her lips.

"Thea! Thea!" he whispered.

She lifted his face to her and looked down into it.

"You see, the Virgin wasn't mad with us, like you thought She would be." He smiled at her translation of his Presbyterian ethics. "Out of all the world She has saved only us. Do you believe me now, little dumb one?"

He reached up and drew her to the bench beside him. For an instant to Johnnie Deautremont they seemed to have become one entity. They had ceased to be persons with names and ideas and memories. They possessed neither past nor future. They had become only man and woman, as the great Rodin dreamed it in marble, held lovingly in the hand of God.

Johnnie Deautremont moved away from the window and back to the edge of the gully where the desolation set in. Such miracles happened in fires. He was woodsman enough to know. Sometimes the suction became so great that all the oxygen would be drawn up out of a place, and the fire would pass over it untouched. He remembered a farmhouse back of Hinkley that had gone, unscorched even, through the holocaust. Oh, yes, those things happened sometimes; not often.

But Johnnie Deautremont had beheld there another miracle greater even than the freak of the fire, a miracle that had left him impotent. Perhaps there existed deep in his soul the spirit of the artist. At any rate, he had seen that night something too beautiful to touch, something too rare to destroy.

When he crossed the Lumber River again, a mile above the cabin, he was not so careful. Perhaps he was too weary this time to fight against the rapids, perhaps he was indifferent. Perhaps he was at peace.

Tell Haley always contended the company never would find another cruiser like Johnnie Deautremont, another man with his endurance, his nerve, his eye for timber. "But a damn' queer Kanuck" he always finished. "I never liked him."

IN APRIL

IN APRIL

JUDGE HADLEY stretched out his legs and unexpectedly kicked over the wicker waste-basket
under his desk. Then he drew in his legs and peered
down with annoyance at the litter of torn papers
sprinkled over the dusty hollow where lived his feet
and his waste-basket in inimicable proximity. In-
stinctively he bent over to pick up the débris. Then
he felt suddenly rather stout and middle-aged and
irritable.

"Hasn't been emptied for a week," be grumbled.

"What, sir?" asked the clerk, a Spanish-American
war veteran who chewed tobacco and had a limp and
friends in politics.

"This waste-basket."

Judge Hadley felt an unaccountable rage toward
this clerk, toward the janitor (an individual he had
never seen and whom, judging from his ministra-
tions, he believed to be mythical), toward the grimy

mahogany-veneered pomposity of the court-room
with its dirty windows, its mud-tracked marble
floors, its torn expensive window-blinds, which followed your hand down yieldingly, but which even
the most adroit coaxing could not persuade to ascend.
Perhaps because the mackerel and coffee and fried
potatoes he had eaten for lunch had not agreed with
him, or perhaps because it was four o'clock and April
with a touch of May in the air—if indeed one could
imagine spring in that court-room—Judge Hadley
felt tired and disillusioned.

"Hurry up that last case, Fred," he said, without
looking at the Spanish-American war veteran.

"They're lookin' for an interpreter, your honor."
Fred expectorated adroitly. "Even Si Wyatt can't
understand him."

"A pretty time to work up his defense," Judge
Hadley grumbled.

He shut his eyes and for a few minutes didn't
think of anything. Then he remembered vaguely
the days he had wanted to be a judge, the days when
he had clerked day-times in Jim Conklin's hardware
store and read law nights. He was mildly amazed
at the whipping enthusiasm that had kept his eyes
open over the tattered Blackstone he had borrowed
from Sam Bellows. As if it were another person,

he looked back on the struggling months after he had passed his bar examinations. It was in that very room he had pleaded his first case—and won it.

He supposed he must have felt very exhilarated and triumphant, but it seemed a long time ago. It had been then, too, that he had planned to marry Clarissa and be a judge. And, someway, linked with the vision of Clarissa was the dream to be a judge the State would be proud of, a judge with heart and insight as well as intellect. But Clarissa had died the first spring after their marriage, and that same year he had mounted the first round on the ladder of politics.

Judge Hadley yawned and opened his eyes. He wished he didn't have a headache every afternoon now. He knew drearily that he needed exercise. He ate too much. Suddenly he jerked forward in his swivel-chair.

"I can't wait here all day," he snapped. "Have that case called now, Fred. I have an engagement." Judge Hadley had decided to play golf.

He watched the Spanish-American war veteran slouch across the room and bawl out his inarticulate orders. Judge Hadley was suddenly filled with disgust for his clerk, for his job, for the ugliness of life. He loathed being a police judge and being forty-five. Then he remembered suddenly that it was April out on the golf links.

As the room filled slowly he stared at his calendar. He didn't have to look at the people then, and, besides, he had discovered that it produced a kind of respect for his dignity in the minds of his watchers. He had himself photographed that way once—only he had been looking at a book of bare-foot dancers, instead, which had been supplied by the photographer, who had exhorted him not to look as if he were enjoying himself too much.

"The case of the State *versus* Stefan Povala for illegal sale of spirituous liquors to United States soldiers," bawled the Spanish-American war veteran.

Judge Hadley scanned the faces around the two tables before him. Povala was probably the one at the end of the table on the left. He sat quietly, slightly bent forward.

Despite the fact that facilities for improving one's personal appearance were not abundant in the city "lock-up," Judge Hadley realized that the man had made an awkward attempt at neatness. With his fingers, perhaps, Povala had combed back from his broad forehead the sun-bleached strands of coarse straw-colored hair. Without analyzing it, Judge Hadley knew that the prisoner's skin and eye-brows, of the same shade as his hair, were a strangely effective background for his eyes, which were deep blue and curiously bright.

For an instant he had caught the fellow's attention; then he took refuge again in his calendar. Povala wasn't the usual type of "bootlegger." Judge Hadley had observed the Slavic face before, but instead of the usual stolid fatalism there was something curiously childlike and pleading in Povala's expression.

Judge Hadley shook himself mentally and turned toward the secret service man who was to testify against the prisoner. He shouldn't let this man hypnotize him—besides, he'd made rather a name for himself cleaning out bootleggers.

"MacNeil and I was in khaki, ye understand, and we met him there at the Walnut Street bridge," the secret service man was saying. "It was about five-thirty but growin' dark already. 'Can ye get us a drink, bo?' says I. He looked sort of startled and pretended like he didn't understand—but he did all right."

"Tell only what happened," interrupted Judge Hadley. "Never mind your observations."

Donovan of the secret service winked the eye away from Judge Hadley, and the Spanish-American war veteran grinned. His Honor's ill humor tempered the whole court-room.

" 'We got money,' says I, and I flashes a dollar bill before him. He sort of cowered, but he begins to take notice, and I knows we're on the right track. 'I no sell,' he says in his lingo. 'Take this,' says I, 'and get us a drink,' and I stuffs the money into his pocket. 'We'll be waiting here,' I says, 'and in fifteen minutes it'll be darker.' "

Judge Hadley stole another look at the prisoner. He was straining to watch the man testifying against him. Evidently the language puzzled him, and he cupped a thick-fingered hand around his ear, believing that if he could hear more plainly he could understand. He seemed to be quite without resentment. He was just waiting. Discouraged at last, he dropped his hand to the edge of the table, and his eyes rested on it. He had given up trying to understand.

"Well, he brought us back the booze all right," the secret service man continued, "and some change beside. It was not bad whisky, either—from the smell." This comment did not pass unappreciated.

The case for the defense progressed haltingly. Si Wyatt's interest in his client was frankly half-hearted—besides, it was a clear case against him, and Si Wyatt was anxious to get home to his garden; he had hired a man to help him dig the sweet-pea trench that afternoon. Moreover, Povala was about as difficult to handle as a sheep that has been dazed by a thunder-storm. It apparently had not pene-treated to him that Si Wyatt was paid by the county to use his talents to defend him and others as unfortunate. Besides, Povala's limited command of English seemed to have deserted him entirely.

It was evident he understood nothing of the reason for his imprisonment or for his trial. This country was difficult to understand—even as Poland had been difficult. Nevertheless Si Wyatt droned through the form of a defense markedly similar to pleas he had made on a dozen like occasions. Indeed, Judge Hadley could have prompted him if at any moment the words had failed. Then he sat down and yawned.

And the case for the defense was ended.

For a moment the court-room was silent. Then an unexpected thing happened to Judge Hadley. He looked down from his desk directly into the eyes of the prisoner. Suddenly he had a curious sense of isolation; it was as if they two were alone in the court-room.

"*To byli soldate*," said Povala.

Then he stopped, dazed, like a child who is blind-folded in a school game. He caught suddenly at the sleeve of the interpreter. Even in Polish he spoke with an effort.

"He says they were soldiers," explained the inter-preter. "He did not want to get the drink for them, but he thought he had to. In Poland, he says, one obeys a soldier or, *pouf!* one receives a beating, or perhaps one's cow is driven off and the children are hungry."

Povala again looked up at Judge Hadley.

"Bo to byli soldate," he repeated. Then he smiled apologetically and made a deprecating gesture with his great hands. After all, when one is understood, language is a futile thing.

The simplicity of the man's appeal was disarming, irresistible. Judge Hadley felt a strange elation. Here was one man who trusted him, even as a child trusts his parents—a devoted, inarticulate sort of trust.

With an insight Judge Hadley did not believe he possessed, he grasped the background of Povala's existence. As if he had been there, he saw the low-roofed Polish village on the muddy highroad along which the oxen labored. He could hear the troopers of the Czar gallop into the tiny square in front of the church and give their orders. There are many faces like Povala's in that little group of peasants—dumb, accepting faces. Yes, in Poland one obeyed a soldier. Judge Hadley was amazed at the vividness of this picture. Surely Povala had needed no lawyer for the defense. For this once, Judge Hadley became the judge he had intended to be back in the long evenings when he had thumbed Sam Bellows' Blackstone, back in the days when he had been engaged to Clarissa.

The approach to number seven on the Fairview Golf links was a steep one. Judge Hadley had always rather dreaded it, because each time it had convinced him that he was short of breath and forty-five and weary. Now he took it like a school-boy. With steady fingers he molded the little pyramid of damp sand and topped it with a "glory dimple," ivory white and glistening. Then, for a minute, he looked westward over the sloping meadows, curiously lovely with the yellow green of April.

"Strange place—Poland," he observed; "or, at least, it used to be."

Sam Bellows was still puffing from the ascent.

"It's nothing to boast of now. Still, I guess some people have got a genius for suffering, for being misunderstood." He dropped down on the wooden bench next to the sand-box. "Go ahead—it's your honor."

Slowly Judge Hadley drew a stick from his bag.

"Anyway, there's America for some of them, and a betting chance of meeting a Yankee who understands."

Judge Hadley drew his club back for a full swing, and clean from his driver the ball curved upward, then down, and he watched it go bounding along the hillside.

THE CROSS-BEAM

THE CROSS-BEAM

I

OLAF NELSON stood by the kitchen window and stared out across the acres of Minnesota prairie. It was November, and the ruts in the roads were already stiff with frost. The sky, too, was low and gray, with a mist prophetic of snow-clouds.

Ever since he was twelve years old Olaf had stared across those acres and he had always hated them. Back in the old country he had lived in the hills. They were green hills with rushing freshets, and the trout stream that turned the mill-wheel in the village was a gay one. Sometimes the trout leaped up into the sunshine and flipped a shower of iridescent drops into the air for one dazzling second.

The village, too, was gay. All day one could hear the distant tinkle of cow-bells on the hills, and at night there was often a dance at the inn. Olaf had been happy there. The people were friendly; there were chickens and pigs to play with in the tiny garden behind the house, and in the evenings his mother had told him stories about the trolls who lived just over the hill. Olaf's mother and father loved each other, and Olaf had been raised with the gentleness of their love about him. For a sensitive boy it was a heritage prophetic both of great happiness and of even greater suffering.

Then Olaf's father was drowned; six weeks later his mother died of the fever; so when the Tegners moved to the States they took Olaf along to his uncle. Swen Bjorkman had gone over in the eighties, and the rumor was that he had prospered. No one had ever cared much for Swen, but no one doubted that he would be successful.

When the village heard that Mrs. Bjorkman had died, they were sorry they had sent Olaf. It would have been better to keep him there and bring him up with the other children, hard as it was already to make both ends meet. Swen Bjorkman was no man to bring up a child. Even Rudi Djursen hated him, and Rudi was the best-natured man in the village.

"He's a hard man, with no blood in his veins," Rudi had said, "not even amiable in his liquor. I will never drink again with a man with fish eyes."

To the child of twelve Swen Bjorkman had seemed like one of the wicked trolls out of a fairy-tale. In the twenty-six years he had spent under Swen Bjorkman's roof this antipathy had strengthened, but it was based no longer on a mere freak of childish aversion. Olaf Nelson had every reason for hating the old man lying in the next room.

For there lay Swen Bjorkman, and Olaf thought he was dying. Luke Weller, the doctor, had been there an hour, and old Mother Lindgren had been called in to help. The stove in the kitchen needed refilling, but Olaf did not move.

He was thirty-eight, too old now to think of doing any of the things he had hoped to do. But he was free. He could sell the farm and move to Minneapolis. Lillah had been once in Minneapolis. Then he thought, perhaps, she wouldn't want to be reminded of any of that. Well, then they'd go to Chicago or maybe to Denver. Denver would be better for her. The old man couldn't now beat him out of the farm, or the money in the squat wooden bank in Black Cloud. Swen Bjorkman had no one else to whom he could leave his property. Thirty-eight was no tender age at which to become one's own master, but it was better than never being free at all.

True, twenty years before, the night that Swen Bjorkman had had his first stroke, Olaf Nelson had made a desperate, baffled lunge for freedom. It had seemed to Olaf like a judgment of God that the cross-beam of the barn had fallen on his uncle as Swen had lashed out at him with the iron-buckled halter. Olaf had planned to leave that night. The flier for Duluth always slowed down at the Christian Bridge. Any man with agile limbs and no fear in his heart could board it—any driven man.

Instead, Olaf had galloped into town on the back of old Walli, the plow-horse, to fetch Doctor Weller. He remembered how exalted he had felt as he rode, the mare jogging him from side to side on her broad back. He had lifted the beam from his uncle's shoulder and had laid him out straight on the wooden floor. Swen Bjorkman's face was gray, and the eyelids did not flicker. As Olaf had drawn the torn buffalo robe up over him, he had thought that would be his shroud.

But Swen Bjorkman had rallied. Luke Weller had never heard of a case like it. The old man was paralyzed, to be sure, but his mind remained unaffected. Strapped to his bed, he became even more diabolically tyrannical than before. He continued to run every detail of his farm with the same unsparing ruthlessness. The old devil seemed to have developed a psychic insight. He would know in some way whether the roof of the cow-barn had been mended, the cattle turned out up on Section Four, the hogs driven in to be slaughtered. There was something uncanny about him, and terrible. In his physical impotence he seemed to possess the boy even more completely than he had as a giant of strength. Because he was dependent on his nephew for every mouthful he swallowed, he had made him just that much more his vassal. Olaf never dreamed any more of the midnight flier, with its white banner of smoke against the starlight, but he dreamed of the time when Swen Bjorkman would cease to breathe.

This day he had had a second stroke, and Olaf Nelson had galloped into town through the twilight of morning to fetch out the doctor. His heart did not beat so fast this time. He was older, and the years had done something to him. They had mocked him out of his birthright. Simple people know no methods for shirking any of the brutalities of duty.

From the room where Swen Bjorkman lay the door opened, and Luke Weller came into the kitchen. He stood a moment, undecided, then he rattled the grate of the cook-stove and put in another stick of wood.

"Kind of cold that gets you," he said. He didn't want to answer Olaf's unspoken question. "Remarkable case," he said finally, "remarkable." He still did not catch the eye of the man beside him, and his words came slowly. "Looks like he might live to be a hundred."

For a long moment there was silence in the kitchen. Luke Weller was used to the heartbreak of life; he had watched suffering often and it had left him untouched. But he didn't want to look at Olaf Nelson now. At one time he had believed Olaf had a future; there seemed a little different strain in him than in the other Swedes in the neighborhood. Olaf had borrowed books from him and from the minister and from Judge Santaline. The judge had wanted Olaf to go to the university at Minneapolis; but Olaf had been caught as surely as though he had been locked up in a prison—caught by the terrible, unescapable exigencies of the poor.

Luke Weller was not a man oppressed by the vagaries of conscience. Life was a fairly simple and brutal affair, on the whole. It wasn't often that any one aroused in him a sense of rebellion against the inexplicable blunderings in the ordering of human lives, but Olaf Nelson had done that. Luke Weller had liked the straight set of Olaf's eyes, the blond curls that fitted close to his well shaped head, the grave forehead, the sensitive mouth, even the chin, which held refinement rather than determination. He would probably never amount to much; he was neither ruthless nor lucky enough. But he possessed potentialities.

Luke Weller was also oppressed by the conviction that he had aided in the conspiracy against Olaf's future. Twenty years before he had promised Olaf the death of Swen Bjorkman, just as surely as he had ever promised anything in his life. The old man was doomed, and if Olaf only waited patiently a little time he would inherit enough to take him away from Black Cloud, put him through the graded school, and later through college. Heaven knew he had earned every cent, too, of that inheritance, for he had drudged on Swen Bjorkman's farm since the day he had come there from Sweden. Why run the chance of losing everything when another six months would see the whole thing finished? Besides, somebody had to take care of the old devil. Twenty years before Luke Weller had begun to say this, and the boy had believed him. The old man might outlive them both.

Then Luke Weller wondered about the Lillah person. She called herself Montgomery, but Sam Dillon, who claimed he had seen her up at the Soo, said that up there she had called herself Raphael. Luke Weller had no reason to doubt Sam, and yet Luke knew that his townsman was a judge only of what meets the eye. Since Lillah had come, from no one knew where, to wait on table at Gus Lieber's chophouse, Luke Weller had formed the habit of dropping in there for supper instead of eating it at the Black Cloud House, where for twenty-odd years he had dragged out a not too desolate existence.

II

Olaf Nelson refused the doctor's invitation to ride to the village with him, but a mile behind Luke Weller's livery team Olaf was driving old Ringer to the spring-wagon. There were three prescriptions he must fill that evening. Old Mother Lindgren left to-morrow. She had to get back to her daughter-in-law, and Olaf Nelson would again be alone. This would be his only chance to get into town for a week at least.

He sat hunched forward on the driver's seat, the reins held loosely in his hands. The mare knew the way in without any guiding. There was nothing now to divert Olaf Nelson from facing his situation. The copper-colored pastures, sloping away to a black, grass-tufted swamp or lifting into the higher land that had been sown to winter wheat, held nothing to catch the eye.

He had ceâsed to see these fields years ago. He lived with only half his consciousness; it was a defense, perhaps, against even greater suffering. The less of him that lived, the less of him there was to be hurt. It was not a very brave philosophy, and he knew it. That was the trouble with him: he didn't have any spunk. If he had had, he would have broken loose long ago. But always there had been the hope that fate would one day rescue him.

To-day Luke Weller had read Olaf Nelson's death-sentence. There was no use going on any longer dreaming of a rescue. All he could do was to farm. He was thirty-eight. He had neither education nor money, nor was there any longer in his make-up the bravado that challenges fortune and refuses to be dismayed. He was tied to a bed-ridden old man whom he had once feared, whom he still hated, as a sailor who has been hurt by the ocean can hate it, as a lumber-cruiser, driven a little touched by the isolation of the forest, can hate the timber.

There was no use, either, thinking any longer about Lillah. He couldn't bring her out to be also a slave to the whimsies of Swen Bjorkman. Besides, there was something in Lillah too delicate, too luxury-loving. True, there was nothing esthetic about Gus Lieber's chop-house, but one felt that she had never belonged. She worked as hard as the other girls,—Gus Lieber saw to that,—but she served the food with a grace that made the task seem easy.

Olaf didn't know how old she was; perhaps thirty, perhaps older. Her cheeks were a little sunken, there were shadows under her eyes, and her body, though still graceful, was thin almost to the point of scrawniness. Her mouth was straight, the lips thin, and her chin was a trifle projecting. Lillah's eyes were gray, and her lashes curled slightly and were very dark. Her hair was an undecisive blond and had been crimped until the ends about her face were stiff and short. Her skin, too, had the unhealthy creamy softness of a skin much massaged.

For Lillah Montgomery the decline had set in some time before, and yet never before had she possessed so definite or so insistent an appeal. Because her loveliness was going, it was recaptured and bestowed anew upon her by every man who saw her.

Just as the face that is almost beautiful makes a creative artist out of every beholder.

But the old fire was gone, for Lillah saw only the face the speckled, square mirror that hung over her wash-stand gave back to her. She did not know she possessed the mystic quality of creating a gracious imagination in all who beheld her. She only knew she was tired and poor and not very strong and that she had gambled away every chance for security.

Olaf Nelson had never told her he loved her. It had not been necessary for either of them to put it into words. Indeed, he had never been to see her more than a dozen times, but she seemed to him a person less fortunate than himself. His feeling for her, however, was not only pity. Her delicacy, her wistfulness, would have conquered alone. She ought to marry some one who could give her all the things the suggestions of which she seemed able to create out of such poor scraps. Lillah Montgomery may not have been either very good or very intelligent, but there was about her something of the artist. Luke Weller knew this through his mind; Olaf Nelson knew it even more truly through his instincts.

With a stolid conscientiousness Olaf Nelson finished all his errands in the village. At the drugstore he had the liniment prescriptions filled. Luke Weller had told him he would have to rub the paralyzed legs and back of the old man. He bought, also, Swen Bjorkman's favorite brand of chewing-tobacco and the licorice-drops, cheaply doped, that Swen thought put him to sleep. At the general store he bought coffee and sugar and tea and flour. He was like a man stocking up for a trip in the Klondike. After all his purchases had been made, he carried them out to the wagon and deposited them safely under the seat.

Across the road from the Black Cloud Emporium shone the windows of Gus Lieber's chop-house. Olaf had not intended to cross over, but he did. Well, he didn't need to go inside. The room had been an old grocery store, the walls of which were still scarred with the marks of the shelves. In the middle of the room was a horseshoe counter of dark-painted wood the top of which was covered with a sticky down left in the wake of some one's old petticoat now used as a mop. On the walls hung advertisements of soft drinks not carried by the establishment, and gaudy calendars with no regard either for pictorial value or date. On the counter stood a scraggling line of catsup-bottles, sugar-bowls of heavy pressed glass, and squat mustard-jars on which the contents had caked so long before as now to have become part of the container. To the left of the door stood a round-bellied iron stove surrounded by a boarded parking of sawdust stained brown with the juice of tobacco. As a background for beauty Gus Lieber's chop-house left virtually everything to be desired.

The counter was full now, for the flier from Fort Pierre was just in, and there were many passengers this evening. Olaf watched the girls as they brought in the orders of beans and hamburg steak and fried potatoes, piled dangerously the length of the arm. Every time the short swinging-doors into the kitchen flickered open he expected to see Lillah stand in the doorway, but every time the door disclosed only Sina, or Annie, whose substantial bulk shut out all view beyond.

A long time Olaf waited. The passengers from the flier bolted their food and left. Sina and Annie stacked the greasy plates and bore them off to the kitchen. Finally Annie swabbed the counter, leaving great untouched scallops along the outside edge, stuck a toothpick from the pink glass dish into her mouth, and went away. The room was empty now, but Olaf did not move from the square of light outside the window.

Finally the kitchen door opened, and Lillah came out. She wore a soiled kitchen apron too big for her, and she was carrying a tray of glasses. Olaf saw her stop and her whole body tremble. Then she made an effort to reach the counter and deposit her burden, swayed again, and her body shook with a paroxysm of coughing. Off the tray reeled the heavy tumblers, like things maliciously endowed with life. By the time Olaf reached her the coughing fit had passed, and she smiled at him across the tray, half empty now of its burden.

"Lillah——"

"Gosh!" she said, "this is the second time I've done this. Yesterday it was soup." She smiled again, shyly.

Olaf took the tray from her and put it on the counter. When she leaned over to pick up the broken pieces, he stopped her.

"Sit down," he said and he pushed her toward a stool. Then he knelt down before her, and put the jagged fragments into an empty peach-basket he found behind the counter.

"Yesterday," she repeated, "it *was* soup. No kidding." She waited a moment. "To-day they put me in the kitchen, where it don't make such a scene if you—sneeze."

Still on his knees before her, he looked up at her. "Lillah!"

A long moment they stared at each other. Then, very gently, she reached out toward him and drew his head against her side. Her arms were so soft he could hardly feel them, but they were warm and they held him with a strength he had never suspected. Then his arms groped their way around her, and he could feel her lips against his forehead.

"Lillah!" he repeated, "Lillah!"

Her fingers stroked his hair as though he had been a child. He had no idea there could be so much gentleness in the world.

"Olaf," she said at last, "I'm not good enough for you. And yet I'm not sure it matters. I love you."

Again there was a moment of silence, while their arms gave each other the reassurance their words would destroy.

"You know all about me," he said finally, "and old Swen."

She nodded.

"I know. It's a damn' shame."

They were both standing now, but their hands held each other with an agony of tenderness.

"It will be hard work out there even with me to help. You'd be tied, just like me. And you'd hate

him. And he'd hate you." Again he stopped, struggling to hide nothing from her. "I've got nothing
of my own. It's all his. And Luke Weller says he
might live to be a hundred."

Lillah Montgomery smiled.

"Luke Weller don't know everything." Then she
drew toward him softly, and her arms sought the
curve of his shoulders. "It's even Stephen," she
went on. "I reckon there are those that wouldn't
think you were getting a prize package in me."

"Don't say that!"

She pressed her temple against his cheek.

"Oh, it don't matter, does it, so long as we've got
each other?   We've got more than our share, I
reckon, right this minute."

"Lillah!" he repeated, "O Lillah!" There seemed
so little to say when one was happy.

Luke Weller knew he would be late for supper.
Still, Gus might get the old woman to fry him up
something, and Lillah might bring it in to him—
Lillah. He was a fool to think about her the way
he did. Then, before he pushed open the door to
Gus Lieber's chop-house, he looked up. A long
moment he stood there. They had not heard his
footsteps, he decided, or his hand on the latch. Well,
perhaps it was lucky he had looked up just in time

before he had pushed the door open. Yes, perhaps, after all, it was lucky.

III

There was a great deal to say in the village when Olaf and Lillah were married. Sam Dillon still insisted she had once called herself Raphael and that he had met her up at the Soo. But no matter what the men of Black Cloud may have thought of Lillah's past, there was no one who spoke unkindly of her. There was no one who didn't wonder how she happened to choose Olaf Nelson, who from every worldly point of view was the poorest bet among them. There was no man, too, who was not in his heart a little jealous of Olaf, for Lillah Montgomery had the trick of doing something to a man's imagination.

The day of his marriage Olaf went in to tell old Swen. Over Swen was drawn a red quilt, frayed and soiled where his beard and chin had rested upon it, and over his useless legs lay summer and winter a robe of rusty-looking buffalo-skin. Twenty years before the room had been added to the shack. The walls had been plastered, but they were still unpapered, and on them had been pinned the chromos and calendars of the early nineties. Nothing in the room had been touched, for Swen Bjorkman had developed an invalid's irritability with even the slightest innovation. Olaf had once started to straighten a picture of the Swiss Alps that hung above the whatnot facing Swen's bed, but the old man had screamed at him to let it alone.

"Tanklös varelse," he said, "cannot you mind, perhaps, your own business? That is as I have looked upon it forty months now. That is as it shall always be."

On the table stood a jar filled with cattails. Olaf remembered how he had brought them home from the swamp, and his uncle had laughed at him and ordered him to throw the weeds away, but he had put them in the front room. No one ever came in there then. Now they had become as immutable a part of the room as the Swiss Alps. Olaf wondered sometimes if the things would not endure forever. He remembered the marsh had been dyed with sunset where he picked them, and they had looked like elfin wands. He thought now he had never seen anything so ugly.

That Saturday Olaf brought Swen his dinner of beans and bacon and black coffee as strong as a drug. Swen seldom spoke now, though his speech was unimpaired. Some day the paralysis might reach his throat; he might go that way. Luke Weller had predicted it. But, as Lillah said, Luke wasn't always right.

Before he took the dishes away Olaf waited. He still wore his overalls and the coarse Mackinaw jacket. .He would have to hurry if he got to town by three o'clock, and yet he could make no move to speak. Old Swen would have to know this evening, anyway. It would be better to get through the scene now. All the time he knew Swen's eyes were on him—the eyes that were the cold light blue of a moonstone. "Fish eyes" the folks in the village called them. Finally the old man stirred, and his voice had all the resonance of twenty years ago.

"I won't have two fires burning," he said, "and you can't bring her in here."

Something went cold around Olaf Nelson's heart. The old man was uncanny, and the blue eyes became at once like nothing human.

"We'll sit in the kitchen," he said finally.

There was always a terrible moment of waiting before the old man spoke—a moment in which one awaits the words, as a traveler at sea waits the shriek of the fog-siren.

"You cover the kitchen fire at eight, as always."

A terrible flush of humiliation crept from Olaf

Nelson's throat to his temples. That any man should dare to speak to him like this! At that moment he could have strangled Swen Bjorkman. But he did not move. It was better to answer nothing. The old devil might take it out on Lillah. No, after all these years, it was too late to make a stand.

As he drove into town he saw dirty-looking snow-clouds lumber across the sky. There had been a few flurries already, but it was too cold to snow. At any rate, it would be warm back in the kitchen. He had brought in some boughs of spruce and evergreen to make it festive, and there was a new red table cloth on the table. Also he had bought some cakes and cheese and a bottle of spiced wine. He remembered the weddings back in his village in Sweden. He wanted his own to be like them in some way; only, of course, there wouldn't be any fiddle or dancing.

At Pastor Nordlie's house he met Lillah. Gus Lieber and his "old woman" had come, too, to be witnesses. Pastor Nordlie had put on his Sunday coat, and Mrs. Nordlie wore her dress of black silk. But Olaf Nelson saw nothing but Lillah. He thought she looked pale, but her eyes were on fire. He wondered suddenly how she could care for him as she did. He knew for the first time the humility of one who loves with completeness.

"Lillah," he said, "are you sure that you love me, dumb ox that I am?"

She did not touch him, but her eyes were caress enough.

"I am sure," she said.

After the service Pastor Nordlie said a blessing, and then Mrs. Nordlie invited all of them to come into the dining-room and drink coffee before they started back. She even used her china cups that had come all the way from Stockholm. Olaf hoped he would not break his before he could set it down. He had never touched anything so fragile before. Lillah, he noticed, held her cup as easily as though she had never drunk out of the great white mugs in Gus Lieber's chop-house.

"Luke Weller's gone to Minneapolis to-day already," Gus Lieber offered. "These Yankees don't like us Germans drink. They got no sense. It will be a week already before he comes back." He made an explosive gesture. "Whoof! Then he be for a year sober maybe."

When they started home it had begun to snow. Olaf wrapped the buffalo-robe around Lillah and bunched the straw up thick under her feet. It was twilight now, but still light with the flakes of whiteness. Olaf watched them fall upon the ragged lap-robe, upon the sleeves of Lillah's coat, upon her gloves.

"Put your hands here," he said, "where the snow can't get at them," and he drew the robe up closer around her. "I am jealous, I think, of the snow."

She laughed softly, and leaned her cheek against his.

"It is very nice here," she said. "I hope we have a long way to go."

"It is as white to-night as a night in the old country. In my village in winter," he said, "it was twilight all night long, like some nights here in the summer."

Again she laughed softly.

"Go on; tell me any old thing. I'll believe it."

"Lillah!" Their arms held each other fast, as though they had found each other for the first time. "Lillah! Lillah!" he whispered.

Her hands pressed his head against her cheek, and her lips touched his eyes and his temple.

"Silly!" she said. "You are happy, and you're not very used to being it."

At last they drove into the farmyard. There were no lights from the windows, and the house looked black against the new whiteness.

"Want to come out and help me unhitch?" he

asked finally. He knew he did not want her to be without him in that house, but he did not want to depress her with his own apprehensions.

Lillah felt the concern behind the question and also the gallantry that prompted his lightness.

"Surest thing you know," she said. "I reckon you'll be having me do it all alone soon, eh?"

They both laughed, and he kissed her, as light-hearted at once as a school-boy. After all, things weren't so bad. They had each other. What did all the other things men set their hearts on matter?

Lillah sat in the wagon while Olaf found the lantern and lighted it. The barn became at once a place of fantastic, lunging shadows as the lantern swung slightly from the nail against the cross-beam. Olaf Nelson looked up at it.

"It was that beam fell," he said, "the night I almost caught the flier." He stopped a moment. "That was twenty years ago."

Lillah Nelson looked down at him.

"Help me out," she said at last. He lifted her over the wheel and held her to him. For a long moment neither spoke.

"Except for that cross-beam we never would have met," she said. Silent, he looked up at it.

"I used to think it was me it fell on," he said

finally. "What if it should fall on her, too?" he thought, and his arms drew her to him again in an agony of apprehensive tenderness.

"Come on," she said at last, "we're never going to get these birds unhitched at this rate."

Olaf set about the business, letting Lillah delay him with mocking attempts at assistance. Finally, the horses were led into their stalls, fed and watered, and the sticking door rolled almost shut for the night. On the way back to the house they walked slowly, Olaf with Lillah's trunk on his back. They were happy now, but inside those walls lay a helpless man whose strength was as baffling as the whirl pool.

At the kitchen-door he stopped. It was warm inside, and the air was fragrant with the smell of the cedar-branches. He wondered if Lillah would think he had been silly to try to decorate the place in this way for her. He put down the trunk, and on the kitchen table he lighted the kerosene-lamp. The room was different at night. She came toward him and looked around.

"Olaf," she said, "it's just like Christmas." She sniffed exquisitely. "And, golly, how it smells!"

A flush of pleasure mounted slowly on his cheeks. She didn't think he was silly. She never would. It was a moment of perfect reassurance, as complete as it was trivial.

She took off her hat and coat, finally, and he shook down and refilled the cook-stove. It was pretty nice here, he thought. He would get some red calico curtains for the windows, and he would buy a caster set, with pale pink bottles, for the center of the table. After all, he had a little money of his own. He earned at least as much as the hired man.

Suddenly there came a sound like the tapping of a blind man's stick. Lillah looked up at him, sharply.

"Old Swen," he said. "He wants something." He opened the door out of the kitchen and stood an instant in the doorway. "What is it?" he asked.

For a moment there was silence.

"Bring her here," he said at last. "I want to see her." His words came slowly, full of malice. "I want to see the woman that would marry you."

"Lillah——"

She joined her husband in the doorway.

"Get the lamp," the voice commanded. "I want to see her face."

Olaf brought the lamp and held it high in the doorway. The old man lay like a log on his bed, but his face gleamed out of the shadow. He and Lillah greeted each other only with their eyes. It was a moment of unendurable silence when anything monstrous might happen. It seemed to Olaf at once as though Lillah were no longer breathing, as though she were an image from which all life had departed. He wondered if the moment would go on forever, if indeed it had always existed.

Then the old man's eyes blinked again in the shadow. They were like the eyes of a cat caught for an instant by a lantern at night on the highroad.

"That will do," he said at last. Then, after a moment, "I will live longer than she will." It sounded as though he chuckled, but perhaps it was only the rustle of his wiry beard against the bed-clothes.

Slowly Olaf closed the door behind them.

"Lillah——"

She took the lamp out of his hands and put it on the table. Then she set her hair to rights and drew up a chair toward the stove. Finally she looked up into his face.

"Gosh, he certainly can throw a scare into *you!*" She laughed, and tried to believe that her laugh sounded natural. "Cheerful old party, ain't he?" Finally she drew Olaf over toward her. "You ought to stand up to him, silly. Why, I'm not afraid you can bet."

This time his arms did not answer her entreaties, and he shook his head dully.

"I know," he said finally. "I don't stand up to him. It does seem sometimes for sure like it was on me the cross-beam landed."

IV

For the first winter since his childhood Olaf Nelson was happy. He was not so busy out of doors but he could do most of the work for Lillah. He liked to think her cheeks had rounded out a little and that the lines of fatigue had gone from around her eyes. Old Swen he still tended like a baby. He had forbidden Lillah ever to enter the front room. It seemed, in some way, with the door always closed between the two rooms, that the old man's curse must lose its power. The food Olaf took him Lillah had cooked. It was better than Olaf had ever prepared, or old Mother Lindgren. Olaf wondered sometimes why she fussed so to have the napkin on the tray clean and to warm the plate in the oven. She at least owed him nothing.

About the woman Olaf Nelson had brought back Swen Bjorkman never asked. Olaf wondered if perhaps he might not have forgotten her, and his heart gave a bound of relief at the thought. But old Swen had not forgotten.

"She was coughing this morning while you were gone to the cow-barn," he said. "Put some more ointment on old Hulda's neck where she rubbed it against the stanchions." The old man's eyes had a way of never quite focusing, and his face remained always as inscrutable as a mask.

With slow precision Olaf smoothed the sheet and readjusted the bedclothes. His face, too, did not betray him, but there was cold fear in his heart. It was true about old Hulda and the stanchion, and yet no one had ever told Swen Bjorkman. It must also be true about Lillah and the fit of coughing. He wondered whether, after all, he might only have imagined she looked better. She seemed so happy! All afternoon as he mended harness in the corner by the stove he would steal long glances at her. Sometimes she was sewing. Sometimes she read out loud, foolish romances, cheaply written, but from her lips they became the songs of poets. He anticipated for her every wish. When it seemed she had no appetite, he brought her twelve oranges from Black Cloud for which he had sent all the way to Minneapolis. When she saw them she turned away her head, and he knew there were tears in her eyes.

One night at supper he suggested they invite Luke Weller out some time to eat a meal. Lillah neither met his eyes nor answered.

"It's some trek," she said finally, "no matter how swell the food."

For a moment Olaf was silent.

"It might perhaps be that he was coming this road, anyway."

"It might perhaps be," she mocked. "Maybe a breath of fresh air, now that it's twenty below, would be just what he's wanting. He gets so little chance to be out!" She laughed.

Olaf blushed foolishly, but he refused to be dissuaded. He was only afraid she might force him to put into words the reasons he had for wishing Luke Weller to come. At once the thought occurred to him, "What if old Swen might be the reason for the doctor's journey, what if at last the paralysis might one day creep as far as his throat?"

But it was no use hoping any longer for a miracle. Old Swen was as well as that first day. He was enchanted. Like the king with the red beard, he would go on living, perhaps, forever. A spasm of anger passed through Olaf Nelson, and his hands shook so violently that he was ashamed. How easy it would be to do murder in such a moment! One would simply perform the act, as detached and un-moved as a professional pig-sticker. It is not safe for men whose blood is cool and runs slowly ever to give way to passion. They have no temperamental defense against its mercilessness and its madness.

Lillah Nelson watched his face.

"Tell Luke Weller to come," she said, "as soon as he's called out this way." Then she laughed, and it was a valiant attempt at naturalness. "I reckon he misses me to put a brace of fried eggs in front of him every now and then."

It was February when Luke Weller appeared, one of those days that has within it the mocking prophecy of April. The snow over the fields was soggy, and here and there black, wet patches of earth showed through. Back in New York State, Luke Weller thought, one might find to-day the first crocus. Funny thing, his being out here. He had stood second in his class at the medical school. It had been predicted that he would go to Syracuse or may-be Buffalo and become a great surgeon. But here he was in Black Cloud. He was almost fifty. The facts of his life were so dreary that he refused ever to review them: his hideous, uncomfortable room at the Black Cloud House, the outrageous, greasy food he ate three times a day, the complete lack of gentleness or beauty or intellectual stimulation. And yet he was neither bitter nor scarred with self-flagellations.

He played as good a game of poker as any man in the State; he had never gone back professionally. Indeed, as a doctor he had little to his discredit and much to his advantage. He was conscientious about his work and interested in it. Once every six months he disappeared to Minneapolis and there were never in Black Cloud any questions asked. From the point of view of his endowments his life was a failure, but from the point of everyday living it could not be said, to him at least, to be without interest.

He had never been a man who cared for women, even though the facts of his life were by no means above criticism. Only one woman had ever captured his imagination, had ever caught at his throat when he drove back at night from a late case, alone beneath the stars. She was the only woman who was to him more than a biological function. She was some one who could give significance and beauty to existence, who by her very presence bestowed a magic over all the grossness of living.

Luke Weller knew why Olaf had sent for him. It would be the first time he had seen Lillah since that night he had almost burst in upon them at the lunch-counter. He had thought about her often. He knew in some way that she was one of those women whom marriage would not change. He knew, too, that she was one of those even more rare persons capable of only one tremendous and complete adventure. She belonged in that same group of women who can love with artistry and without restraint, with Rachel and Isolde.

Olaf was at work in the barn when Luke Weller arrived. He was early, and Lillah met him alone at the kitchen-door. He knotted the reins about a poplar sapling and knocked the mud stolidly from his boots on the kitchen-step. Then he and Lillah looked a long moment at each other. Finally, she lifted her shoulders with quaint irony and smiled.

"It's no good, is it?" she said.

But Luke Weller's expression never changed.

"Do you cough much?" he asked. She shook her head.

"Not much. I feel pretty good." Again she stopped. "But it's no use hoping, really, is it?"

He refused to meet her question, and his eyes retreated, beaten.

"Well, I was invited here to-day," be blustered. "Aren't you going to ask me in?"

"Luke,"——she forced his eyes to meet hers again,

—"Luke, before he comes, tell me." It seemed in some way as though her eyes were the only things in the universe. "It's no use, is it? Tell me."

"Look here,"—he made a brave attempt at swagger,—"I'm no soothsayer. Besides, my job is full of miracles. Things happen all the time, amazing things. Not that I do them. They just happen."

"Luke——"

The swagger was all gone now. She was stronger than his will. Still her eyes held his with hypnotic earnestness.

"How much time do you give me?"

It was no use trying to evade her.

"Another six months," he said, "in this damn' climate."

She did not move, and her face did not change expression.

"Another six months." It did not seem that she was speaking to him. "That's a long time, a long time." Then at once she came down the steps toward him. "Luke,"—her fingers touched his sleeve, —"don't say anything to him. See? There's nothing he could do, and he's happy, and so am I. I feel fine, honest. Not weak or anything."

It was unbearable to face her pleading.

"He could send you West. Perhaps in Colorado ____"

She laughed suddenly, and the sound of her voice startled him.

"Send me! Luke, you're crazy. He's no bank president."

Luke Weller's eyes wandered to the jutting ell where old Swen Bjorkman lay.

"He could," he said, "damn him!"

Lillah Nelson's hand dropped to her side, and all the tension went out of her body.

"Well, I reckon that's out."

When Luke Weller left that evening, Olaf Nelson came out to the buggy with him. After the doctor had clambered in and Olaf had tucked the robes around him, he still held his hand on the driver's box. Luke Weller could not see his face, but he could feel his presence as distinctly as though he could watch every change of expression.

"I heard what you said to Lillah this afternoon," Olaf said finally.

Luke Weller knew the darkness covered his surprise.

"*He* told me when I took him in his supper."

"He told you?" A strange feeling seemed to lodge around Luke Weller's heart. And only this afternoon he had said that the world was full of miracles. But it was always terrifying to have one happen. "He did, eh?"

Again there was an interval of silence.

"He laughed, too." Olaf Nelson's voice had the dead level of one telling a monstrous tale he does not expect to be believed. "It's been a long time since I ever heard him laugh." Still he did not take his hand off the seat of Luke Weller's buggy, and yet it was by more than physical contact that Luke Weller was bound. Had he lifted his whip and lashed at his team, he had a conviction that they would not have moved until Olaf Nelson was willing to let him go. "Sometimes it seems to me"—Olaf's voice came as steady as a pastor's reading the lesson—"there can be nothing sinful in murder."

As Olaf walked back to the kitchen he did not hear the tell-tale click of the cautiously closed door. Lillah was standing in front of the stove when he entered, her hands behind her and her slim body struggling not to betray the agony of shivering.

Olaf walked over to her.

"You're cold."

She did not let him touch her.

"I—I just took the butter and eggs down cellar. It's no Palm Beach down there, you can bet."

Olaf's eyes narrowed; he was puzzled.

"Why don't you use the box in the pantry—like always?"

Lillah shrugged her shoulders.

"Oh, it don't matter, does it? Besides, I thought I heard the cat down there." She stopped, frightened lest she overdo the plausibility of her story. Then she turned toward him. "Olaf!"

He stood facing her, the light of the lamp behind him. Never had he seemed so large to her or of such potential strength. What if he really intended to do the thing he had hinted at to Luke Weller! "Olaf!"

She drew close to him, and her arms wound about his neck. He hadn't done anything yet, she thought. Perhaps she could still save him. "Olaf!" she repeated. His arms held her against him, but there was no passion of response in the gesture. He was not thinking about her. It was the first time Lillah had not been able to make him forget all the rest of existence in the joy of her body.

"Olaf," she said, "big goof, listen to me." She shook him sharply in an effort to concentrate his attention. "Olaf, sweetheart, do you ever think how many months we have been happy? What a long time there still is for us? Olaf,"—her hands swept over his hair and shoulders; she strained to him with every part of her mind and body,—"remember, we have been happier in one year than lots of people who live to be a hundred. Olaf, it isn't the years that matter. It's the moments."

He untwined her arms from about his neck and put her from him gently.

"Olaf!"

He could not see the terror in her face.

"Don't touch me," he said. "I don't want to think about you to-night. I don't want you to make me forget—something."

His words came slowly, but with terrible distinctness. For a long moment there was silence in the kitchen, and Lillah Nelson looked at the man who stood opposite her. For the first time she had been unable to control him with the hypnotism of her love. For the first time his will had been stronger than hers. She was beaten. In that moment Lillah Nelson accepted the inevitable.

"Olaf," she said at last, "you must go out and see the new calf." Her voice was calm. "Put down plenty of straw and cover it with gunny-sacks." He got up slowly to obey her. "While you are gone I will set the bread and then I think I'll—turn in."

Half an hour later, when he came back to the

kitchen, she was no longer there. Late that night, as he stared up into the blackness, it occurred to him that he had not noticed the big yellow bowl on the kitchen-table in which the bread-dough was always raised.

The next day Luke Weller made the same journey across the prairie from Black Cloud to Bjorkman's farm. It was winter again, as bleak as though yesterday's mocking promise had never been made. Luke Weller shivered, and closed the eyes of his mind against the gray sky and the level acres cheerless under the dirty snow.

Swen Bjorkman was dead. One of the Lenning boys had ridden in to tell him. Olaf Nelson had met Rudi Lenning on the way into town, and had asked him to fetch out the doctor. It was too late for the doctor, though. The old man was cold. Rudi Lenning reckoned no one would miss him and that it would be a good riddance. He said Olaf seemed sort of dazed, but he didn't seem sorrowful. Well, Lord knew he had no reason to mourn the old devil.

No one answered his knock, and Luke Weller pushed open the door into the kitchen. It was empty. Then he heard footsteps outside, and Olaf stood in the doorway, a pile of wood in his arms.

"You—" Olaf said. He still stood, as though all power of motion had left him.

"Yes, me." Luke Weller looked away from his eyes. "I—I suppose I had better look at your uncle." He put his medicine-bag on the table and attempted to appear casual.

"Yes," he said, "he's there. Where he's been for twenty years." Then suddenly he came forward. Olaf Nelson was a big man, but now, with the great pile of wood in his arms, he seemed like some character out of a Norseman's legend, some one fabulous and terrible and elemental. "If you don't understand it,"—his eyes indicated the room where the dead man lay,—"remember all the time I can explain."

Luke Weller closed behind him the door of the front room. He heard Olaf Nelson tumble the wood into the woodbox by the stove. Then he heard him cross the kitchen and close the outside door behind him. After a moment Luke Weller walked over and looked down into the face of Swen Bjorkman. He was dead, that was obvious, as dead as the Ptolemies. It looked as though it had happened easily; his fingers still touched the frayed edge of the quilt, and the bedclothes were smooth. Yes, it had surely happened without any struggle. Luke Weller bent over to draw down the blanket when the door from the kitchen was opened, and Lillah stood in the doorway. Her eyes were the color of iris, and her cheeks were white. She closed the door quickly behind her and came a step into the room.

"Where is he?"

"Olaf?"

She nodded.

"I don't know. Gone to take care of the animals, probably." Luke Weller came close to her. He was afraid she might fall.

"I'm all right." She held up her hand to ward him away. "I'm all right. I tell you I'm strong enough to take on somebody twice my size." Her eyes glittered strangely, and two spots now glowed on her cheeks. "You're all wrong about me, you and Olaf. I've got more strength than you take me for." Her eyes finally sought out the dead man. "More strength than he took me for. He said he would outlive me. He yelled it." Again she stopped, and her breath came in gasps. "Well, he didn't. He didn't. He's dead now, and I'm strong. He's dead now because he couldn't struggle against me. I did it. It was easy, honest. He didn't even whimper. Just one little squeak, and he was gone."

"Lillah!" Luke Weller was beside her now, and held her in his arms. He could feel the quiver of her body and the sobbing of her breath against his throat. "Lillah!" he repeated, "Lillah!"

"Olaf hasn't come near me all day. He won't even look at me. He don't know anything—definite. He's only afraid for me; and all the time he acts like he was the one that's guilty. But he ain't." Again she stopped. It took so much energy just to speak now. "He ain't. No matter what he says he ain't."

He carried her out of the room and up to her bedroom, and he covered her over with a blanket he found in the closet. Then he returned to his work. This was not the first autopsy Luke Weller had made. He was clever at that sort of thing. It was twilight when he went out to the kitchen, and Olaf Nelson had just lighted the kerosene-lamp on the table.

"Go get Lillah," he said; "I want to speak to both of you."

He wondered at first whether Olaf would obey him, and whether Lillah would. But she came. In the shadow-filled room Luke Weller faced them, and this time he knew Olaf would believe him.

"It was very simple," he said, "and understandable—a broken blood-vessel. Not unusual at all in this sort of case." He turned to Olaf, suddenly,

"You said he laughed yesterday, laughed heartily for the first time in years." Again he stopped. "Well, he paid for his joke. He paid for it." Luke Weller snapped his satchel together, and put on his coat. At the doorway he turned toward them; they had not moved from the table. "You know, I told you strange things happened sometimes, miracles. Well, this is one of them. You're free now, both of you. Free."

Lillah slipped her arm through Olaf's, and in her face was the peace of complete self-forgetfulness.

As he drove home that night under the starlight Luke Weller, too, was at peace. He had seen her for the last time, but he had held her once in his arms. She said he hadn't struggled any when it happened, old Swen. He had only given one little squeak, one little tiny squeak. He remembered Olaf with the pile of wood in his arms. Olaf would have done it differently, very differently. Lillah knew this, too. Both knew that this time Olaf Nelson would have taken a stand, and Olaf would have had so long a time to go on living.

Then Luke Weller remembered some pictures he had once seen of the Colorado mountains. They said the air was clear out there, and the sky was as blue as June's, and there were purple shadows in the gorges. They would get a cabin somewhere high up in the sunshine. There they could see the dawn turn the gray rocks to coral. They could watch the crimson ball of sunset and the first star come out of the blue beyond the ridges. Yes, a year, two years; that was a long time in which to be happy. A long time.

APRIL FLOODS

APRIL FLOODS

A CROSS the rusted looking, Minnesota prairie, where it seemed only yesterday the snow had lain, slanted the first warm rain of April. There had been other rains already that had eaten away even the ice drifts in the shadow of the river banks, but they had been as cold and as bleak as November. To-day's rain was fragrant and whimsical. Gustaf Franzen, trudging head down along the muddy path above the river, shut his eyes and breathed deep.

He thought suddenly of the little flower shops in Stockholm filled with rose trees for the Easter festival. He thought of the city pavements on a wet spring night dappled with shifting pools of silver from the street lamps and from the lamps of cabs. He thought of himself in one of those hansoms. He had been to the opera and he was on his way to the Norstedt's or to the Wenström's to smoke, to gossip, to rejoice indolently in a sense of deserved well being. Waldemar Norstedt's library was charming.

The tapestries had come from Italy, the great bronze candlesticks from Innsbruck. All of Stockholm foregathered there, professors, journalists, editors, scientists. How long ago it all seemed and how mercilessly clearly he could remember it.

He opened his eyes again and stared dully across the acres of Minnesota. Some of those acres belonged to him. If he worked very hard there might some day be more of them. Abrupt as a wart on a chin stood his wooden box of a house. It was bleakly ugly and still unpainted but it boasted storm windows and the flue in his stove was a good one. To the south lay a wide brown stretch sown to winter wheat, across which trembled a veil of green. West was his pasture, east the red painted barn, more pretentious than his house, the fenced in barnyard miry with the trampling of cattle, the huddle of machinery under the slanting roof of the shed. North was the river and the mill Olaf Swanson had started when he thought the railroad was coming that way. Nothing was left now but the dam and the race. The water was black and very deep in the flume where no wheel had ever turned. Gustaf Franzen had used the remnants of lumber from the mill for his sheds and fences. Gustaf owned land across the river too, but it was hard to get at, for the section bridge lay a half a mile down stream. When the water was low he could cross on the dam. Even now any one with steady nerves—and good luck—could effect a passage. In two weeks, even in one, the sluggish stream would have become a torrent plunging recklessly westward.

With the apathetic interest of a man dull with loneliness Gustaf looked across the river, then at once his eyes focussed. Some one was crossing on the dam. It was a woman, her short full skirt swirled around her by the wind. Her head was bare and she was bent forward to counterbalance the weight of something heavy in a bag she bore upon her back. Stooped as she was, Gustaf knew even at that distance she was young. Her shoes and stockings were off and she was making her way carefully but rapidly across the wet boards. The stream as yet carried little current. She would be safe enough until she reached the narrow, rotted plank above the flume. One false step there and she would be sucked down hopelessly into the black water. He was too far to shout to her, nor did he wish to startle her. With eyes narrowed to slits with intensity he waited.

She had reached the middle of the flume now, then she stopped and looked down into the pool of black water as innocent of danger as a child leaning over a garden fountain. Fear in Gustaf changed at once to anger. What a fool she was to take a chance like that. What was she doing there any way? Who was she?

Slipping along the mud of the path he raced to meet her. She had reached the bank now and stood, gravely regarding her bare feet, wet and streaked with mud. The bag on her back jerked and emitted shrill screams of terror. In spite of his anger Gustaf smiled. Suddenly she looked up into his eyes and a scarlet flush swept from her throat up to her temples. She was like a solemn child that has been caught at a boisterous game.

"Gee whiz," she said, "you come too damn quick." Gingerly she lowered the shrill burden to the ground. She was embarrassed but not awkward. It was only her eyes that pleaded for mercy.

Gustaf Franzen was no longer angry but he managed a show of severity. "You were a foolish woman to come across on the dam." He was speaking to her in Swedish and his eyes never left her face. "It is very unsafe, do you understand me, very unsafe. I forbid it."

Again she smiled up at him. She knew now that she had frightened him and that his severity was only the reaction from apprehension. "I am strong," she said, "and sure footed like a goat." Then after a moment of silence "I am from Walli Lenning's—with the pig you buy yesterday." Again she smiled up at him, shyly. "He is a very good pig," she spoke deliberately, "but too damn frisky to carry long way."

Gustaf watched her intently. She was probably younger than she looked, seventeen perhaps, for the peasant type develops early. Her shoulders were broad, her breasts low and her arms looked strong. He liked her low forehead, the gray eyes set far apart and the dark, straight brows that grew close above them.

Gustaf had been born an aristocrat but he resented suddenly the fact that this girl had been sent five miles across country afoot to deliver his pig. Walli Lenning was a swine himself to do such a thing. No man would have obeyed him. To walk five miles with that load. It was outrageous. Because Gustaf Franzen was angry with Sina's uncle he was brusque with Sina.

"Come into the house," he said, "and get warm. You're wet as an otter." She made a motion to resume her burden but he pushed her aside and swung the bag to his shoulder.

"Let me," she protested, "I am used to carry things."

He started to speak, then checked himself and walked on up the slippery bank, never looking back to see if she followed. At the kitchen door he stopped. "Take off your jacket here and dry it," he ordered, "and dry out your shoes before you put them back on. I shall take the pig around to the sty." He hesitated a moment and when he spoke again he did not look at her. "I shall drive you home."

For a second Sina stood motionless in the kitchen. It was a bare room, furnished as a room is only when a man is its sole occupant. The walls were still unceiled and the floor unpainted. In one corner stood the stove and piled at one end of it and thrust into the opened oven door were the utensils he used to cook with. A rough deal table stood against the wall, a chair was drawn up beside it and on the table were a knife and fork and spoon, from which the imitation silver plating had already chipped away, and a heavy white plate and a cup. Beside the stove stood a rocking chair, low hung and upholstered in carpet. The room was clean and sweet smelling with the fragrance of the white pine, but it possessed a bleak masculine untidiness. A pile of harness lay in one corner which he had evidently not finished mending. In another stood three lanterns, blackened with smoke and rusted. Unlike most homesteaders he did not sleep in his kitchen. Sina noticed that the door into the other room was closed.

She took off her coat and hung it on a nail near the stove, then she sat down in the rocking chair. Her feet were muddy and she would have preferred to wash them before she drew on the coarse wool stockings. But Gustaf Franzen might return any moment and she was embarrassed to be found bare footed. Many times in the old country she had worked barefooted in the fields with the men. Over here even she had taken her shoes off when she scrubbed the floors and she had never minded who saw her. Gustaf Franzen was different. His house, to be sure, was not better than the Lennings' or the Nelsons' or Swansons' and not nearly so gay inside. She even felt sorry for him, and then at once she smiled at her presumption. Who was she to pity a person like Gustaf Franzen?

Then she heard his foot-steps at the doorway and she stood up, shy and startled. An instant he looked at her.

"Oh," she said, "I take your chair. Forgive me."

This time it was on Gustaf's face that the slow

color mounted. "Child, don't be foolish. Sit down."

She knew some way that his brusqueness only covered embarrassment. "But I must go." She sat down gingerly. "Gee whiz, I can't keep old Grimpel waiting for the milking."

Gustaf Franzen replenished the fire. "You can't go before you are dry again." Then he drew up the other chair, filled his pipe and lit it. For a long moment there was silence in the kitchen. Gustaf did not look in her direction. He relit his pipe twice. At last he cast a quick glance at the woman beside him. Her head lay against the back of the chair and her body was relaxed. Without being observed he could look at her profile. There was a beautiful quietness about her. He liked the way her hands did not move in her lap. Her breath came evenly and her brow was serene. He wondered who she was. She was the first woman to step into his house since he had built it. Indeed she was the first woman with whom he had talked since he had come to the new country. Outside the twilight deepened against the panes of the windows. The bleakness seemed to go from the room with the evening. The only white in the place finally was her face, pale against the black of the chair.

At last she sat forward, "Gee whiz, it is late. I must get back for the milking."

Gustaf Franzen stood up. "Put on your shoes while I hitch up. I shall be back in a moment."

Sina looked up at him shyly. "It is bad going on the roads," she said. "The slew by Olsen's has overflew. You go up to the hubs in mud." She stopped helplessly, realizing she was not gaining her point. "That was why I walk over with the pig instead of one of the men bring it in the wagon."

Gustaf smiled at this defense of her employer's variety of sex discrimination. Women were meant to serve. That was the way the world was run.

On the way back to the Lenning's farm they journeyed a long time in silence. Finally Sina asked him about his crops. What would he do with the acres across the river? They would be good for grazing. Then she told him about the Lenning's and the cheeses she made. She was starting a garden too and perhaps she would have a border of *bläklint*. Olaf Nelson's cousin, who was coming over on the *Kung Oscar*, had promised to bring her some seeds.

When he let her down at the kitchen door he asked her if she would be in church Sunday at Black

Cloud and she told him she would. Gustaf Franzen had never, since he had come to the new land, been inside the church of his countrymen.

That night he sat for a long time in the darkness of his kitchen. He could go into the other room, of course, the closed door to which Sina had remarked. But he did not move. He remembered a dozen times how her face had looked against the back of the chair beside him. He remembered her hands in her lap. They were large hands with strong white fingers and the nails were worn short with labor. He remembered the hands of the women he had known back in his uncle's drawing room in the *Drattninggatan* in Stockholm.

It was cold in the kitchen now and the rain slanted sharp against the windows. Suddenly Gustaf dropped his face into his hands and he did not move. He could never go back. It seemed now he would never go forward. He was lonely, so lonely it was a physical ache—like a sickness.

On Sunday he saw Sina at the church. The next Sunday he called on Walli Lenning, her uncle, and in another seven days he and Sina were married.

Spring had come in earnest when he drove her home the evening of their wedding and the west was still warm with a reluctant, gold pink sunset.

Along the roadside the leaves of the aspens, full grown now but still of a fragile, transparent green, fluttered and whispered in the warm May twilight. It was a bleak country at noon, flat and bearing yet the scars of the fire that had swept across it twenty years ago. Against the sun still rose the charred trunks of the forest giants, gaunt and black as the crosses on calvary. The after growth of blueberry thicket and scrubby aspen had been allowed to follow only the roadways and the streams. Most of the land had been cleared for grazing and for wheat by the Swedish and Danish farmers who had homesteaded the region.

It was a lean soil, grudging and backward. The prodigal farmers of Illinois and Iowa would have held it land worthy only to raise brambles and squinties. But the peasant farmers from the Old World knew how to thrive even where the land was thinnest. Along either side of the railroad tracks, where the company had cleared a narrow margin of ground, they planted gardens of cabbages and onions and sowed the rest to timothy. They harvested too not in the careless, free handed manner of farmers no more than a hundred miles to the south. After the cocks of hay had been carried, high overhead like tattered banners, to the carts, the ground was reraked and recocked so that no strands of hay, like retreating lines of foam, still lay on the stubble.

They could not know how bitter their labor was for life in the Old World had been hard too. Only Gustaf Franzen realized the heart breaking unevenness of the struggle but he too had been caught in the net of circumstance. And now, surely, that he was married there existed no way out.

As they rode on toward the sunset he looked at her curiously. She still had on her wedding dress of white percale. It was stiff and awkward—like the first communion dress of a Bavarian brewer's daughter. Her hair had been ruthlessly crimped for the occasion, but it hung now in straight, thin strands against her warm forehead. She sat very quiet beside him, her eyes far ahead and her hands motionless in her lap.

"Sina——"

She looked up at him suddenly and her lips parted in a smile of pleasure because he had spoken. With timid persistence her eyes fastened his until he should finish.

"Did you have a good time then," he went on, "at the wedding?"

Her whole face lighted up like a child's. "Oh gee, yes." She spoke often in English. In Swedish she knew he remarked always her dialect. "It was good Cousin Rudi came in time, too, bringing the *torta*. It was just like old country with the *präst ost* and the spiced wine." She was silent a moment, her eyes watching the reins as they flopped up and down on the mare's broad back. "They will miss me, gee whiz, at the harvest. I am as strong as a man." Again she stopped and her eyes lifted to his gravely. "But I work for you this harvest, eh? And the next one? Maybe always—till you get rich and move down to Black Cloud?"

He looked away suddenly from the pleading in her eyes. He felt at once guilty and unconvinced of his guilt.

Again her eyes forced his to meet her. "You like me to do that?"

With a repentant gesture he put his arm around her and drew her face against his shoulder. "You are a stupid child," he admonished, "to make yourself so humble. Who am I but a 'Scandahoovian' farmer—and not so good a farmer as Walli Lenning at that. You are as much a person as I am." In a half guessed way he was building up a defense in his own mind against the Olympian regard in which she held him. It was not only unjustified but it was dangerous.

He bent his cheek against her hair. It was soft to his skin but he could smell the course soap with which she had washed it. As a rebuke to his æsthetic snobbery he touched the crimped strands with his lips.

Sina Franzen did not move, but her eye-lids lowered slowly over her grey blue eyes. It was cramped to lie there with her head drawn sharply against his shoulder, but it was a torture she would wish to endure through the eternity of a Swedish Lutheran heaven. The touch of his hand held a magic that left sensitized all of her body. No matter what the future brought there would always be this moment. Nothing could ever quite blot out that memory.

With a swerve the mare turned in at the farm house. The windows were black against the twilight and a bat, at their coming, was startled into its circling, ugly flight. They both looked at it but neither spoke.

"The bat is lucky, like the black cat if it comes of its own will to your house," she said finally. He knew some way she didn't believe this.

They drove the horse into the barn and she helped him unhitch, taking great care not to let the harness touch any part of her dress. It was done in a trice, the mare fed and watered and the sticking door rolled, almost shut, for the night.

As they walked back to the house their shoulders touched often. She was too shy suddenly to reach out toward him and he was moody and silent.

"Gustaf—" She stopped on the step outside the kitchen. "This is our house."

He smiled at her gravity. "Not as good even as your Uncle Walli's. After awhile," he grinned again, "you will grow accustomed to these frontier hardships."

"Oh gee," she said, "aren't you the fun maker." She had wanted to retort in kind—but this was all she could muster. Gustaf lighted the kerosene lamp on the table and she noticed his eyes were grave.

An instant they faced each other in the gloomy kitchen. There was so much she could do here. She could make it as gay as her uncle's, as the Swansons'. "What did you do with my box?" she said finally.

"In there." He pointed to the closed door.

"Our bed room?"

She threw back the door and he stood behind her with the lamp. It seemed empty at first, except for her box, a cheap bed of pine and a wash stand. Then she noticed the walls of the room. They were lined with books, dozens and dozens of them in orderly rows. Uncle Walli had had a Bible and an almanac and a book about dreams.

Curiously she crossed the room and drew a book out from the shelf. For a second she puzzled over it, turning the pages slowly. Finally she came back to the center of the room. "It is too dark to see the words there. I can't quite make it out." Again she studied the pages, turning them at first slowly and then in a frenzy of haste. "Gustaf," she said at last. "I can't read it. None. Not one damn word." She looked up at him with eyes of terror.

Gustaf Franzen smiled. "It is French."

A long moment she stared at him. "French," she repeated. "Oh, not Swedish or English."

He nodded.

"Can you read it?" she asked.

Again he nodded.

Slowly she looked away from him around the room. "And the other books?"

"German and Swedish," he said, "a little English. I am sorry now there are not more. I had never supposed I would have the same occasion to use English." He smiled again, grimly. "In those days I had never anticipated this departure for The States."

Very slowly again Sina's eyes came back to his face. "Where did you get those books?"

"Here and there." He shrugged his shoulders. "Most of them while I was at the university." He put the lamp down on the wash stand and drew a volume from the shelf above it.

"Gustaf——"

Instantly he turned around and looked down into her face.

"Gustaf, Gustaf——" Her arms were around him and she held him with a strength he had never suspected. At once their lips found each other and she kissed him with a desperate passion that knows neither fear nor embarrassment. His response to her was at once as reckless as hers. He did not suppose she could arouse in him, even for a moment, this strangling, primitive emotion.

"You do care. You love me." She spoke this time in Swedish, slurring her words together in the manner of her province. "Care for me—more than for these." Her arms were flung out in a gesture.

Again he seized her to him. It seemed to him she must cry out with the strength of his arms, with the hurt of his lips against hers. "I do." It was almost a sob. "I do."

The summers of the north are tropical and fierce and farmers have to labor with the frenzy of soldiers during an attack to keep abreast of nature. All in a day everything has burst into life. All in a day, too, comes the harvest with its anxiety of rains that rot the hay, of vicious thunder-storms following hot noons that turn the wheat sour, of early frosts that can bring to naught all the heart breaking labor of the summer.

Sina was right when she said Walli Lenning would miss her. But never had she worked on Walli Lenning's farm as she did on Gustaf Franzen's. Up every morning before sunrise she baked and scoured before it was time for the milking and the long labor in the fields. The kitchen was a different place now, bright with curtains of red calico and a scarlet cover for the rude deal table. She was happy in the kitchen. The room with the books she never entered except when she had to.

All day she was silent and contented. Evenings sometimes she and Gustaf discussed the farm. But they were too tired to talk much. Mostly they sat on the kitchen step in silence, watching the twilight change the bleakness into gentleness and mystery. Over head there sometimes curled a flock of swallows, venturing away on long sorties only to return to the eaves of the red barn. Gustaf looked at them sadly and each time he wondered whether he should ever wander even as far as they did. But he was too fatigued to speculate long. Always as soon as the twilight had faded they went to bed.

After the first frost comes Indian Summer. This is the glory of the whole year in the north land. The birch and cottonwood leaves turn yellow, the sun seems closer, some way, to the earth but its warmth is kind and the twilights are long and refreshing.

One Friday in October Gustaf drove into Black Cloud. He told Sina there were things he must buy, wire, new tugs for the wagon and she ordered him to bring back sugar and coffee and flour. It was all bought at one store and not until after he had fulfilled every duty did he go back to the partitioned off cubby hole that was labelled post-office.

"Is there anything for me?" he asked finally.

"A package." Mark Dick stooped down and lifted something heavy onto the shelf before him. "Looks like it come all the way from 'Scandahoovia'," he gossipped. "Thirty-nine cents due."

Gustaf Franzen paid it and loaded all his bundles into the wagon. The package he placed on the driver's seat beside him and he glanced at it often. What a fool he was to go on caring. Why couldn't he sever every emotional tie that bound him to the old life as he had every physical one? He could never go back—anyway not for years and years. He was poor. He was married and the woman who bore his name was a farmer and the daughter of peasant farmers. He had bolted a door behind him and thrown away the key. Why should he go on dreaming he should one day find the same door open? It was unintelligent to torment himself longer with memories. He was a fool and a coward. He would stop.

And at once he dreamed back to the old days at the university when he had planned to become a writer, when his first story had been accepted. How young the world had been then and how credible every miracle. El Dorado lay just around the next corner—and he was certain to pass by that way.

As he rounded the turn below Christian Bridge the mare started at something and swerved to one side of the road. Gustaf was startled into ill temper. Then he noticed the woman who stood by the road side. She wore a suit of dark blue, too warm for the day, and her shoes were covered with dust. She was carrying a small black bag which was also dust covered. He saw that her face was pale and oval, the forehead narrow and the chin small and rounded. She made him think of an old picture he had seen once in Florence. The paint had faded and the canvas had been maltreated—but the eyes persisted.

A long moment they stared at each other.

"I'm sorry I startled you," she said finally. "After all, is it such an anomaly to walk in this country?"

A red flush mounted under his bronzed skin. "I think it is rather." He was speaking in diffident English. "But more of an anomaly that you should use that word."

She smiled. "I don't know why I did. I was sorry the moment I said it." She shrugged her shoulders. "Perhaps I thought that you wouldn't understand English and that it wouldn't matter."

Gustaf Franzen hesitated a moment. "Let me take you the rest of the way. It is still too hot for walking."

She sensed at once the eagerness that lay behind his reserve. "You are very kind." He was beside her in a moment, he lifted in the little black bag and then he helped her over the dusty wheel.

"It's affectation to treat this costume with so much respect," she said. "Look at it. I've come all the way from Minneapolis to-day on the day coach."

Then after a moment. "I'm Jeanne de Royer, the new country school teacher."

Again he looked at her speculatingly. He felt no longer shy but he was curious and he knew his interest would cause her no embarrassment. "Oh yes, this democracy prides itself on its rural schools," he said, dryly. "It is so stated in the geographies back in my country."

She smiled at his raillery. "You are a man of great reading." Then she looked at him with the same intentness with which he had studied her. "I am going out to Olaf Swanson's," she said. "I'm to be boarded there it seems. He did not meet me at the train. After all, I am only a woman and a teacher—third class."

"Olaf Swanson's is not out of my way," he said— and then he wondered at once why he had lied to her. What if it was out of his way, was it not his duty to drive her there? Instantly too he knew the reason for his falsehood. He would want to see her again and he would wish the meeting to appear casual, unpremeditated. "You have never taught before?"

She shook her head. "Without influence, or luck, you can't get a city school until after you have had rural experience. I've got to earn a living—and fellowship beggars can't be choosers. I've another year at the university ahead of me." After a moment she looked up at him narrowly. "How strange that I should be telling you all this. How strange that you should be here at all. You're not the type of Swede I expected." She stopped, embarrassed at her frankness. "Don't misunderstand me, please. And don't think I am trying to invade your confidence." Then she laughed softly. "I am, of course. What woman doesn't try to explore any man who interests her?"

Gustaf Franzen smiled down at her. "And what man would not be disappointed not so to be explored?"

Suddenly her eyes focussed on something ahead and her brows drew together in a line. "That—" she pointed, "is Olaf Swanson's."

He followed her gesture to the unpainted house. They had dug a cave in which to store the butter and cheese and the earth was still scarred with the excavating. Chickens wandered about, even in and out of the open front door, and a pig nosed along in the weeds beside the boarded up mud foundation. He could feel her body tremble and he heard the half sob that escaped her lips. He too understood the desperation she must feel at its loneliness and squalor. Without thinking what he did his hand reached out and closed over hers.

"It isn't so bad, really," he said. "You get used to it. You do, indeed." He was amazed at the conviction his voice had taken on.

"Used to it," she repeated and her voice was thin with scorn. "But I'm young now. Things matter to me." Her face was white with rebellion. "What have I done to be banished to this—but be poor? Is poverty such a sin?" She had been caught unawares and her outburst was the cry of a child that has been hurt. In an instant she had control of herself. "I'm sorry. Forgive me. It isn't your fault."

He got out and helped her again over the dusty wheel. There was no sound from the house. The Swansons were at work in the barn or the fields.

"Good-bye," he said. She put her hand in his. "Remember—if it gives you any satisfaction—there are two of us."

It was a long moment before she answered. "I shall remember it," she said, gravely, "but I don't think it's the better part of wisdom."

That evening they sat as usual on the doorstep. Sina looked up at him often when she thought he would not notice. He was a handsome man, different from the other Swedes because his features were clean cut and narrow.

"Gustaf—" She stretched out her hand toward him and touched his sleeve. "It seemed a long time you were gone to-day, gee whiz. But I bring in all the tomatoes and cabbage. And I go across to the cows in the pasture. Brindle's neck is almost cured now where she cut it, big old fool." She waited a moment. "The salve I make up is not bad, eh?"

He could not look around some way into her face. "Sina," he said finally, "did you cross over by the dam?"

She slipped her hand into his and her fingers pleaded for mercy.

"Sina——"

She leaned her head against his shoulder with the same wordless appeal as a whipped shepherd dog that wheedles around the legs of his chastiser.

"It is not dangerous for me," she said, "and it is so long a walk clear by the bridge."

Gustaf knew this was so. He was sorry for her suddenly. Her life was harder than his—and if there should be children!

"Gustaf," she said again. "I won't do it if you say not to." She wanted to tell him she would give her life rather than displease him. She wanted to tell him that his glance was more to her than all the warmth of summer, that the magic of his touch had only grown more potent as the months had passed. She wanted to tell him she yearned toward him as the winter wheat does toward the sun of April. "Gustaf," she said at last, "there were lots of rotten ones among the cabbages, no good for keeping, so I give them to the pigs."

While Sina was undressing Gustaf opened the package in the kitchen. There were two of Anatole France in it, an Ibsen, a copy of Bergsen. He fluttered the leaves slowly. They had cost him fifteen dollars. He was crazy, like the man who dropped dead from hunger standing at the opera.

Then he thought of the girl with the eyes like the Florentine painting. Outside a hoot owl called into the silence, and the night wind drew into the open door bringing with it the smell of dusty leaves and wood smoke and the damp low fog of autumn. Well, he would not anticipate. She would be here, whether he saw her or not. He felt suddenly the richness of a man who decides not to go to the opera but to sit at home and smoke his pipe. He felt less lonely to know there was some one who could dispel his loneliness—even though they should never meet.

On a Sunday early in November he and Sina drove into Black Cloud to church. Already the ruts in the road were stiff with the frost and the country was ragged where the harvest had been made. Over the pastures stood yet long stalks of copper colored weeds that rattled against each other. Sina wore a shawl of grey homespun over her head and her lips were blue with the chill. On her lap she held the hat she would put on just before they should drive into town. The straw was rose colored and faded and it was trimmed with a wreath of cotton cherries interspersed with porcupine quills. Gustaf remembered the first time he had seen it. It was as though some one had struck him. But, curiously, it seemed to him he had never seen her face so lovely. She was like a child that has been dressed up for a prank and is being jeered at by its tormentors.

"Swell," she had said, "you like him?"

Gustaf had looked away from her eyes. "I like you," he had answered.

To-day he looked down at the ghastly thing on her lap and at the hand that held it there. How hard she had worked. Her hand was the hand now of a woman of forty,, muscular, already a little cramped, with blackened, work ruined nails. But her face was still young. He remembered a girl on his uncle's estate back in Sweden. They had mouths alike, large, slightly opened and with a gentle short upper lip.

"Sina," he said, "are you happy?"

She smiled up at him. "Yes." Then after a moment. "It has been a good harvest."

"A good harvest," he repeated to himself.

Sina Franzen had not the gift of speech but she was not without her intuitions. He had asked her whether she was happy because she knew that he wasn't. She knew even before he did that he was playing a losing game against contentment. To her it was like a mother's knowledge that a child has within it the germs of a fatal malady. But the hours had not yet run out of the hour-glass. Sina Franzen hoped for no miracle. She belonged to a people that was used to the rigors of fate—but for the hours that still remained she could love him. After all, she had already been a long time happy—eight months now. And some of that time had been ecstasy.

"Look at Olaf Swanson's field," she said. "It is as though the pigs had rooted it."

In church Gustaf knew the girl from Minneapolis sat behind him. One Sunday in the month the minister spoke in English. This was the Sunday.

Gustaf wondered what she was thinking of the pastor's naïve acceptance of every Evangelical incredibility, of his unmasked satisfaction in the wrath to come. Sina listened with childlike gravity. Gustaf wondered how much she believed of this—or whether she was thinking about the winter wheat and the weasel that had gnawed a way into the chicken coop and the coyotes that beset the nomadic flock of turkeys.

Gustaf supposed the new teacher must know by this time that he was married, that she must also know the kind of girl he had chosen as his wife and yet, somehow, he disliked the thought that she was looking at the two of them together, speculating, explaining to herself with a smug feminine superiority the none too exalted motives that had driven him into this marriage. Well, let her wait until she had spent a winter here. She didn't know yet what tortures of loneliness a northern winter was capable of.

After church they came face to face in the narrow entryway. Sina stood beside him and he knew that her eyes were fastened on the stranger's.

"How do you do?" Jeanne de Royer said. Then after a second, "It is a great treat to be told occasionally of what feats of vengeance the Christian religion is possible. You Norsemen are still worshipping your Thor and your Wodan." Her mouth held an elf-like malice.

Gustaf knew she was tantalizing him deliberately and he was not unflattered. "Our deities are not so worldly as the Gods of you Normans," he retorted, for Jeanne de Royer was Canadian French. Their eyes held each other as though they alone stood in the crowded vestibule. Then he turned to the woman beside him. "Miss de Royer," he said, "this is my wife."

The two women shook hands in silence. Then the girl in the blue suit turned back to Gustaf. "Country school teaching," she said, "is nothing to write home about." Her words were spoken lightly but her eyes belied them. He could see already the look of desperation. She was caught too, just as he had been. "Oh, will the winter be long?" she asked finally. He was not sure afterward whether she had spoken or whether he had read the question in her eyes.

And the winter was long. By the end of November the snows had set in. The young men who went north to the logging camps had already departed. In the town of Black Cloud the snow lay two feet deep and the woodland roads were impassable. But across the prairie it had drifted. Here and there lay great barricades of snow, writhing and twisting across the meadows.

Life on a winter farm is stagnation, varied with arduous tasks. The path to the barn must be kept open even during the blizzards, the stock must be watered and fed, the stove must be kept filled with fire-wood. Over the windows formed a fuzzy blanket of frost that would not go away until February. Sina, idling away the short twilight, made an intricate series of chains by pressing her wedding ring against the white dampness.

Four times that winter Gustaf saw Jeanne de Royer, once by chance in the village. Once, when it was his turn to distribute the mail along the Christian Bridge road, he brought her a letter at the school house. It was after school when he arrived but she was still sitting at the desk. The air in the room possessed the frugal warmth generated by human bodies and carefully guarded against outside freshness. He noticed her face was pale and there were shadows under her eyes.

"You don't get exercise enough," he said bluntly.

She regarded him a moment. "No, I suppose not. But I can't seem to face striking out into that terrible prairie alone. It puts you so on the defensive."

She was embarrassed at her confession. "Do you know what I mean?"

"Yes."

He picked up a book on her desk. "Mistral—" His face glowed with interest.

"Yes," she said. "I'm working for my thesis."

"I've got the other volume," he said.

"Oh——"

He looked at her an instant. "Friday I drive into the village again for the new harrow. I will bring you the book on my way back."

It was seven days till Friday, seven days whose monotony had taken on new significance, seven days that were made longer because of that brief moment at the end. They were both too well disciplined to yield to the temptation of creating their meeting in anticipation. A hundred things might happen to prevent his coming. She was a fool to set so much store by the half hour they would be together. Something would surely happen. But on Friday he came.

It was after school and the room was deserted. As he pushed open the door the wind carried in with him a thousand sparkling flecks of snow dust. Overhead the sky was as blue as July's and the air was a heady tonic.

"I brought the books," he said, "and something else." He pointed to the doorway.

"Snow shoes——"

For a long moment they looked at each other. They were like truant children on a school day. It was unsafe to make a comment. Words might give the episode a significance they could not face.

"Let's——" she said.

It was twilight when they returned to the school house. The paleness had gone from her cheeks and her eyes were the color of iris.

"Shall we hide them here," he said, "behind the birch pile in the wood-shed?"

She nodded. It meant then he would come some day again.

"Good night," she said.

"Good night."

They had not even shaken hands.

In two weeks he returned. It was a day in February when one begins to imagine the snow will one morning be gone from the hillsides and in the black soggy earth will be violets.

For a long time they walked in silence on the path that led to the birch grove above Christian Bridge. One could get into quite a glow with the going and on the edge of the wood they waited a moment for breath. Below lay the fields that belonged to Gustaf Franzen, level and snow covered through which twisted the moonstone blue of the frozen river. Up the river he could see the dam where he had first encountered Sina. How long ago that too seemed now.

"Tell me," she said at last, "why you are here."

It was the first time he had ever recounted the story, the political intrigue in which he had become involved at the university that had ended in his expulsion, in his being cast off by his uncle, whose ward he was, and finally in the diplomatic insinuation by the government that the land of opportunity lay in the New World.

It had come at the beginning of a promising career and it was a punishment over severe in comparison with the crime. But the memories of the '48 revolutions on the continent, all of which had been bred within the universities, did not lead a monarchial government to look leniently upon the electoral reforms blatantly promulgated by a group of university students. Bitter, disgraced and without money Gustaf had come to the States and he had followed the trail of his countrymen away from the sea coast and down the Great Lakes to the land they had wrung from the forest, to the homesteaded farms of Minnesota and Wisconsin and Michigan.

Jeanne de Royer looked down on the acres Gustaf Franzen had broken to the plow. How curious the two of them should be here. Then with a giddy lightness of relief she knew this desolation could not last for ever. She at least could go back.

"In three months it will be spring," she said, "and I shall be gone." She had only half intended to wound with her remark. Woman-like she wanted him to discover in advance whether he was going to miss her and she wanted also to discover how much she cared to have him care.

They walked back to the school house in silence. There were many things she had wanted to discuss with him about her work. He was better informed than the professor under whom she had studied. There was much too he had treasured up during those weeks to say to her. He had begun a translation of "Blades of Grass" into Swedish. He wanted to explain to her why the great Russians translated better into German than into English. She was the only link he possessed between a past that had taken on a fantastic blessedness and a present as bleak as the fields before them. Had Gustaf Franzen lived only a few years longer in the

old life he might have known in it either success or
failure. The torment lay in a banishment that had
come too soon.

Even in the new land he might go on with the
career he had dreamed of. Other strangers had
come to these shores and had learned to write
English in a way that demanded the esteem of the
most jealous of Anglo-Saxons. In Minneapolis he
might find something at the university or on one of
the newspapers. After the first step it would not be
difficult. What a fool he had been to come out to
Minnesota just because his countrymen had come
here, because he had been shy of his English. Because he had believed every man's hand was against
him. It was not too late now to make a start.

At the school house gate he said good-bye. It
was never easy to leave her and he did it awkwardly,
even rudely, and he tried not to think of her face
as she stood there in the twilight on the dreary trek
homeward. So she was leaving in the spring. Well,
he was too. He could sell the farm to Olaf Swanson for enough to take Sina and himself to Minneapolis. He would not have to take the first job that
offered. He would have enough to live on for a
month or so—if they were careful. He was young
yet. It was ridiculous to stay on here in this back-

water. All the way home he forced himself into a
passion of conviction. There were letters he could
get from friends in Sweden to persons of influence
here. What a fool he had been to have bungled so
at the beginning. Well, there was still time to
change.

When he reached home he hurried out to the cow
barn. He would be late with the milking and he set
about unhitching the horse with a guilty haste.
Down in the basement where the cows were kept
there shown a pale radiance. At the bottom of the
ladder steps Gustaf stopped. Sina had preceded
him and the task was all but finished. She was at
work now on the last cow, her temple pressed against
the beast's side, her strong hands working with
rapid evenness at the udders. She glanced up at him
and a look of shy tenderness softened the gravity of
her face.

"Old Hilda holds up to-night on the milk," she
said. "It is the weather."

He entered the stall and looked down at her.
How broad her shoulders were and her hips. She
had gotten stouter since they had been married and
more muscular. Her clothes smelt of the barn and
her shoes and her hair. It was impossible that it
should be otherwise. She had labored for him like

a hired man and she had done a woman's work in the house beside. Her face too had changed he thought. It was more mature, graver and there was a look in the eyes he had seen in the eyes of pioneer women who have had children die in their arms forty miles from the nearest doctor.

"Sina," he asked her a second time, "are you happy here?"

She lifted the pail of milk safely out of reach of the animal's heels but she did not get up from the low stool. It was a long moment before she answered and he saw she chose her words with difficulty.

"I am used to work like I suppose would kill the women you knew back in the old country." She held out her hands before her and looked at them. "I am strong. I like animals and hay and to walk in the black mud behind the plow." Again she waited a moment. "I am not smart like—like the new school teacher. I am afraid of folks, even the folks in Black Cloud. But I am not afraid of cold or the heat of August when strong men flop down in the fields like babies. It is harder for you. But for me it is easy—like breathing." She spoke very slowly. "I could, I think, not breathe in any other place."

He picked up the pail of milk and he followed her out of the barn, through the twilight and into the house. Well, it was settled. There was no use dreaming any longer of a miracle.

After supper they still sat at the kitchen table. It was getting late, almost seven o'clock. "This spring," she said, "you buy from old Larson some more land across the river. It is better than here, eh?"

He nodded but he did not answer.

Sina scraped the remnants from the supper plates into a crock for the chickens. "Gustaf," she said, and she came toward him, the crock still held against her side, "I know what you mean by happy. When you came it was like a spring that sets in in April after the winter has been hard." Again she stopped and she shifted her weight awkwardly, embarrassed before him. "Gustaf," she repeated, "I am grateful. See? For that April even though the winter should set in in October."

The snow went early that spring and before they knew it farmers were plowing and planting, pasturing the cattle out in the open, mending fences and bridges. Gustaf like all the rest was up before daybreak and he worked with a panic of haste not only because there was much to do but because it was easier to drive back the tortures of longing when one was all day too busy to think and at night too weary. Gustaf was a better farmer than he used to be. He was learning. Some day he would be prosperous. Some day. Well, there were many whose lot in life was less pleasant than his. Sina watched him often when he did not notice but she seldom spoke. There was nothing to talk about.

Jeanne de Royer he determined never to see again. In six weeks she would be gone, in a month, in two weeks. With a subconscious accuracy of which he was only half aware he kept track of the days. Once the thought came to him she might be gone already and it seemed for an instant his heart had stopped beating. Well, it was better so. They would be to each other only a torment and the pleasure in it was not worth the pain.

Late one afternoon in May Gustaf came back from the wheat field to work in the garden. It was going to rain soon and he wanted to get the sweet corn and cabbage seeds in before the deluge. Sina had gone across the river to inspect the cattle and he hoped she had noticed the black clouds to the west. Yes, it would surely rain fiercely inside of an hour.

As he trudged along the path toward the house he was startled by the sound of a horse's hoofs. Some one was driving in at the gate. It was Jeanne. "You." He ran toward her, at once as gay as a school boy. "I thought you had gone." It was a gasp of relief as crude as it was unexpected.

From the driver's seat she looked down at him. She had on the same suit she had worn that first day he had seen her and the small blue hat that fitted close to her delicate, beautifully modelled head. She was lovelier even than he had remembered her.

"Gone," she said and her eyebrows lifted in quaint sarcasm, "and bearing off with me all these books of yours?" She pointed to the pile on the seat beside her. "Oh, Mr. Franzen, you do me an injustice." For a long moment they stood looking at each other. It was enough some way that the other one was near.

"Won't you come in?" he said finally. "You must be stiff after the long drive." He hesitated an instant. "My wife will return shortly." How blunt and ill-bred it sounded, like a servant's intrigue. "She went across the river to see the cattle. She is as clever as any stockman in this part of the country."

Jeanne de Royer stood up and he helped her over the wheel. "Thank you."

They faced each other a moment undecided. "Show me your books," she said finally.

She followed him into the kitchen and he opened the door Sina always hesitated to enter. They did not close it, nor had they the outside door of the kitchen. They had nothing to hide.

"Oh—" An instant she looked around her, her eyes bright with curiosity and surprise. "I didn't have any idea. I thought you might have brought over a dozen or so, not all this wealth." She walked about the room, touching the books with her fingers, opening one here, reading a name plate, an inscription. Suddenly she turned toward him. "You can never be lonely, can you?"

A long moment they stared at each other.

"Yes."

He had not meant to speak but her question had startled him into honesty. At once she could see in his face all the hunger and longing any effort of will could no longer fight down. He was old suddenly, old with the sense of defeat that foreshadowed the battle.

Outside the storm had come but they did not notice. Jeanne de Royer looked away from his eyes but Sina Franzen, in the kitchen doorway, watched his face as a mother watches the face of a child.

They had not heard her enter, for already the noise of the wind rocked the house.

"I know——" Still Jeanne de Royer did not meet his eyes. "I know." Then suddenly she turned toward him, her own eyes black and her whole body tense with emotion. "But why should it be this way? What have you done to be banished off here? It's cruel and it's unintelligent. You've got everything, youth and background and ability. You could go a long way, I know it. You could be a great person some day." She made a little desperate gesture with her arms. "Oh, you're a fool to defeat yourself this way. It's only a half life you're leading, a shadow life, full of heartbreak and loneliness."

"Jeanne——" He seized her wrists and they stood there breathless, their eyes burning into each other. "Jeanne," he repeated, "why do you say these things? Don't you know they cut like a lash?"

Still her eyes never faltered. "They're the truth." Then at once the tension went out of her body and her eyes were no longer defiant. "Oh, Gustaf, they're the truth," she repeated. "I know it—because I love you."

Sina Franzen crept out of the kitchen and closed the door softly behind her. Already the rain drove across the prairie in great slanting sheets. It was the first fury of a spring storm. After a while it would settle down into a gentle patter full of low, pleasant noises and the prophetic smell of new grass and blossoming woodland.

Sina drew a deep breath and closed her eyes. For a long time she stood there. Yes, spring had come early this year. She knew how the ground felt as it soaked up the downpour. The beasts out in the fields liked it too. Slowly she walked away from the house. It was like the caress of gentle fingers as it fell upon her hair and her cheeks and her shoulders.

As she passed the barn she saw that the gate to the chicken coop was drawn closed. The old weasel had been busy again there. Then she went on down the path across the field. At last she stopped and a smile crossed her lips. It was here that she had first seen him and how ridiculous she had looked in her bare feet and with the grunting pig in the sack on her back. She remembered too how he had looked. He had been angry with her for crossing over the dam. How handsome he had been and how her heart had beat because he had been disturbed enough to be angry. How handsome he still was.

The water in the flume looked black as night and the river was high this year. No one but a fool would think of trying to cross now by the dam. Surely, no one but a fool. And still, with the storm coming on, one might easily imagine she had tried to take that desperate short cut to safety. Yes, one might easily imagine.

JOHNNY GERALDY

JOHNNY GERALDY

JOHNNY GERALDY was born in one of those nameless lumber villages up along the St. Lawrence. His father was a Frenchman, powerfully built, as the Frenchmen in the colonies seem often to be; blunt, unimaginative, of tremendous physical endurance. Cold meant nothing to him, nor heat, and hunger, fatigue, and loneliness were unchallenged parts of normal existence. He was the true type of pioneer that nothing can hurt because nothing can cut through the callous of his commonplaceness. Marie Tremont, whom he married, was of another planet. The pioneer endures the present because he never projects it into to-morrow. He never sees the future as more days of heartbreak and loneliness, even as to-day and yesterday. It is not that he is doped with optimism; he is simply of the temperament that does not torment his imagination with a hundred baleful chimeras.

Marie Geraldy was afraid of the wind in the forest, the hoot of the night owl, of the evil spirit that made the flame flicker in the lantern and the puncheons creak even when no one stepped upon them. During the long days when she was left in the cabin she conjured up calamities that might overtake her: the timber wolves might come, a marauding band of Indians, fever; but most often of all that ghost that stalks by every woodsman—fire. A thousand times she would start up from her sleep at night with the smell of wood smoke in her nostrils, only to discover it was a phantom a dream had invented.

When she knew she would have a child a new dread possessed her. She was afraid, not for herself or because of the agony of pain that awaited her, but for the new life that was to be born into this wilderness, to be oppressed as she had been, perhaps even to be destroyed.

Johnny Geraldy grew up to look like his father. His shoulders were broad and his hands were large and his eyes were set far apart. Physically he resembled the other chaps in the country. They were strapping fellows, as acceptant of hardships as the average man is of comfort. He could swing an ax along with the best of them; he could trek the long miles to the northward when the cold froze a man's beard to the rough wool of his woodsman's jacket, and when the sky at night held the eerie magic of northern lights. True, Johnny Geraldy was the son of a pioneer, but he was also the son of his mother, who was afraid when the puncheons creaked and who woke up at night with the smell of wood smoke in her nostrils. As the peasant people say it, Johnny Geraldy was marked.

In a country where physical prowess is the touchstone of a man's existence it is, indeed, a curse for a man to suspect himself of being a coward. Johnny Geraldy looked so much like the others that he hoped none of them guessed the secret that made him a man apart. He hoped nothing would ever happen that would make patent to all the world the thing that was so pitifully known to him. He hoped that some kindly angel would lay out his path in safety and protect him from ever revealing this thing that to him was more obvious than the yellow sun of midday and the moon at night.

He prayed that the saints might spare him from any crisis where a man must make an instant decision, where a moment unwittingly reveals him for all that he is and hopes and tucks under—for the man that his fellows see walking about and joking and lighting his pipe, and the man that sleeps underneath that can make a fool or a knave of the other, or can make of a commonplace fellow for one little moment a god.

One of these moments came to Johnny Geraldy the first fall he went up ahead of the loggers, the summer of the drought.

It was the last of October, and Devil's Creek licked its way like a tongue of fire between the banks. It was difficult to remember how, after the spring rains set in, the creek became a river down which the Tamarac Lumber people floated the winter cut to the mills at Pierre Fonds. It was easy business then, for the floods of April buried deep the boiling current with its treacherous pulls and eddies and the deadly bowlders. But till the rains came there was never a man who could run that stream in a boat. Rumor had it there had once been an Indian who had shot down the creek at sundown; old Jacques Morceau saw him, but, as Jacques said, it was sundown, and the Indian might, after all, have been only a log. Funny thing, but a log could often make the trip in safety without being either sucked under by the current or tossed ashore or up on to the rocks when it struck the white water.

"It's the devil's own creek," said Jacques Morceau, "and whoever would run it safely must first give his soul over outright—and then never lift a paddle."

That seemed to be the way of it, but what man would have the courage to sit stark in his canoe and trust even to the Angel Gabriel to lead him over the rapids and safe to the lake at Grandes Forêts, where the Devil's Creek smoothed out?

Grandes Forêts was the outfitting village from which the Tamarac Lumber crew set out. This they left every fall in November, when the first heavy snows were in, and they did not come back until April, when they floated the black logs down to Pierre Fonds.

Perhaps Grandes Forêts was no El Dorado for a man to return to, but it sat in a little clearing, and when the sun shone it found it. It was not forever choked under by the gloomy blanket of pines. In Grandes Forêts there were stores and saloons and a church. One could be almost warm in Grandes Forêts and just as drunk as he pleased. Every man had a sweetheart there, and there were dances sometimes in the tavern where old Jacques played the fiddle—played it very fine indeed.

Every man ached to get back home to a pretty face and a home-cooked stew and as much applejack as he wanted. Even Johnny Geraldy dreamed, though he had never breathed a word to Jeanne Beaumont. But he had watched her through the mass, and she had known his eyes were watching. He had watched her at the tavern, and she had laughed more brightly into the eyes of some other fellow to make Johnny sick with longing for her sweetness. This narrow creek would take him home as fast as though a man had learned to fly—and yet no white man dared to venture on it, and Jacques Morceau's Indian probably had been a log.

Before he tramped back that night to the shack, where the stew was cooking, he strolled down the trail to the water. In a thicket of cedar, in the lee of a shelter, stood a slender birchbark canoe. Johnny Geraldy glanced at it idly. He wondered whether it would not be safer in the cabin. Not for six long months could a man use it. It would be sure death now. Oh, well, he would bring it up to-morrow. Then he trudged along back to the shack. The room was heavy with wood smoke, for the flue in the fireplace was a bad one. Johnny hated the smell of wood smoke, even smoke from a tame old fireplace with three men to watch it. It made him feel strange and ill, and his heart stumbled fast in his breast—but, then, that was because he was marked.

This was the first year that Johnny Geraldy had come up early. It was a promotion, of course, to be made cruiser, to be sent on ahead to blaze the tract that would be cut that winter. It was a matter of some responsibility and prestige; it brought in more money. Many a man had envied Johnny, and said so openly, but Johnny did not envy himself.

It meant going up alone into that forest, hearing all day and all day the sound of the wind in the branches. It meant never seeing the sun; it meant being hemmed in by the black trunks of trees, black regiment of guardsmen in a silent army. It does terrible things to a man if he's not forest-broken. Only a tough fiber can stand up against it. Jean Rébolt was a good woodsman because he was a dullard, and Peter Lafferté because he was a devil-may-care and a swashbuckling fellow. Johnny was neither of these, and he would have wished to be either—even Rébolt, whom children pushed in the street and made fun of.

At the company shack in the timber Jean and Peter joined him. They had come up ahead with provisions, brought arduously over the narrow trail northward that the deer had worked into the under-brush. They brought him news of the village: how the wheat crop was fair, and Rudi Agatin was better of the fever, and how old Jacques Duval was having all the village in to revel at the tavern one night before the loggers were to leave.

"To-morrow it is," he said, "and a fine affair it will be too, with Jacques to play for the dancers and plenty to drink when a man gets hot with his jigging around."

Johnny Geraldy had gone once to this party. Old Duval ran the tavern, and one night each year he stood host to the village. It was the great affair of the season. The girls bought new ribbons to wear on their dresses, and the boys knocked the mud from their boots and brushed their hair down sleek above their temples. Jeanne Beaumont would be there, he knew, and he could see how her eyes would sparkle and red spots glow on her cheeks.

"A curse to be here in the timber that night," Peter Lafferté said. He threw another log of pine into the fire and watched how the flame sprang up to meet it, and how the needles writhed back in the heat. "That's the way the whole woods would go to-night if a spark was to touch them," he said. "The trail up is slippery with needles and dry as tinder. Whoof"—he said—"with a breeze it would be a fine thing to lay eyes on, a fine thing indeed."

They ate their supper on the rough deal table, bent over their stew, their faces only half clear to each other in the heavy light of the lantern. Jean Rébolt kicked a log on the hearth. "She will smoke to-night," he grumbled, "for the wind's from the east."

Then they rolled their blankets around them and lay down in the narrow bunks to sleep. In a twinkling there was no sound in the shack except the deep, even breathing of healthful fatigue and the soft falling of ashes on the stones of the hearth. . . .

Johnny Geraldy never knew what time it was when he was awakened. He only knew that suddenly he was sitting bolt upright, his heart pounding like a woodchuck in a trap, his eyes staring full into the darkness, and the smell of wood smoke in his nostrils. This was fire, just as Peter Lafferté had predicted. He had said the trail back through the pines was slick with needles. How the woods would go on a night like this! They would be a devil's chimney, spitting their flames up to heaven.

Without any act of volition Johnny Geraldy got out of bed and tiptoed to the door. He was careful as a fox not to waken the others. It seemed that his feet did not even touch the floor and the latch did not click as he closed the door after him. Then he found himself running down the path to the creek, his boots striking flint from the pebbles as he raced. There was one way to escape, only one, and that was by water, by the Devil's Creek, alone in the darkness. It was just one chance in a million, but it was better than being caught by the fire. There was just one way, and that was in the canoe under the cedars. That was why he had stolen out of the shack so quietly, so that not one footfall sounded. There was room for only one in that shallow boat of birchbark. Jean Rébolt and Peter Lafferté could burn up to a cinder, back there in the cabin, perhaps even without waking. Johnny Geraldy did not stop to give them warning.

From the cabin to the cedar clump was the work of a second. Dazed with fear he plunged into the thicket. Then his head struck something. He could see no longer. But he did not have to depend on his eyes now. With a strange new sense he groped his way until his hands found what they were seeking, then he dragged the birchbark shell down to the water. All around him he could hear its broiling. He was wet now. He must get in before the current sucked him outward. Like a seal he slid his body into the canoe and he lay down flat on his stomach. He was blind as a bat, but it didn't matter down there in the darkness. He was moving out now, very rapidly. It seemed as though he had leaned his ear against the heart of the river. He could hear the thing grind under him and shudder and tremble. He was tossed from side to side; he was plunged head foremost. Then it seemed at once as though he had been caught from motion, as though strange fingers snatched the sides of his canoe and held it an instant still. Then they pushed it off again, and he thought he heard the river laugh.

He had no idea of time any more. He was wet where a wave had lapped over him. Still he lay on his face in the shallow bark, his blind eyes shut fast against the blackness.

It was dawn when he finally came to. He was swinging, gently now, for there was no current. Tiny waves lapped around the sides of the canoe and talked in a low voice. Very slowly he turned over. There was light against his eyeballs. Finally he opened his eyes and saw the gray sky overhead and the thin gray clouds of early morning skudding over it.

For a time he lay there staring. He could see. At last he sat up straight. Not two hundred yards before him lay the village, built up against the wall of forest. Smoke was rising from some of the chimneys, but there was no one yet upon the street. It must be very early morning. At last the sun came up behind the wall. It was as peaceful as a Sunday. At once he thought of the forest fire—that awful thing from which he had driven. But the horizon was clear and the air was fresh with the morning sharpness. Could he have been crazy and dreamed it?

Slowly his thoughts groped back to his awakening and his stealing his way out of the cabin. He had left the others in there—to die for all he cared —and he had escaped in the canoe and had blinded himself before starting. Here he was now in the lake, safe as an otter drawn up sunning himself on a log. He had done something no man had ever done before him. He had shot down the Devil's Creek rapids in a canoe when the water was low. He had done a deed not the most reckless man in Minnesota would even dream to do. And he had left two men back in a cabin, sleeping, to be burned up in the fire. He had left them there to be murdered because there was a chance for only one man to escape.

Rudi Agatin saw Johnny Geraldy as he walked up the street of the village. He looked at him blankly, and then he brushed the broad back of a hand across his eyes. "Name of a name," he said, "or do I still dream?"

Johnny Geraldy came a step nearer. "It is I, and I am here," he said.

Rudi Agatin still gazed at him. "But how are you here?" he demanded.

"By the Devil's Creek way," he said.

"Name of a name," the old man repeated. Then after a moment: "You have come back for the gayety to-night. You have come back to watch Jeanne Beaumont. Man," he said, "you must have drowned your wits before starting. But you have done something no man has ever done before." The old man's eyes rested on him as the eyes of a believer might look upon a wonder-working image.

Inside of thirty minutes Rudi Agatin had told all the village how Johnny Geraldy was there and how he had come down the Devil's Creek in the nighttime, a thing that no human being, even a redskin, had ever attempted before. And all the people stared at Johnny Geraldy, and the children followed him around the street, at a distance, silently, whispering.

That night he went up to the tavern. He had not wanted to go, but it seemed, someway, a part of this strange rôle he found himself playing. It was jolly in the tavern. A spruce fire leaped up the chimney and threw long tongues of light into the room. The red tiles of the floor were jolly and the flash of light from pewter mugs and plates.

Jacques Duval saw Geraldy as he pushed the door open and stood a moment silent at the threshold.

"Bravo," he cried, "it is Johnny Geraldy and he has come down the Devil's Creek alone in the nighttime. We will drink him a toast in his honor."

Then they passed around a pitcher of applejack, and everyone drank and cheered, but everybody looked at him a little strangely. It was uncanny, that thing he had done. There seemed, someway, no adequate reason for it.

Late that evening Jeanne Beaumont sat down on the bench beside him. Her cheeks were as red as poppies and her brown eyes sparkled. She was a little thing to have so much vitality. She did not stand near as high as his shoulder, and yet he knew she was a volcano of energy. To-night when she sat beside him she was quiet, and he thought she was shy. She looked up at him quaintly. "Man alive," she said, "that was a crazy thing to do. You were a fool to do it of course. But I cannot but look up to you with admiration."

"Jeanne——"

Her eyes did not leave his face, and she looked at him as a woman does who is convinced against her instincts of the quality of a man. It was a mixture of reluctant admiration and retribution. She had wronged him in her thoughts. She owed him, therefore, something more than the acclaim all the village gave him. She owed him affection because in her heart she knew that he held that for her. "Johnny Geraldy," she said, "you are a brave man. When you go back to the woods again I have something for you to take with you, a charm that is very effective against cuts and chilblains."

That night he walked up the road beside her to her father's cottage. She had never seemed so little before, or so yielding—or so unattainable. When they stopped before the white gate that shut off the withered garden she turned her face to him and he knew another man would have kissed her.

"Good-by," he said. "I am going back to-morrow —over the trail by St. Pierre way."

"Oh—" she said; then, after a moment: "You will be back in the spring with the others?"

"No," he said; "I go north still further to blaze the tract for the cut next fall."

Then she went into the cottage and brought him out the tiny figure of St. Anthony that held a charm against cuts and chilblains. "Keep this by you," she said. "Not but what St. Anthony himself seems to go beside you. St. Anthony," she laughed, "or—the devil."

"Jeanne———"

She turned her face up toward him in the moonlight.

"Good-by," he said.

In that moment he knew he might have her. She was waiting for him, as he had never dared dream she would. He might have put his arms around her and lifted her face to his and put his lips against her mouth. She would have come to him then, completely, because he had done a brave thing, because she was sorry she had once held in her heart the thought that this man was a coward.

"Good-by," he said—and he was gone.

The next day he started up the trail before sunrise. It would take him a long time this way, and the pathway of needles was slippery to walk on. He was alone again under the twilight of the spruces. There is a terrible silence up there in the forest, a silence that beats against a man's eardrums like the pressure of air in a mine. He hated it here in the forest. It played such tricks on you, like the trick it had played that night he smelled wood smoke. It had drugged him and blinded him and made him mad—and he had done something in that madness that had turned him into a great man. Jeanne Beaumont had lifted her face to his in the moonlight because she had thought him brave. He could have crushed her softness against him; he could have felt the gentleness of her arms around him; he could have felt the touch of her lips. But up here in the forest he had left two men to be murdered. He had gone off and left them without a warning because he was at heart a coward.

"Oh, God; oh, God!" he whispered, and his hand closed around the tiny figure of St. Anthony that held a charm against cuts and chilblains. . . .

The long winter passed with its hideous cold and its beauty, and spring came, swelling the Devil's Creek to a river, and summer came and fall. Johnny Geraldy went through the routine of the days as he always had. He was a good man with an ax. He was intelligent and reliable. The men he worked with always thought him a little stand-offish. He didn't join in when they sang, and liquor always made him silent. They had sometimes thought him cautious too, discreditingly cautious, until that fabulous exploit of his when he had bowled down the Devil's Creek just to take his girl to a dance.

And, after all, was she really his girl? He seemed only to look at her and wonder. He never slid his arm around her waist, or kissed her ear, or called her "little cabbage." Johnny Geraldy's wooing was not like most men's, if indeed it was a wooing at all. Johnny Geraldy had become a great man, but he had become even more a man apart, and the awe in which his fellows held him was harder to bear than their indifference. It is a terrible thing for a sensitive man to know the craven potentialities that sleep in his own soul.

Another year passed and another, and the Johnny Geraldy story had become a legend. People began to hear about him in other villages. The men of Grandes Forêts made up splendid exploits for him. He could swim a league under water. He had strangled a mountain wildcat with one hand behind him, he could tramp for seven days without food or sleep. Jeanne Beaumont watched him now with a strange look in her eyes. Folks wondered why she did not marry some one else, for it seemed that Johnny Geraldy would never come any nearer with the question than the yearning that was forever in his eyes. Folks said he was a modest man, too modest. Why, he had the world by the tail, and he did not a thing about it. It seemed, someway, a pity.

Jeanne Beaumont once laid her hand on his arm and looked up at him gravely. "Why do you shut us all out?" she said. "You are too much alone. You are lonely."

"Jeanne——"

They were sitting on the bench before her father's cottage, and she leaned toward him, her shoulder touching his. "Why do you shut us out?" she demanded.

It was a long moment before he answered. He did not move in his place, and his eyes stared ahead into blackness. "You would not come in if you knew."

"Johnny"—her voice was sharp with concern, not so much for his words as for the way in which he had said them—"Johnny, what do you mean?"

Suddenly he turned and looked at her, and it seemed as though he were saying good-by to her, as though he were gazing upon her face as a man who is going upon a far journey tries to stamp upon his memory the face of a loved one.

She covered her face with her hands and trembled a little. "Don't look at me so," she said. "I don't understand you. You scare me."

"Listen," he said, and he held her eyes now like a man in a trance. "None of the things that they say of me is true. I'm a coward. That time I came down the creek I thought the forest was afire. I was running for my life. I was desperate. I didn't think of any one, just of myself, and I took the one short cut to safety." He stopped a moment. "Back in the shack I left the others, Jean Rébolt and old Peter Lafferté. I didn't tell them I was going. I stole out, as silent as a wood fox, and I took the one canoe and left. The forest didn't burn. I must have dreamed it and smelled the smoke that curled out from our fire. I was safe, do you see? I didn't need to do it." Again he stopped. "And they thought I had come down just to take you to a dance."

A long moment she sat as though she were enchanted. Finally she moved. "Johnny"—she reached out toward him—"Johnny," she said, "you're dreaming. Dreaming now, not then." Suddenly she drew him toward her, and her hands held fast to his shoulders. "Listen to me," she said, "this is our secret, what you've just told me. Don't tell the others. They'd think you were crazy. They'd laugh at you. Johnny——"

He looked down at her amazedly. She didn't believe him! She too thought that he was dreaming. He could have her now. She loved him. She thought he was a great man still. No, he alone in the world knew the truth that he was a coward.

"Johnny," she whispered.

Suddenly he lifted her face to his and kissed it— but it was as though he had kissed the lips of a painting. It was almost the kiss of a memory. "Good-by," he said.

"Oh—" her voice was a cry of terror.

He took her arms from around his neck. "Good-by," he said. It was no use trying to make her believe him. In all the world only he knew it, but it remained for him more real than existence, more real than her arms and his longing. "Good-by—" It was this time a whisper. And he was gone.

The summer that year was a hot one. The needles fell dry from the pines and spruces, red dust powdered the weeds and the blackberry thickets, and the sumac leaves changed into long scarlet tongues in the first part of August. The sun hung hot every afternoon and disappeared at evening in a black bank of thunder clouds, shot through with lightning tremors. But no rain fell. Devil's Creek was narrowed down again to a streak of current lashing its way around the bowlders and against the sheer walls of the course.

In September Johnny Geraldy met Jean Rébolt and old Peter Lafferté at the cabin. They were early again this year, bringing provisions over the narrow trail from Grandes Forêts. Johnny Geraldy was glad to see them. It was good to smell another man's pipe in the evening, to have some one say: "It looks to-night, as though there surely would be rain," or : "We must find a new place to hide the meal and the sugar, the squinties have found out this one."

Then, too, they brought him the news of the village. It had gone bad with the gardens this year. It had been so dry the bugs had gotten into the potato plants and the cabbage leaves had shriveled. "It is bad, indeed," Peter said, shaking his head gravely. "The cabbage leaves only shrivel as a sign of something."

"As a sign of bad soup," Jean Rêbolt suggested, and he shrugged his shoulders with a grin.

But Peter Lafferté refused to be convinced. "No," he said, "it was so back in the old country the summer before the Germans crossed the border. It was too the year a blight fell on the chestnut trees and all the horses went lame."

The two men regarded old Peter gravely. Old Peter was, of course, talking nonsense, but he talked it with such an air always of revelation that even a sensible man could not but be a little disturbed.

"I wonder," said Jean that evening, "if there can be anything in the old fellow's bad musings." Then he looked, almost shyly, up at Johnny Geraldy. "But you wouldn't care," he said, "would you? There is nothing that you could fear."

Johnny Geraldy made no answer. Jeanne Beaumont had not believed him, and he had told her the truth. How much less would this stripling. "No two men fear alike," he said finally.

Again the boy looked up at him, and his eyes were shy with admiration. "But you," he repeated, "fear nothing."

That night Peter Lafferté lifted his finger to the dog star. "Look," he said, "it is red. We will have a big wind to-morrow."

This time the old fellow's prophecy came true. Indeed, it did not wait until morning. With the sunset the wind set in. It was fitful at first, coming in sudden puffs, twisting, dropping completely, like an animal that crouches to awful stillness before it springs. Then the wind swung around to the east and the gale redoubled. All night it bent the branches westward, pinning them smooth with the even force of its pressure. Like the tide the gale came out of nothing and swept onward into nothing.

"It is a black night," said old Peter Lafferté.

"It is all because the cabbage leaves have shriveled." The young fellow tried to laugh, but Johnny Geraldy saw his lips were blue and his eyes asked a frightened question.

No one had more than fitful sleep that night. Johnny Geraldy lay staring up into blackness, oppressed by those intangible fears one can drive back into submission during the daytime. At dawn he fell into a heavy sleep, nature's toll for the hours of restlessness. He was dreaming when old Peter shook his shoulder. He looked up into the old man's face, drawn into the grotesque keenness of an animal's.

"Smell——"

Johnny Geraldy sniffed at the air as he had been commanded.

"You smell, then, nothing?" Peter's face was eager with longing for a denial.

It was a long moment before Johnny Geraldy answered. "Yes," he said.

Peter Lafferté stood up and pushed open the door of the shack. "It is due east," he said. "The trail north would miss it," he went on: "it has little chance now of working northward." The two men stood there a moment in silence. Peter's voice had come as slowly as a pastor's. It was strange how calm a man could be in such a moment.

"Yes," Johnny said, "the road north would miss it." Still the two men did not move. There was one thing neither had said to the other, but that thing was more real than the peril of the moment. Finally old Peter raised his eyes to Geraldy.

"It is each man's right to decide just how sweet life is to him." He stopped a moment. There was no doubting the humility of his appeal. "But you did it once," he said finally—"you did it on a wager to take a girl to a dance. Now the village lies in the track of the east wind, and the east wind is faster than a man on horseback." Already the little animals scurried out from the underbrush, gophers and chipmunks and squirrels and foxes. "See," he said, "they are flying, but they will not be fast enough. There is only one way to get the news to the village. One way."

Johnny Geraldy did not move. He had done that thing once. He had made the journey down Devil's Creek when it was nothing but a thread of current lashing against the bowlders. He remembered the night he had done it. He had been drugged with sleep, and his eyes were blinded. He had crashed into a sapling thicket and had struck his forehead such a blow that he was sightless as an owl. Then he had lain face downward in the canoe. He had not lifted a paddle, he had not even leaned to this side or that in an effort to direct his canoe. He had sold his soul to the devil that night and the devil had taken him down in safety. What chance did he have of repeating his exploit?

"You are the only man who could do this." The old man spoke the words with the calmness of conviction. "You are the bravest man in Grandes Forêts. You can now become its savior."

Still Johnny Geraldy did not move. It was a moment of terrible silence, a moment when anything might happen. True he had done what Peter Lafferté had said, but how could he establish again the same conditions that had made the other feat possible? It was neither night nor was he dazed nor was he blind. At last had come the moment he had prayed all his life would never arrive, that moment when a man must show to his fellows his soul.

"Peter Lafferté," he said, "I am not a brave man. That was luck, that other time. Just luck. It was only a mistake, an accident that I went at all. This time, if I go, it is deliberate. It is death."

The old man looked at him and shook his head. "A man doesn't do a thing like that by accident." Again he shook his head sagely. "Don't try to fool with me," he said. "I am an old man, and there are some things that I know."

So Peter Lafferté would not believe him either!

There was no one who believed him then. Must he bear this secret all his life alone?

Old Peter started down the path to Devil's Creek. The canoe was in a shelter near the stream, hoarded away until the floods of April. Peter pushed back the underbrush and pulled it out. Johnny Geraldy watched him, but he made no move to help. He was like a man who sees the gallows lifted for him, black against the sky. At the edge of the stream Peter Lafferté dropped the birch bark. Johnny Geraldy saw how bubbles of water rose from the damp sand around the old man's heavy boots. Funny that he should be noticing this now.

"If you don't get there," said old Peter, "I shall tell all the world what you attempted. If you do get there"—his lips drew into a droll smile—"you will tell all the world it was 'just by accident, just luck.' "

Johnny Geraldy faced him finally and spoke. "Turn your back," he said. "I want to be alone." Then he gripped his hands together in an agony of pleading. "God," he whispered, "make me blind. Make me blind." But the sunlight sparkled on the waxy leaves of aspen, and the waves swirled and broke at his feet. He could see everything, everything. "God," he said, "be merciful. Make me so I cannot see."

Old Peter, with his face still turned away, stood waiting. "There is no time to pray," he said. "Anyway, the dear God knows what is in our hearts."

In a final agony of concentration Johnny Geraldy shut his eyes. "Dear God," he whispered, "make me blind, make me blind." With his eyes tight shut he stood there. That was it! He must keep them that way. He must stumble now into his canoe and lie there, face downward; he must lie there as he had on that night so long ago when he had sold his soul to the devil.

In a blundering panic of haste he felt his way to the canoe, slid it into the stream, and threw himself into it. In an instant it took a leap forward, then it shuddered and seemed almost to stop. Johnny Geraldy did not move; he still lay there, face downward, his eyes tight closed against the blackness. At once the bark staggered forward again. Sometimes it pitched him from side to side, sometimes it jammed him forward until it seemed his head would crash through the delicate walls of birch bark. Sometimes the spray dashed in, stinging like dust swept up from the prairie. Sometimes the canoe dipped so far one way as to ship in water.

He wondered suddenly how far he had gone, whether he had already struck the white water, whether ahead of him loomed up the Devil's Reef, like the teeth of a monster. It was inhuman to lie still, like a log, and not lift a paddle to steer clear of destruction. It was incredible. "God keep me blind," he whispered; "God—or the devil keep me blind."

In an agony of torment he lay there. His muscles ached until he could cry out with torture. Finally all sensation seemed to go out of his body. "I have become a log," he thought, "for only a log can do this. The devil has turned me to wood." Then, finally, the woodenness crept to his brain. He had no sensation at all now, no emotion. What would happen if he could not move when he came to the smooth shallows of Grandes Forêts? What would happen if he could never deliver his message? Suppose he had been struck dumb? And then suddenly all thought left him.

Rudi Agatin, in a fishing boat trolling for pike, came across him. The canoe had been shot far out by the catapult force of the stream. Rudi Agatin had rowed over to him. He had thought the canoe was a derelict thing, broken loose from some wharf in the village. Inside he had found a man, asleep it seemed, maybe dead. He towed the canoe to shore, very gently, and lifted the body within it. Johnny Geraldy opened his eyes. It was hard to look against the sun; still he could see everything, all the queer, weather-etched wrinkles in the face of Rudi Agatin, the way his shirt was open at the throat, and the bronzed skin of his neck.

"Name of a name," gasped Rudi, "it is you."

Johnny Geraldy sat up, and, finally, he stood.

Rudi still looked at him as though he saw a ghost. "You have come down Devil's Creek for the second time, and you are not dead."

Yes, he could see and move and breathe in the air of autumn. He was not dead. He started walking, slowly at first, and finally trotting. At last he broke into a speed that had in it desperation. Like a madman he raced through the village. People stared at him as though he were crazy—or they were. He bowled into a group of children playing on a corner, and one of them burst out crying. At Jeanne Beaumont's cottage he slowed up and pushed open the gate. Jeanne Beaumont stood at the doorway.

"Johnny—" she called out.

He stumbled to her side and stopped. "Johnny," she whispered—"Johnny."

Fumbling, his hands seized her apron, her dress. At once she put her arms around him and drew him to her. "Speak to me once," she said. "Speak to me." Then she looked up into his face. "You have come," she said, "with a message."

He nodded.

"You have come by the creek. You are wet." She was struggling to read him now as a man who is lost in a blizzard strains his eyes to conjure up some object with which he is familiar. "You have come with a message. Something terrible." She stopped a moment and then her lips said a word she had not even thought of. "Fire——"

Again Johnny Geraldy nodded.

Suddenly she lifted her face, and the wind swept across it. Yes, it was a gale from the East, from the tamarac country. She fancied for a moment she saw tongues of flame above the tossing branches of forest.

"You came to warn us to cross over the lake to the clearing."

He nodded.

"Johnny," she said, and her eyes held the gentleness of wisdom, "it was true what you told me once. You once were a coward. But you are not a coward now. You are greater even than the stories that men told of you before." She stopped a moment. "But no one but me can ever know how great, for you can never tell it—and I never shall."

FREDA WALDENSEN

FREDA WALDENSEN

FREDA WALDENSEN pulled on the worn buffalo mittens over her black woolen knitted ones and buttoned up the coonskin coat.

Douglas Harting looked at her a moment curiously. "It's a terrible evening to go out in," he said finally. "Why don't you stay in town to-night, Mrs. Waldensen, and wait until the roads have been broken a bit first?"

Freda Waldensen knitted her brow in annoyance. "I should have ridden in a-horseback"—she was thinking out loud rather than talking to the man opposite her—"but I wanted to bring in the feeder and fetch back the stacks and provisions."

Douglas Harting smiled, half unconsciously. "Then I can't flatter myself that the little arrangement we have just settled was enough to bring you into town?"

Freda Waldensen's eyes narrowed as she looked at

him. "It is not often that I come in in winter and
there were errands I should perform." Then the
scowl drew her black eyebrows into a straight line,
and Douglas Harting knew she was no longer speaking to him. "But I was a fool not to ride in a-horseback."

Without another word she turned toward the door
and he followed her, confident in the belief that she
would pay no more heed to his words than if he had
been one of her own farm hands. "Seriously, Mrs.
Waldensen, this is a brutal storm. Is it after all
good sense to venture out?"

"All the more reason why I should get back," she
said. "Those fools are bound to do something
stupid without me. It will be a hard night on stock."

Again Douglas Harting smiled. In no capitalistic
stronghold had he ever heard more outspoken con-
tempt for the mentality of the working class than
from the lips of this peasant Viking. "Too bad your
daughter isn't home," he suggested. "She must
surely be a happy understudy in authority."

Freda Waldensen looked at him, he thought,
scarcely tolerantly. What he was saying was to her
frankly nonsense, but she must be at least discreetly
polite. This gentleman, after all, represented one of
the great packing houses of Chicago, a concern with

which she had just put over a deal to be reckoned with in six figures. Freda Waldensen had, moreover, another reason for tact, a personal reason. Douglas Harting knew a world she did not know. The time might come when she would have to ask a favor of him, and that favor was going to be connected with her daughter.

Douglas Harting had deliberately brought up the subject of the daughter. He was curious about her, about the relationship between this gaunt and able woman and the girl he had once seen sitting in the spring wagon in front of the county recorder's office waiting for her mother. He was curious because, for some quite unaccountable reason, for perhaps no good reason at all, he, too, had a suspicion he was going to be drawn into the drama of these people's lives.

He thought with interest about his one encounter with Ingra. It was summer, he remembered, and she had on a pink dress of some light material and a big white hat that drooped down spinelessly over the pink and white prettiness of her face. She was what the country louts would call a "baby." She was soft and gentle and warm, and the skin of her cheeks was like peach bloom. Douglas Harting had suggested she witness one of the documents, but her mother had ignored the suggestion as though she had not heard it, and Duck Libb had been called in from the neighboring hay and feed store instead.

Ingra Waldensen was about twenty, Douglas Harting supposed, the sort of girl no man can look at with equanimity. She made no motion to attract, she sowed no seeds of conquest, but in her static composure lay a generic appeal as potent as it was unconscious. To Douglas Harting she represented everything that was banal and obvious, and yet even he could not look on her stolid prettiness without a disquieting quickening of every pulse. It was humiliating to realize how close to the primitive even a man who was supposed to be matured and sophisticated could be.

She was better dressed than the other girls of the countryside; and, despite Freda Waldensen's Lutheran traditions, Ingra had been sent to the convent at Montreal. "It's a good school," Freda Waldensen had said, "and they teach a girl how to be a lady."

Ingra Waldensen could be patted into any mold, but she could not be chiseled. She would hold her form only as long as the sculptor stood by to knead the damp clay into existence. The best teachers in the world could not change the material out of which she was made.

Douglas Harting wondered what Freda Waldensen thought of her daughter. She had made of her an heiress certainly. Ingra Waldensen would be well off, even as great cities reckon money. Freda Waldensen had not labored twenty years for nothing. Douglas Harting wished he might have seen the mother when she was younger. He knew the main facts of her life, but it was difficult to visualize her as anything other than the gaunt, indomitable person she had become, shrewd, relentless, fiercely ambitious. He knew that she and Oscar Waldensen had pioneered that country, coming there before the railroad and the survey. He knew they had lived in a mud hut, and that it was a year before there had been even boards laid upon the dirt floor. He knew that Ingra Waldensen had been born in that hovel.

The next year Oscar Waldensen died of fever. The neighbors had urged Freda to sell out and go back to the old country or perhaps move down to the settlements. A woman with a child could get a job as cook in a hotel or lunch room. But Freda Waldensen had not even heard the words that they were saying. Next year, instead of selling out, she bought more land. The people thought she was crazy. She could not break the land she had already. And then, one day, she went to Grundy Center and bought five cows. They were rangy, big horned things with great hollows at their hip bones. She drove them back herself the forty miles to home.

A fantastic parade it must have been across the swinging prairie, gray sky above, the gray-green grass beneath, forever rippling like the waves of a placid inland lake. And silhouetted against the grass and sky that herd of cattle, looking like the offspring cast by famine, and a tall, thin woman, slightly stooped, on horseback, driving her famine flock toward the west.

Those five long-horned, thin brutes represented the beginning of the famous Waldensen herd. Freda Waldensen was among the first to realize she had settled on grass country. It was thin soil that would never pay back in wheat or grain for the agony and labor that would go into the planting.

It was range country and she knew the land must forever exceed the herd upon it. So Freda Waldensen bought large and always the increase in her herd would repay her buying. Now she had sixty men who drew wages from her, but when she started she had ridden herd alone. Winter blizzards she had faced to drive her flock to safety when a man would have made up his mind to stand his loss on the morrow.

She could even lasso and brand her animals, though she did not continue this practice long. "It's bad on the wrists," she said.

Freda Waldensen was the first, too, to make a deal with the big Chicago packers, and she made it very much on her own terms.

"If she were a man," Douglas Harting thought, "being President of these United States wouldn't strike her as a fulltime job."

There was something fabulous and yet terrible in the fight she had made. She had gone a long way from the peasant's hovel on a Swedish nobleman's estate, where she was born, to be sole owner and proprietor of the Waldensen herd, but she bore all the scars of her battle. She was lame where a colt had kicked her. She had frozen a hand once in a blizzard. She was gaunt and stooped shouldered, and her face had the hardness of metal. And beside her was the gentle Ingra, tame as a kitten and stupid as a mole. Small wonder that even a less curious person than Douglas Harting should be interested in the situation.

From infancy Ingra Waldensen had been pretty

and placidly contented. As a child she had played on the doorstep of the shack, good naturedly removing from molasses-coated thumb and index finger to thumb and index finger a gray and sticky chicken feather. It was a joyous and half-witted occupation, and the child gurgled with amusement. Freda Waldensen, returning from her labors, used to look at the little girl, first with gentleness, because she had been caught off guard. But the gentleness soon gave way to determination. Freda Waldensen knew what she intended to do about her daughter. It was not for herself that she had stayed on alone to fight it out with the prairie. It was not simply to make more money that she had staked her life against the odds of nature. It was not to be known as the richest woman in the state that she had braved tempest and drought and pest and stampede.

The peasant daughter of peasant farmers, Freda Waldensen had been born to kneed and to eat the bread of labor. There was no task too menial or too severe for her to accomplish. There was no labor on her estate that she would not and could not perform; and yet underneath she held a brutal scorn for all who served her, for all those who are destined through their days to be hewers of wood and drawers of water.

Ingra Waldensen should never know what it meant to struggle, what it meant to be oppressed not only in spirit, but in body. She should never know the bitterness and heartbreak that had been Freda Waldensen's through all the years. Ingra should be no peasant farmer bearing always about with her the smell of earth and stables. Ingra Waldensen should be a lady.

Ingra was beautiful as a lady, surely. Sometimes Freda looked at her in wonder. How was it possible that this soft-cheeked girl could be her daughter? Nature had played a trick on her, but a trick that had in it a touch of the sublime. Around the beautiful face of her daughter Freda built up a legend. Ingra was a prince's child left in a peat digger's hovel. Ingra was a precious loan.

So Freda Waldensen made her fight alone. She never told little Ingra anything. As soon as prosperity started, Freda hired a housekeeper who took charge of the farmhouse and the dairy. Ingra never even darned her own stockings or made her own bed. When she was fourteen Freda sent her away to the convent. She would have liked to send her East, but she did not know the names of any schools and there was no one whom she could ask, unless it were her Chicago bankers or Douglas Harting, and a curious strain of peasant shyness so far had prevented her doing this. So Ingra was sent to the Sisters of the Sacred Heart at Montreal.

Ingra had stayed there longer than most of the girls. There were two reasons why Freda had insisted upon this. In the first place she was still undecided about where in the East to send Ingra, and in the second place she was afraid to let Ingra come home. She dreaded the long vacations just as though they had been a prison sentence. Only Freda was not the prisoner; she was the jailer.

Until Ingra was seventeen, Freda had always regarded her as a child, almost as a chattel, something that was exquisite, but something toward which she needed to exercise no particular mentality. Ingra was not a problem; she was a symbol. She was something her mother had lifted up out of a mud hovel on the wind-beaten prairie and made into something apart, something beautiful. Ingra, as a personality, did not exist to her any more than Douglas Harting or her bankers in Chicago.

Then came the evening she had happened upon Ingra and Sigurd Larson in the summerhouse under the cottonwoods. It was August, cruelly hot and rainless. Freda had had trouble with the hoofs of her animals that summer. She had had veterinaries come from Freemont, even from Chicago. They had all experimented and prescribed, but the trouble persisted. Day by day the animal's feet became more desperate. Finally old Peter Larson, her neighbor, hit upon a remedy, an old peasant method of packing in mud to draw out the inflammation.

Peter came over often that month and with him the boy Sigurd. Sigurd was twenty-one, handsome and awkward and country. But Sigurd had a way with stock, and Freda respected his ability. She even admitted he was "right smart" in the slew of clay he had made on the willow lot into which the herd was driven and corralled until the medicinal property of the mud had had time to take its effect. Sometimes Sigurd stayed for dinner, sometimes even for supper. Freda talked to him always as one stock-man to another. Ingra they both ignored. Freda from intention and the boy from shyness.

What the girl thought about while the others talked land and feeding and weather Freda never bothered to conjecture. Ingra never seemed to think about anything. She was a quiet child, always placid, always gentle. Once Freda had caught her in the dairy, her sleeves rolled up above her elbows, molding butter into little pats with dexterous, rapid neatness. On her face was the half-smile of the artisan who is at peace with his handiwork. Freda watched a moment, then she ordered Ingra to stop and to go back to the house. Ingra obeyed her. She always obeyed, but the half-smile vanished from her mouth.

On this night in August Freda said good-by to Sigurd Larson at the front door of the farmhouse and returned to her accounts. She was behind in the work on her ledger, and she lighted the kerosene lamp in the parlor and opened the heavy, leather-bound volume. It was stifling in the room. Bullet-winged beetles and moths beat against the screens and a wilful mosquito sang continuously and viciously close to her face.

Freda Waldensen finished her task. She was gray with fatigue and the perspiration ran off her face and dropped down onto her hands and the pages on which she was writing. Finally she stood up and walked out of the farmhouse. It was brilliant as mid-day outside. There seemed that night to be just two things in the universe, the great moon overhead and the rolling, endless prairie. Earth and sky, earth and sky, without end, without beginning, flat for a million miles, and over it the velvety dome of heaven with that great, blazing lamp in the middle.

Not knowing in which direction she went, she walked toward the grove of cottonwoods and the summerhouse. Suddenly she heard voices, low at first and too indistinct for her to recognize single words, but the tone was the tone of intimacy. They were talking as people do who are at peace with each other. There was no attempt to entertain, to be smart or amusing. Finally there came a silence, and overhead flickered and rustled the leaves of the cottonwoods in a windless, breathless evening.

Freda Waldensen came a step nearer. She could see them now. They sat on the steps of the summerhouse, Ingra with her hands quiet in her lap, the boy with his arms around his knees and his head bent forward.

"Do you think your mother'd let you go to the circus?" he said finally. "It's going to be Saturday in Freemont."

Ingra Waldensen turned her head. "I know," she said. Then after a moment. "I wouldn't dare to even ask."

They were silent again.

"Ingra—" he was turned toward her now, his arm on the step behind her and his body bent toward her. "Ingra——"

The girl did not move, but his arm touched her

back and tremors of response shot forth from her to meet it.

"Ingra—" his arms were around her now, and her head lay against his shoulder. Then he kissed her, timidly at first, finally with all the turbulence of passion, and her arms clung to him with the unguessed fierceness of instinct.

Freda Waldensen did not move.

After a while the two young things loosed each other, but their hands clung together.

"There's goin' to be a man in the circus Saturday that jumps blindfolded through a hoop of fire onto a running horse," he said. "I saw it on the billboard."

Ingra Waldensen did not answer.

"Ingra"—she turned her face toward him slowly —"do you love me?"

"Yes."

Again there was an interval of silence. Finally he lifted his face to the sky. "Funny how those leaves keep going all the time," he said, "ain't it? When there isn't a breath of air."

Ingra followed his eyes to the cottonwoods. "It's on account of their stems being flat and at right angles." Then she stopped. "I learned about it's being that way at the sisters."

He laughed and drew her sharply against him. "You know a lot," he said, "don't you?"

She lifted her face and he kissed her. Then finally he stood up. "I've got to go, but I'll see you to-morrow. So long."

"Good-by." And she watched him run across the yard toward the barn where his pony was tethered.

Freda Waldensen stepped back into the shadow. A fear she had never known before crept over her, a premonition of her own impotence. Then anger succeeded fear. The game was not over yet. Indeed she had not even begun to fight. Let them watch out, those two.

Finally Ingra left the steps and walked slowly to the farmhouse. Freda did not move until she heard the screen door of the house slam.

Next day she drove into town in the wagon, although it was only Thursday and she had no purchasing to do. On the way in she stopped at old Peter Larson's and told him Sigurd needn't come any more. She could manage now without him. In the village she drove directly to the station where the Western Union office was. Then she wrote out a telegram to Douglas Harting. She didn't puzzle long over the wording—Freda Waldensen's methods were direct :

Wire name and address of most expensive school in Boston.   F. WALDENSEN.

Douglas Harting asked his sister, a smart young matron living on Chicago's South Side, and wired back:

The Misses Selby's School, Number ——, Pine Street, on Beacon Hill.

Then Freda Waldensen telegraphed to the Misses Selby. The answer was a very unbusinesslike long time in coming, and when it came it turned out to be a letter. It was suave and gracious, and it regretted that there were, unfortunately, no vacancies left for this year.

Then Freda Waldensen sent Douglas Harting another telegram. This was a harder one to compose, and he could only suspect the humiliation it had cost her. He would have to help her; he would have to use his influence to get her daughter in.

Douglas Harting took his sister into his confidence. "She's a little peasant puppy," he told her. "I've seen her once. She's pretty as a picture, but peasant—absolutely earth-bound. The mother," he went on, "is stunning—a regular Viking." Douglas Harting's manner partook almost of excitement.

"You ought to see her. She's magnificent and"—he smiled shrewdly at the well-dressed woman across from him—"she's one of my best clients. If I keep her, I keep that whole district. Would you mind, now, doing this little favor for me?"

Mrs. Roger Landon smiled amusedly. "I've done a lot for you, Douglas," she said, "what with entertaining your long-horned employers and all. And now you ask me to perjure my soul and my social standing?"

He nodded. "Your standing will stand it," he laughed. "Anyway, I'd like to do something for Freda Waldensen. She has always done me out so nicely."

But even Mrs. Roger Landon could not maneuver Ingra's entrance for that year. So Ingra went back to the convent and Freda kept her there through Christmas vacation and as late as she could manage into the summer. In the fall Freda sent her East. She was a pathetic little thing as she stood on the platform of the dirty local. Freda was taking her as far as Chicago.

On the station platform stood Sigurd Larson. He had on his Sunday suit, and his hands were rough and red from the severity of recent scourings. He did not even speak to Ingra Waldensen. Freda

never left her side. But his eyes watched her helplessly, and when the train had gone he stood for
a long time looking down the track, even after the
smudge of smoke had drifted far over the prairie.

In Chicago Freda saw her bankers and the men
in the great packing house with which she did business. She stayed only a day. Freda didn't like
Chicago. She thought she disliked the smoke and
the noise, but Douglas Harting suspected that there
was another reason for her distaste. Everywhere
she was treated with respect, almost with deference.
She was not only an amazing woman, she was also
a valued customer. But in Chicago Freda Waldensen was not a czar.

She refused to lunch with Douglas Harting at the
La Salle Hotel, which had at that time the smartest
restaurant in Chicago. Instead she ate at the counter
in the station lunch room.

More than once Douglas Harting had been
prompted to say something about her daughter, but
each time a sort of respectful tact prevented him
from gratifying his curiosity. Mrs. Waldensen
obviously did not want to talk about Ingra. She had
thanked Douglas Harting in a short and difficultly
written letter for the trouble he had taken in her be-
half. As far as he was concerned, then, the incident

was closed. Douglas Harting never knew she had just put Ingra on the train for Boston. It was, distinctly, no longer any affair of his.

When she said good-by she thanked him for a business favor he had done for her. He had given her a market tip that would be of distinct value to her next spring. "You are a friend," she said quite simply.

A sensation of something akin almost to affection went through him. She was a Spartan woman, but she did catch the imagination. "Any time that I can be of service to you—" he mumbled. The bromidic commercialism of his remark angered him. He really meant the spirit behind the words and not the trite phrase.

Freda Waldensen passed over his offer without comment or without even any acknowledging change of expression. "Good-by," she said. She did not go through the ceremony of shaking hands.

Douglas Harting showed her to the door; but long after he had closed it behind her he still thought about her. He thought, too, of Ingra in the Misses Selby's School, on Beacon Hill, Boston. "Quaint world," he said to himself, "very quaint indeed."

Fall stripped the yellow leaves from the cottonwoods and birches. The days grew raw and cheerless and over dun-colored, close-cropped prairie, hung a gray, forbidding sky. Then winter came with its barbaric fierceness and its beauty. Drifts piled across the prairie like frozen waves of a wind-lashed ocean and the frost on the windows was fuzzy with thickness.

Freda Waldensen went about her business as usual. Winter was a period of monotony varied with crises of desperate struggle. There came times when every ounce of a man's ingenuity and courage were put to the test in the unequal battle of man against the elements. Freda Waldensen enjoyed these crises because she won in them so often. She did not become careless through over-confidence, but she had become accustomed to success. Freda Waldensen was both able and lucky.

Once every two weeks she got a letter from Ingra. That had been the agreement. Ingra's letters could not be said to contain much color. She told what time they got up and went to bed, what they had to eat at meals, and what the names of her teachers were and what she studied. In one she wrote, for example:

We went out to another town yesterday to see the homes of some authors. They were Emerson and Alcott and Hawthorne and several others. On

the way back we got caught in the rain and one
of the teachers' umbrellas blew inside out.

Your loving daughter,
INGRA.

Toward Christmas the letters grew more and
more brief. Freda decided Ingra should stay at the
school during Christmas vacation and conveyed her
intentions to her daughter and the Misses Selby with
her usual blunt directness. Then came a letter from
Ingra, no longer than most, but containing a color
the others could not have been said to possess:

Don't make me stay. I think I shall die if you
do. Rember the coyote that Jake Foster caught in
a trap and locked up in a stall in the barn? Well,
he fed it and everything and it died of hunger because the food just wouldn't be swallowed. Well,
I'm that coyote.

Your loving daughter,
INGRA.

Freda Waldensen wrote to the Misses Selby; and
they responded that Ingra's appetite was good; she
looked a little paler perhaps than when she had come,
but that was because she was leading, possibly, a
more cultivated and less wind-swept existence.

In January on the prairie winter sets in in earnest.
Freda Waldensen did not trust the man who was in
charge of the stock on the range, so she rode herd

herself to be sure her orders were being obeyed. It was bitter work and for the first time she had a touch of rheumatism.

On the twenty-first of January a blizzard set in that was destined to remain unparalleled not only in the history of Rising Sun County, but in the life of Freda Waldensen. By four o'clock in the afternoon the air was a fog of stinging, wind-driven snow-flakes. You could not see from the farmhouse windows even as far as the cottonwood clump and the summerhouse. Freda Waldensen decided it was a good time to look over her accounts.

At six o'clock she got up from her ledger and walked to the window. It was dark outside, but she could hear the sharp lashing of snow against the pane and feel the quiver of the house in the wind. This blizzard had not been entirely unforseen, and Freda Waldensen had already taken precautions with the herd. To-night she felt reasonably safe.

At a quarter-past six she heard footsteps on the porch and the heavy stamping of snow from heavy boots. She walked sharply at once to the door and opened it. Peter Larson stood in the doorway.

"You," she exclaimed. "Come in."

Peter Larson came in, and she shouldered the door to behind him. A moment he stood there dazed by the light, his flesh tingling in the sudden warmth and the cessation of the wind's fury.

"Well," she said, "is somebody sick or what is it then?"

"This." He took out of his pocket, lined already with snow, a folded piece of yellow paper.

Freda Waldensen unfolded it—the purple typing was beginning to blur where the snow was melting upon it—and read:

> Leaving this morning for Chicago. Will marry Ingra Waldensen there tomorrow. Home Saturday.
> SIGURD.

"He was in Freemont yesterday looking at some steers," the old man said. "This is sent from there. I only got it two hours ago, and here I am." He looked at her as a conscientious but blundering servant might look at an unlenient master.

For a long moment Freda Waldensen stood there, the telegram stiff in her hand. "Yes, here you are; here you are." She laughed unpleasantly. Then she roused herself into action. "Go out to the barn and tell Alec to saddle Piney."

Peter Larson looked at her in amazement. "You're not goin' out in this?" he said.

"I'm going to Chicago to-night."

It was madness.

In five minutes Freda Waldensen stood in the door of the barn. Alec and old Peter looked at her dumbly.

"You can't make it," Alec said. "There ain't even a road."

Freda Waldensen walked past him, tightened the girth on the horse and got on. "I bought him from Duck Libb, in Grundy Center," she said. "He'll go home."

She was off.

Stinging as spray, the snow whipped against her face. The horse whinnied weakly, but she gave him a cut with the whip. He jumped forward, trembled and then stopped. They could not move against that wall of wind and snow. Then at once the wind shifted.

Freda put her head down against the horse's neck. She talked to him, half words, half just sounds. It was up to him now. He would have to get her in. He would have to save her. "You, you," she said, "old Piney, go on, go on, go, go, g——"

Her face where the wind touched it was blistered with cold. Her arms were numb with the strain of holding. She was lashed at and torn and buffeted, but her body had no consciousness of any of it. Her will alone was living. Finally she saw two lights, blurred and yellow, but near—the railroad station. This much at least she had won.

At the station she wrote a message and pushed it in to the operator. It was addressed to Douglas Harting:

Stop marriage of my daughter Ingra to Sigurd Larson in Chicago tomorrow Thursday. Arrive noon Thursday.   F. WALDENSEN.

In Douglas Harting's private office Freda Waldensen sat waiting. She had taken a cab from the station, upon the arrival of the storm-stayed train, directly to Harting's office. Harting had not been in since morning, they told her. He was gone on a personal matter, and they did not know when he would return. Freda Waldensen said she would wait.

As she sat there, it seemed as though she did not even breathe. Her hands, in their shiny black kid gloves, were held fast together in her lap. Her bonnet with the black porcupine quills had been badly treated indeed by the storm, but one seemed, some-way, not to notice it. The smart stenographers in the outer room had looked at her covertly as she passed in, but they had not tittered. Grotesque as she was, she possessed a grim, unmistakable dignity.

At last the door of the office was opened, and Douglas Harting stood in the doorway. Freda Waldensen rose, but she did not take a step toward him.

He closed the door and came halfway across the room to her. Then he stopped. "Mrs. Waldensen" —it was terrible to have to watch her face; it was terrible to have to tell her the news he brought— "Mrs. Waldensen," he said again.

"They're—married."

He nodded. "At noon to-day in the city hall. I missed them by just forty minutes. I'm—sorry."

She lifted her hand in a gesture. "You're not to blame." Then she looked away from him, out of the window and over the roofs of buildings. It seemed at once to Harting as though to her he no longer existed, as though she were alone.

"Mrs. Waldensen—" if there were only something he could say to her, some way he could reach her.

Finally she turned toward him. "It isn't your fault, Mr. Harting. You've been good to me, very good. I'm sorry I have been to you so much bother." She made a little helpless gesture with her hands.

It was all so futile, everything that she could do now. She was beaten, beaten by a country bumpkin she had hired by the day, by a common Swedish peasant—and by nature. For the first time in her life she had lost.

"Perhaps, after all"—he had a notion that whatever he said would be wrong—"it's for the best. Perhaps Ingra knew what she wanted, what suited her."

"What she wanted!" Freda Waldensen caught hold of the phrase, and her voice was sharp with satire. "Look at me," she said. "I'm a peasant. I know what it is to work with my hands till they're bleeding. I have pitched hay onto a wagon until the skin was torn. I have bent over a field of potatoes until my back was hunched. I have got up before daybreak and broke the ice in the trough to water the stock. All night I would sit up in the barn watching a sick calf—sit up when to keep awake was an agony. Single-handed I fought it out—friendless—to make my daughter a lady. I wanted her to know people in the grand world, to mix with them. I wanted her to marry a man like you, a gentleman." She threw her thin arms out in a gesture. "And what does she do? She runs off with old Peter Larson's son. Peter Larson that I could buy and sell and not miss it from my petty cash account!"

Douglas Harting looked at her. There was something terrible and magnificent about her in her revolt. Freda Waldensen was no peasant. She belonged to the most ruthless aristocracy of all, the aristocracy that rules out all those not endowed with talent. Freda Waldensen had not hated her struggle; she had gloried in it.

Douglas Harting faced her. "Look here," he said. "You've got this all wrong. Ingra isn't you or anybody like you. You're made of steel, refined and burned to the highest, finest tension. Ingra's pig iron. Ingra's peasant. But she's lovely. She'll be happy. She fits in that country, and she'll love her husband and her children. And she'll be kinder to them, and not so stupid as you have been toward her." He met her eyes squarely. For the first time he was talking to her as a peer, as his mental and social equal, not as his valuable, capricious client. "Maybe this hurts, but you've got to look it in the face."

For a long time Freda Waldensen made no answer. He had not known what her reaction would be. He could not even predict, but he would have to run the risk of her anger, perhaps even of her enmity.

Finally her hands dropped to her sides, but she

did not move. "It's—not easy to find out that the thing you've worked for all your life long can never happen."

She took a step toward the door, but Douglas Harting intercepted her. "You won't be hard on them," he said, "those two. Remember it's Nature. You can't beat her. You can't trick her. Mrs. Waldensen, you, of all people, ought to know that."

She motioned him aside with a gesture. "All right," she said. "Then let Nature finish up the job." She laughed, and it was not a pleasant thing to hear. "Let Nature help 'em out then—like she helped me"—she held out her gnarled hands towards him—"like she helped me. I'm quit of them."

It was five years before Douglas Harting saw Freda Waldensen again, though their business relations had continued unaffected. Finally she telegraphed him to come out to see her. It was about the new contract. She had been thrown from a horse a month before, and her arm was still in a sling. Otherwise she would have gone to him in Chicago.

Douglas Harting was not loath to make the trip, in spite of the execrable local trains he would have to travel on. He seldom went out on the territory now.

He was first vice president of the company and his clients as a rule came to him.

Freda Waldensen met him in the village. She looked older, and the white linen of the bandaged arm made her skin the shade of ashes. He was shocked to see her looking so, and his face betrayed him.

"Mrs. Waldensen," he said, "why did you bother to come in town to me? Why didn't you let me come out to you?"

"The courthouse is here," she answered. "Besides, I had other business."

She had not changed, he thought. She was the same indomitable Spartan.

They went through their business as usual. It was a pleasure to work with her. She knew exactly what she wanted, and she knew how to go about it. It was five o'clock in the afternoon when the final points were settled, and they walked down the courthouse steps together. It was April, gentle and indolent.

"Mrs. Waldensen," he said—he was like a boy caught by an impulse—"won't you ask me out to your house for supper to-night?"

She looked at him a moment in amazement. "I thought you took the six o'clock train south?"

"I won't," he said, "if you will let me come."
There was something very boyish in his urging.

She waited a moment. "All right."

Together they drove out from the village. It was
beautiful that evening, soft toned and delicate. The
hoofs of the team sank agreeably into the soft mud
of the road with a pleasant plosh. Along the sides
of farmers' ditches the willows were already faintly
yellow with foliage, and over the earth lay an evan-
escent shimmer of new green.

"It's not bad to-night," he said, "this country."

Freda Waldensen made no comment.

Finally they approached a frame house, set a narrow distance back from the road, the ground in
front still scarred with the yellow clay of the excavation. It was bleak and white and unassimilated, but
it looked ambitious and modern.

"The newest thing in farmhouses I suppose," he
said. "I must say the æsthetic values still don't
mount high with the modern farmer."

Freda Waldensen was silent a moment; then she
made a gesture with her thumb: "That's Ingra and
Sigurd's."

"Oh!" Douglas Harting made no attempt to
soften his remark. There had already been too much
plain speaking between them.

As they drew abreast of the house Sigurd Larson stepped up on the porch, and Ingra Larson opened the front door for him, and a little child lurched forward with a delighted scream toward its father. Sigurd lifted the youngster to his shoulder; then he caught sight of the team on the highroad, and Freda Waldensen. Sigurd waved, and Ingra. Freda Waldensen nodded. There was neither reproach nor scorn in her attitude, only acceptance. Then Sigurd Larson slipped his arm around his wife, and the door closed on the three of them.

After a long moment Douglas Harting spoke. "They're happy, aren't they?"

She nodded. "I suppose so. I don't see them often."

Again there was a moment of silence. Finally Douglas Harting spoke again. "Mrs. Waldensen," he said, "I wish you wouldn't work so hard. Why don't you take it easier, slow up a little?"

For another space the team jogged on in silence, and Freda Waldensen's eyes were on the distance. Finally she spoke and her voice sounded like one who speaks from a long way. "Did you notice the child at the farmhouse we just passed? Well, that's the reason I keep on working. She's not like the others. She's not—pig iron. See?"

He nodded.

Douglas Harting's eyes too were on the future. He thought of the toddling child with her scream of baby laughter. How could anyone tell about a youngster? But, after all, what did it matter what symbol it was to which Freda Waldensen tied up her Spartan courage? All that mattered was her courage. "I suppose we all trick ourselves with a motive," he thought, "that may not be the real motive at all."

Again Freda Waldensen spoke. "She's a different run from the others, that baby." And again her eyes had the look of one gazing into the future.

"Yes"; Douglas Harting nodded. "I see."

BIG CLUMSY SWEDE

BIG CLUMSY SWEDE

I T was a quarter of six by the clock in the station lunch room and the train for Duluth was due in sixteen minutes. Vanda Terschak scrutinized the counters as the hostess of a smart dinner party might satisfy herself of the rightness of her table. In sixteen minutes fifty hungry travellers would pore out of the grimy day coaches and devastate her counters with the thoroughness of a visitation of locust. But now the room gave her a genuine æsthetic satisfaction.

She liked the white squares of paper napkin laid neatly upon the rough, scoured wood, the precision of each knife and fork and spoon and the jaunty fan of napkin that sprang, triumphant, from each heavy, polished tumbler. She admired the pyramid of polished apples, the cake-plates piled with crullers, the mound of buns and ham sandwiches. Then she inspected the water gauge on the new nickel coffee boiler and smiled at the grotesque caricature of her own slenderness its convex smoothness sent back to her.

"Gee whiz," she said, "he is boiling like fit to kill already." With quiet fingers she adjusted the valves. Vanda Terschak was the only one of the girls Hans Schwartz allowed to tamper with the mysterious new percolator. "The rest of you Bohunks all thumbs." Hans's tact was Prussian. "The both hands of Vanda *sind* right hands once."

It was true Vanda handled everything with the nice precision of an artist. Her movements were never hurried and she gave little impression of the physical strength most Bohemian girls possess. Her whole body still moved with the unconsciousness and grace of a child and yet she was a woman. To the power of her physical charm she appeared as unawakened as a girl of twelve, though she was essentially maternal. Perhaps she had always been mature, as is the way with many peasant women. She was absolutely without vanity. She only thought it was good to be alive and busy and pleasant never to be clumsy. Perhaps, after all, Vanda Terschak did possess one minor frailty. She was proud of her hands.

At five minutes of six the door from the waiting

room was pushed open and a big man in a mackinaw jacket blocked the doorway. His cap was off and his tousled blonde hair fell over his forehead. His shoulders were heavy and he stooped as do most men physically overdeveloped. Vanda turned around and the man's blue eyes rested on her shyly.

"I ban hurt a little." He made an awkward gesture with his left hand to the hand that hung stiffly at his side. "Get burn by welding machine. Boss say you put something on. Please—" He smiled at her but his skin was gray under the weather beaten bronze.

Vanda took his wrists and examined the burn. "Gee whiz." Her brow contracted with concentration. "He sure hurt, eh, big Swede?" She looked up into his face and smiled. Then she pushed him into a chair by the counter. "Seena," she called, "fetch the soda and a glass of water." From a cracker box under the counter she selected a frayed clean napkin and tore it into strips. Seena brought the water, slopping a little on the floor as she walked. Vanda said nothing but the big Swede saw her frown of annoyance.

Then he held out his hand to her and he watched her daub on the soda and wrap the narrow white strips around his big calloused fingers. The white of the bandage made his skin as dark as an Indian's. He was ashamed suddenly of his great blunt hand. He was the biggest man in the Northern Pacific Wrecking Gang No. 27. He had earned for himself the title of the "Terrible Swede" but now every inch of his height depressed him. He shifted his weight from foot to foot and hunched his shoulders even more in an effort to cheat his tallness.

Suddenly the warning shriek of an engine at the crossing shrilled into the room. It was the 6:01 for Duluth. Vanda led him to the corner and pushed him gently into a chair by the stove. "Wait," she said. Then she went back to the counter. Hans Schwartz elbowed open the door from the kitchen, a pie in each hand.

Vanda nodded to him. "That old train ahead to-night, Gee whiz," she said. Her cheeks were glowing with the excitement of having to meet an emergency and her eyes looked black. "Quick, Seena, two pitchers of water. There is no time for star gazing."

From his corner by the stove Waldemar Jenssen watched. Sometimes he could not see her as the crowd of men from the train clustered dense around the counter. Dishes clattered, men barked out their orders and Hans Schwartz's commands became more German and more guttural. There was something barbaric in the eagerness of this hungry pack. They gulped their coffee and swallowed their buns as though food was something they had not known for days instead of hours. Men elbowed each other and then eyed the offenders with savage resentment. In ten minutes the fury abated. Soiled balls of paper napkins littered the counters and the floor was wet with the melted snow on heavy boots.

Vanda cleared away the dishes, great piles of them adroitly balanced in her arms. Behind her the swinging door into the kitchen flicked back and forth like an aspen leaf in midsummer. Finally the counter was reset for to-morrow and Hans Schwartz mopped up the wet floor. Then Vanda came back to her patient.

"Hurt now?" she asked.

He shook his head. "Very fine now. I thank you." He stood up awkwardly. "I go now. Goodby." But he did not move.

Vanda Terschak smiled up at him. "Eat a bite here," she said, "with me. I save out something good for you."

A flush of pleasure and embarrassment reddened the bronze of his cheeks. "No," he repeated doggedly, "I go now." And again he did not move.

This time Vanda laughed. "You big bluff," she challenged. "Come here."

He followed her to the counter and she set before him a piece of steak, a great mound of mashed potato and an oat-meal dish full of apple sauce. "There," she said. "Better than the grub at camp, eh?" It was a candid bid for admiration, as naïve and as charming as a little girl's.

The man's eyes lifted to hers slowly and in them burned the defeated longing of one who would speak and has been cheated of words. "It's fine and dandy," he said at last, but Vanda Terschak looked away from the speech that was in his eyes.

"Here," she said. "I cut him for you. You are like a leetle baby." She laughed delightedly and her elbow touched his coat as she leaned over to reach his plate. "Shall I feed you too?"

He blushed at her raillery. "You tink 'big awkward Swede' maybe," he said, "but I ban strong. See." He doubled up his arm in childish defiance.

Vanda pursed her lips and laughed again. "Boo," she said, "you think to frighten me?"

He shook his head. "Not frighten but make you like me a little."

Again she looked away from the yearning in his

eyes. "You talk nonsense, big Swede," she said. "It is time you go now. I close up."

He rose obediently and followed her to the door. It was February outside, bitter cold and starlight. Across the road the wind had driven great barricades of snow and the ground between lay bare and stark as a crater. He waited a moment in the doorway, his cap in his hand.

"I see you again sometimes?" he asked finally.

She shrugged her shoulders. "If you have eyes!" Then she smiled up at him, repentant of her flipness. "Sure ting, big Swede."

"Sunday," he said, "I get whole day off." He waited a moment, twisting the rough cap with his fingers. "I take you snow-shoeing in birch forest if you let me. We see big wolf, maybe."

"O-oh," she laughed and pretended to be impressed. "Well, perhaps I go, perhaps. Now, beat it."

For five days he remembered her as she stood there, laughing. But her eyes had not laughed. Her eyes were kind, as kind as her hands had been. A thousand times he admired the dexterous bandage. All week he wore it. It became grimy and torn, inspite of the care he took, but he would not remove it.

Finally Sunday came and he called for her at the

lunch room. They walked to the edge of the village before he suggested they put on the snow-shoes. Then Vanda sat down on a log, her head bent over, her eyes intent on his awkward fingers that struggled to fasten the straps.

"Here," she said, "go way." Their hands touched as she seized the narrow thongs of buck's hide. "You no good at this business. N.G."

Still kneeling before her in the snow he watched. "There," she said and she laughed down at him. "Now show me a wolf track."

The snow was as fine and as soft as dust, the snow of the bitter cold. It shook down into their faces from the branches of the spruce and fir trees. Overhead was a sky blue as July's with long streaks of white cloud across it. Above the snow rattled branches of underbrush to which still clung withered leaves and red berries. Against the low, smooth hills in the north lay the blue shadows of winter and the air was very still.

They had little to say to each other. It was not necessary to speak words in order to fend off the embarrassment silence brings upon the less unsophisticated. For miles they tramped and the shadows grew bluer. Finally Vanda turned to the man beside her.

"Gee whiz," she said. "It is late."

So they turned around and followed their own trail back to the village. Vanda unfastened her snow-shoes but Waldemar carried them. At the station door he stopped. "Our camp move on to-morrow seventeen miles up the road. A bridge, she is busted." A railroad wrecking crew takes orders as unprotestingly as a soldier. "But I come back again next Sunday." His words were bold, but the eyes that searched her face pleaded for permission.

"All right," she said and again she laughed. "Next Sunday we hunt for lion tracks, eh?"

Next Sunday Waldemar Jenssen came again and the next and the next. Timidly, stupidly he told her about the farm back in Sweden. There had been too little land and too many sons, so Waldemar had been pushed out. He went to sea then, on the *Nun,* but the Jenssens were no sailors. At New York he skipped his boat but he signed on again, this time in Buffalo on one of the old fashioned whale-backs that used to carry cargo up and down the Great Lakes. At Duluth he again skipped ship. A labor scout for the Northern Pacific picked him up in a Finnish saloon down on the point and hired him. For two years he had followed the railroad south across the desolate prairie, still charred and blasted by the great fire that had swept it twenty years before.

And Waldemar Jenssen hated the railroad as he had hated the ocean. He belonged to a race of farmers and he wanted a farm. All around him lay the little estates of his countrymen, patches of sandy potato land and thin pastures through which showed the red clay of the soil. Often he had talked with these farmers and they explained to him how the country was homesteaded. It seemed at first he could never understand them. How could a government be so generous as to give away land? He remembered the little farm back in Sweden. It was not as large by a third as the land he could have here for the asking. But at last he believed and in March he filed his claim.

A fellow countryman in the village of Black Cloud trusted him for the lumber and he started to build his barn. Life is simple up in the north country. Only a hundred miles from the city of Minneapolis is land as remote, as foreign as the Steppes of Russia, owned by people who seemed to have come, some way, blindfolded from a village in Russia or in Sweden, or in black hilled Bohemia. And the sons and daughters of these strangers go to the state's university and, later, some of them to the senate.

By July Waldemar had finished his house, he owned two milk cows and the sandy ground had been sowed to potatoes. The last Sunday in July he drove back to the village for Vanda. On the rough seat of the wagon he spread broad sheets of newspaper and the box was filled with sweet smelling hay.

Vanda laughed at him as he lifted her over the wheel but there was something appealing in his clumsy tenderness. She bent over and rubbed her ankle elaborately where he had scraped it against the side of the box. "You are too damn strong, big Swede," she said, still laughing. "Next time I help myself in."

Down to the road on both sides pressed the birch forest, flickering and flirting in the sunlight. Here and there still stood a charred shaft of tree trunk like a black column against the sky. Meadow larks and Bob Whites chirruped in the underbrush and great gaudy tiger lilies bloomed along the roadway.

Vanda Terschak was happy. She laughed at the funny, jerky way the horse trotted, she laughed at the partridge whose dust bath in the warm sand they had intruded upon. She laughed because she was young and healthy and the sun felt warm upon her back, for summer in the northland is a heady wine poured into a small bottle.

After a while they came out of the forest and passed miles of barren pasture, stretching east and west for ever and north toward the low curved hills. Finally Waldemar pointed.

"See!" he said.

Vanda wrinkled her nose and squinted. "That black dot?"

He nodded and his eyes glowed with pleasure. "My house that I build. See, too, another dot? My barn and the yellow is my potato patch."

"Gee whiz," she said. "So tiny. How could a big man like you get in that house and your barn is built for one small chicken."

He smiled down at her. "You will see. He is not so damn small."

They did not speak again until they drove into the farm yard. The house was unpainted and the sward in front still blotched with the red clay from the excavation.

Waldemar was like a mother exhibiting a precocious but homely child. "He not very nice yet, I tink." But his eyes pleaded for her approval.

Again she laughed. "Pretty good for you. Now

I go inside," and she made a comic grimace. "That will be fierce, eh?"

In the doorway she looked at the one room. The floor was swept and the air was still sweet with the smell of the lumber. In one corner stood a bed and she knew he had tried to draw the rough blanket up smoothly. In another corner was a cook stove, cluttered with pans and crocks. On the rough deal table by the window were a mason jar with a branch of wild cherry, a mail order house catalogue and a Catholic prayer book printed in Bohemian. Vanda picked up the prayer book with curious fingers. She knew he was watching her but she did not look at him. After a while she put the book back on the table.

"Now show me the barn," she said.

He explained to her where he was going to store the hay and the extra stall he was going to build for the yet unpurchased cow and he led her around to the shed for the plow and the cart and that galaxy of curious, shapeless things one finds only around farmers' barns. Vanda listened in silence but he knew that her eyes were seeing only the blunders.

Behind the barn was a hen tied to a log by a tangled piece of cord. The man's cheeks flushed with embarrassment. "She gad about like a silly woman," he said. He knelt down to unfasten the string, bound tight now around the hen's legs. The bird struggled and fought, beating her wings against the ground in an agony of terror at his roughness.

It was a ridiculous scene and they both knew it but Vanda Terschak did not laugh. When the bird at last was free he looked up at her and there were tears in her eyes.

"Vanda," he whispered.

For a long moment they gazed at each other. Finally she walked over to him. He was still on his knees, his hands at his sides. A second she stood there, then she put both hands on his head and drew it gently against her. Timidly his arms were lifted around her. She knew he was afraid of the strength that lay in them.

"Big, clumsy Swede," she said. "I come. You need me, eh?"

Vanda Terschak gave Hans Schwartz at the lunch counter one week's notice and she and Waldemar were married in the little Catholic chapel by the Bohemian priest. Late in the afternoon they drove out again to the farm. Twilight had melted sky and land into a common gray, soft as a pigeon's breast and the hills to the north were as thin as the paste board back drop of some tremendous, empty play-house. Birds still chirruped in the underbrush and against the sapphire now of the evening sky swerved and curled a flock of swallows.

Waldemar watched them in silence. Finally he spoke. "They are for good luck, the swallows." Shyly he reached over and touched her hand. "They know you come."

Vanda patted the calloused hand in her lap but her eyes were on the reins, one of which had been crudely mended with a piece of wire.

"You are my good luck," he said, "my swallow."

For an instant she faced him but the yearning, the dumbness of his pleading choked her. He was so humble, so timid in his great strength. Then she saw that the seam of his sleeve was torn and that he had mended it with great, rough stitches. At once she was glad she had come.

"To-morrow I fix that," she thought, "and the harness and we put up some shelves in the kitchen."

In the six weeks that followed Waldemar thought he had been right. She was his luck bird. Everything she touched prospered. Under her direction he finished the house, rehung the doors, closed up the cracks in the barn. She discovered, too, how the blade of the plow should be adjusted so that it would cut less deeply into the sandy earth. Finally he built her a shed for the chickens facing the south, and screened it in neatly with fine wire. Vanda had arranged with Hans S_hwartz to supply him with eggs and poultry as soon as she should be prepared to. It was to be her own enterprise. Waldemar's hands were too heavy to handle the tiny chicks.

Though his awkwardness often provoked her it gave her a sense of importance. He was dependent upon her, she was his benefactor and she liked the superiority of her position. If she patronized him it was with the gentleness of a mother who coaxes along a blundering child. She was ten years younger than he but she treated him with a mixture of tact and bossiness that was both adroit and naïve.

It was enough for Waldemar to obey her, to know she was in the kitchen baking, in the cow shed milking, to steal a look at her profile as they sat summer evenings on the kitchen step and watched the blue night smother the long sunset. He loved her with a desperateness that had pain in it and he never quite believed his luck that she was his wife. When the ache was hardest he would lean over and pat her hand and she would smile and talk to him about the water barrel they must mend to-morrow and the ditch he must dig so that the rain would not seep into the cow shed.

The first Sunday in August Vanda drove alone into the village to mass. She had on her wedding dress of white percale and a big white hat with red roses. The skin of her face and throat was wind bronzed and red with health and her teeth were very white. In her eyes lay unawakened contentment.

Seated high on the driver's seat her body yielded to the rough jolting of the wagon with something that was almost grace. At the corner by the Lutheran church she drew up sharply to avoid running into a man. For an instant they looked at each other searchingly, baffled. In that moment something terrible had happened and something beautiful. It was as though out of two different worlds they had come together—and as though each had known all the time of the other. There were no defenses, no escapes. Something stronger than either one had gripped them.

With hands that trembled for the first time Vanda drew in the reins. "Gee whiz," she said. "Better look where you're goin', eh?"

The young man took off his cap and smiled up at her. He was tall and straight and good looking. Brown curls, cropped short, fitted close to his head which was beautifully modelled. His eyes were blue, his mouth large and turned up a shade at the corners and his teeth were as white as hers.

"Yes," he said. "I shouldn't want to be laid out —now." His cap was still off and she saw the way the sun glinted in his hair.

Another moment they stared at each other, then Vanda's horse, impatient of the delay, started on. She did not draw in the reins to stop him nor did she look back. At the church she got out of the wagon and tied the horse with a rope halter to the wooden paling of the fence.

Inside the church she knelt down and her lips said over the Hail Mary. All through the mass she did not look behind her but she knew he was there—watching. She did not feel self conscious, or even excited but, when she knelt for the benediction, she knew it was of her he was thinking. To her had come at last the terrible power a woman possesses who knows herself to be desired.

After mass she came out slowly. There were many people she knew and Father Manardi stopped to greet her at the door.

"You are prospered then, my daughter?" he asked her.

Vanda smiled and nodded. "But it is too hot for

the potatoes." She made a little mocking gesture with her shoulders. "Whoof—the bugs come to eat them before we do."

At the fence by Vanda's horse stood the stranger. He was as well dressed as any man from Minneapolis who ever came into Hans Schwartz's lunch room and his manner proclaimed his assurance. With a deftness Vanda could not but admire he untied the rope halter, slipped it through the bridle ring and retied it in a knot she had never seen before. Then he cramped the wagon around and assisted Vanda in so that not a fleck of dust from the wheel touched her skirt.

Again from the driver's box she looked down at him.

"There is a dance to-morrow night at the Rudolfs' barn raising." His words were neither command nor entreaty. He knew simply that she would be there. Then he took off his cap again and the sun once more turned the close cropped locks into glinting bronze.

They did not even say good-bye, for his presence did not leave her. All the way back to the farm it seemed as though she were powerless to move and her eyes saw nothing. She thought suddenly of a fairy tale of her childhood and she smiled to herself.

"I bet I am enchanted," she whispered finally. "Gee, how funny."

When she came into the one room of the farm house Waldemar looked up suddenly and blushed. He was sitting at the little deal table and before him lay a dozen pieces of paper, torn and ink blotted. It was coarse grained paper and the pen he wrote with tripped maliciously and left little sprays of ink in its trail. Waldemar's brow was wrinkled and beads of perspiration stood on his upper lip.

"Oh," he said, "you are back too soon." He was like an honest child, caught at a knavish trick. "It was to be a surprise."

Vanda stepped nearer and looked at the arduous scrawl. "What is it?"

"I write those folks in Minneapolis, like you read about in paper—that send you little chicks that are just hatched so you not have to wait for old hen to lay and hatch them herself."

"Oh—" Vanda slowly took off her hat and unbuttoned her dress. She stood there before him in her petticoat, her arms and neck bare, her young breasts held firm by the smooth linen of her bodice. "Oh—" she repeated.

He watched her put on the blue gingham work dress and rebuild the fire. He was stunned at her indifference, her casualness. Finally she looked at him. He was like a dog that has been scolded for an unknown offense. She came over to him and patted his shoulder.

"That will be fine and dandy," she said. She was the mother again, humoring her child. "How many did you say for?"

Waldemar's sun again rose in the heaven. "Six hundred. See?" He was aghast at his temerity.

Vanda nodded. "Good. I can manage so many damn easy."

The next afternoon Vanda put on a clean blue gingham dress, shimmery with starch, and harnessed the horse to the spring wagon. She walked to the edge of the potatoe patch where Waldemar was working and called him. With questioning eyes he came toward her. She met him squarely.

"Look," she said, "I take the clock into town to get fix and I buy sugar and tea and coffee."

He nodded his assent dumbly.

"Then I have supper at Hans Schwartz's and I go to the dance in the Rudolfs' new barn. I think I stay all night with Seena afterward. It will be late."

Again he nodded.

Vanda smiled at him pityingly. He would be lonesome without her. She was sorry. "I have not seen the folks since—since I come here," she said. "To-night by Rudolfs' we have two fiddles and a zyther, like in old country." A far away look came into her eyes. She was homesick, not for the dirty village in Bohemia that she scarcely remembered, not for the gaiety and excitement of the lunch counter. She was homesick for something intangible, nebulous, something she had never known. She felt oppressed and at the same time exhilarated.

Vanda Terschak came of a people whose feelings were simple and strong. The folk stories of her childhood had been a meaty food, as unashamed, as primitive, as vivid as the colors the women wove into their broideries. Their humor partook of the grotesque and the vulgar, their hatred and their love were elemental, their conventions the feast days of the church. The wrath of God meant little in comparison with the carnival of living.

Waldemar rubbed the sleeve of his shirt across his face. He was embarrassed at the contrast between her trimness and his grime. He did not want her to go but it would never occur to him to prevent her. She was young and he was thirty. He must remember that.

"Tell Seena she must come here sometimes, eh?" He wanted her to believe he understood, that he shared her social cravings. "Soon you can show her your chicks. You will be proud then, eh?" he beamed.

Vanda smiled and nodded. "You will see to-night there is clean straw for the cows and the door to the chicken coop is fastened tight and plug up the weasel hole beneath the fence."

He smiled slyly at the unflattering minuteness of her directions. "I will try to be as smart like you," he said finally.

For a long time he stood in the potato patch, his hoe on the ground, his eyes watching a speck of blue high on the driver's seat of the old spring wagon. Even after it had become lost in the birch wood his eyes held the far place where it had gone. Then he took up his hoe again and went to work. He would have to hurry if he were to finish before sundown.

With each mile of the way to town Vanda's heart grew lighter. She was anxious to see Seena and the other girls, to go into the stores, to admire the local jeweler's assortment when she took him the clock. Suddenly she wished she had put on her best dress and the red sash. She might at least have worn the sash. How plain she looked and her skin was as dark as a half-breed's. But even as she despaired she knew she was lying to herself. She knew she was beautiful and that it was good to live.

Some way the hours passed until all the girls at Hans Schwartz's piled into Vanda's wagon and started for the dance. They were a noisy crowd, as fresh and light-hearted as though they had not worked since six o'clock that morning. Vanda was more plainly dressed than they and she was glad. She was no village flirt at a street fair. She would not coquette for his attention. But beneath her hauteur lay another reason. She knew that—for him—her beauty would shine through a thousand dresses of gingham.

Along the fence at the Rudolfs' there stood already a half a dozen farm wagons and a pretentiously shiny new roadster. Seena noticed it and pointed.

"See," she said. "He's here. The new boss of the construction gang." Then she turned to Vanda. "Whoof—" and she made a comic, extravagant gesture, "he's a swell guy. A fellah told me he been in Chicago and Minneapolis and Winnipeg and Boston and China. And he's rich." Her voice shrilled with emphasis.

Vanda looked at the girl beside her. "Oh—" So he worked for the railroad. Well, she supposed he had to work for some one. It was strange. Perhaps Isolde never wondered either what it was Tristam did. "Come on," she said—but she walked more slowly than the other girls.

The door of the barn stood wide open and a broad avenue of light stretched across the roadway, throwing the pebbles and the weeds into exaggerated silhouettes. Already there sounded the thin, delightful discords of violins being tuned. Then some one ran up the chromatic scale, ending in a wild, high flourish. Something in Vanda's heart stood still and she stopped. "Gee," she whispered, "gee."

True enough, a little apart from the group near the door, was the stranger. His hands were in his pockets, his cap off and his eyes watched the doorway. He stood apart not from snobbishness but from preoccupation. He was like a man on a crowded city corner who catches a memory of April trees and broiling trout stream. When Vanda entered he came over to the giggling, pushing group of country girls. He and Vanda looked at each other but they did not speak. When the fiddles struck up a tune he slipped his arm around her and led her into the dance.

The big room with its rough pine rafters was lighted by a dozen lanterns that gave the place a shadowy vastness even greater than it possessed. In one corner sat the three musicians, Bohemians, their black eyes fastened on the dancers, their white teeth gleaming, their feet beating the accent of the rhythm. They had no music before them. What they played were the tunes of the old country, strange, gripping things full of a savage, desperate joyousness. Most of them were in the minor, for even the dance music of a peasant folk has its moments of heart-break.

Vanda and the young man from the construction gang danced as though out of all the millions of people in the world they alone possessed reality. Their response to each other was as simple, as complete as the joining of two raindrops on a window pane. After the dance they followed the others out into the moonlight but they did not loiter near the door so that they might come trooping back the instant a new dance was begun. Instead they walked on across the pasture, blanched and still in the moonlight. It did not occur to them they had come far, that the dance tunes reached them only as crippled melodies from which distance had shorn all but the accented notes. Vanda could supply the lost notes from memory, but Michael Collins had been raised on other tunes in another land.

Finally they stood, their eyes looking out over the prairie, level now as a glass.

"I have seen the sea like that," he said. "Once I shipped to Rio. I was sixteen. When we started I was the boy that was there to let the cook bedevil him. When we came back there wasn't a mast I couldn't reach the top of. It's great business, bein' up there with nothing but the sea and the sky and St. Anthony to keep you from plungin' headlong." He shrugged his shoulders cynically but his smile was as ingratiating as a boy's. "Not that I count much on the saints."

She looked up at him gravely.

"No," he went on, "the world's a fine rose growing on a thistle. It's yours for the picking." He stretched out his hands toward her. "See, my fingers are agile and strong. I can get you the rose—without a scratch, without a thorn prick." They looked at each other in silence. The wind stirred the long grass of the pasture, it caressed their cheeks and foreheads like the touch of a phantom lover. "Vanda, Vanda——"

Suddenly her arms sought the curve of his shoulders, her temple pressed against his cheek, the smell of her hair was in his nostrils. They never knew how long they held each other. The breeze fluttered her skirt around him, the pale moon grew higher and smaller. Three tunes were begun and finished in the Rudolfs' ballroom and they still stood there. Finally his lips touched her hair and her eyes and her forehead.

"Vanda," he said.

She lifted her face to him and their lips met. It was as though all their lives had been nothing but a preparation for this moment. Nothing before had mattered, nothing to come mattered. All the reality of existence was crowded into that moment.

"Listen," he said at last. "Next week I go up to Winnipeg and from there to Quebec. I'm the boss of the division." He held her away from him and looked at her. "I'm always going to be the boss. You're either born that way or you're not. I knew it that first trip I shipped to Rio." This was no theatrical bravado. He was as honest with her as though he were in confessional. "Come with me to Winnipeg. It's a big world and I can show it all to you. I can give you everything you want. I'll take you to San Francisco and maybe to China. There'll be big ships and big cities and big oceans. It's the keys to the world I've got here in my pocket."

She stared at him with the wide eyes of a child and she knew he was speaking the truth. He would always be boss of his gang. Someday he might even start in business for himself. He was one of those men whom it is as impossible to defeat as it is inevitable that others shall be defeated.

For a long moment they looked at each other. She did not move and her arms hung motionless at her sides. "I'll come." She held up her hand suddenly. "No, first listen." He was standing close to her but he did not touch her. "It is not because of the big cities, or the things you could give me. It is, I don't know—" she lifted her shoulders with a quaint wistfulness. "It is as though the sun told the willows it was April. Is it a big foolishness that I speak?"

Suddenly they heard voices across the pasture. She wondered idly whether they had been missed but neither was oppressed by regret or embarrassment.

"Come," she said, "it is late"

Slowly they walked back toward the barn, their hands holding fiercely to each other.

"Sunday," he said, "after mass I shall tell you where to meet me."

She nodded. "Sunday. That is six days from now. Six years." She laughed, softly. "What if I hadn't nearly run over you, eh?"

He shrugged his shoulders and drew her against

him with desperate tenderness. "What if there hadn't been any world whatsoever?"

They clung to each other like frightened children.

"I love you," he whispered.

She pressed her cheek against his and their arms held each other with the fierceness that has in it the knowledge of parting.

"Gee whiz, gee whiz," she whispered.

All that week on the farm Vanda went about her work with feverish intenseness. She baked and scoured and churned. She even tried to show Waldemar how the curded cheese of the Bohemians was made.

"Why for should I learn?" he demanded. "Is it not enough that you are a master?"

Afternoons she helped him with the potatoes. She showed him how to raise the oat bin so that the rats could not molest it. She had a hundred plans and Waldemar humored her, amused at her childish tyranny.

"Next spring," she said, "you should dig a ditch the length of the potato field. The soil to the east is better. Can you remember that?"

He looked down at her and smiled. "Next spring," he said, "you can remind me."

That Sunday they drove in together to the village. At the door to the church Waldemar drew up the horse. "I come back when the mass is over."

Vanda puzzled a moment. "No," she said, "meet me at Seena's. I walk a little way with the folks."

He nodded but he did not drive on. For a minute they looked at each other. "Vanda," he said, "there is no one so pretty like you in all Minnesota."

A flush stained her cheeks and crept painfully down her throat. "Oh, go on," she said. Strange how difficult it was to smile then.

During the mass Vanda did not look around. She neither prayed nor listened to the service but she felt at peace. What she intended to do she could explain to no one, so why harass herself with a thousand potential confessions.

After the service he was waiting for her on the sidewalk. Quite as naturally as though he had been her brother she left the Rudolfs and went over to speak to him.

"To-morrow night," he said, "I shall leave here at seven o'clock and drive out to your place." He waited a moment but she did not interrupt him. "I shall wait for you at the edge of the pasture where the red rock is. We can make Duluth by morning. You can buy all you want there. Then we're on to Winnipeg." He was speaking as calmly as though he was telling her the weather would be fine for the harvest. They did not even shake hands. "Vanda," he said, "it will be to-morrow the beginning of the world."

Their eyes burned into each other. "I know," she said.

Then they said good-bye and neither one looked back as they walked down the village street.

As soon as Vanda returned to the farm she put on her work dress and started for the potato patch. Waldemar, returning from the barn, met her half way. "Vanda," he protested, "you work too hard. Like a horse. Leave a leetle for big man like me, eh?"

But she shook her head grimly. "To-day he is fine weather. To-morrow?" She shrugged her shoulders. "Go in the house now and smoke." She turned him around, as one would a child, and gave him a little push. "Shoo—" she said. "Beat it."

It was sundown before she returned. "To-morrow," she said, "I finish my garden." She dropped down onto a chair by the table and the light from the lamp fell upon her. There were shadows under her eyes—one seldom sees these on a country girl

—and her hands had fallen into her lap with the stillness of exhaustion.

Waldemar knelt down and tried to unlace the coarse boots but his fingers only knotted the cords.

"Clumsy one," she said, but she smiled at him.

He was chagrined, even more at her smile than at her rebuke. "Is there nothing I can do for you?" he asked finally.

But it seemed to him as though she had not even heard his question.

The next day was misty and cold, one of those August days that come sometimes in Minnesota, gray and raw with the prophecy of winter. Vanda shivered and put on her shawl when she went out to feed the chickens. By afternoon it had begun to drizzle.

"Perhaps it will snow yet," she said. Waldemar was getting ready to go to town. A wave of apprehensive tenderness swept over her. "Why go to-day," she said, "you will catch bad cold, sure ting."

Her interest pleased him but he only laughed. "I cannot work out. It is good time to fetch the wire and plow-blade."

After he had gone Vanda put her house in order. It was different now from that first time she had seen it. Curtains of turkey red calico hung at the windows. On the floor was a bright colored rag rug, such as the Bohemians make. The copper pans that hung above the stove shone like the tiny clouds that flecked the sunset. On one wall hung a metal crucifix, hand wrought and very old, on another an enormous sent-free calendar depicting a scene in the Swiss Alps. Vanda looked at it now. "I will see that with him," she thought. Then she whispered, "Gee," and she did not move for a long time.

At six o'clock Waldemar's supper was ready. Vanda had put on a clean blue calico dress and combed her hair again. Her face was pale but her hands went about their work with the swift efficiency they had always known.

At six-thirty he had not returned or at seven. A quarter before eight she heard the grinding of wheels on the gravel. In an instant he appeared in the doorway. His hair was tousled and tiny drops of moisture clung to his face and to the coarse wool of his jacket. She could tell at once he was laboring under great excitement.

"What is it?" she said.

"Vanda, Vanda," he repeated. "They have come, the tiny chicks from Minneapolis. I got them at the station. It is so cold now, like winter. They will die, maybe."

Vanda pushed him aside and went out. Under a corner of the dripping canvas she peered into the crates. It was almost dark but she could hear a curious murmur, made up of dozens of infinitesimal flutterings and peepings. "Oh my God," she thought, "there must be a thousand. Oh my God."

Then she lowered the canvas flap again and came back to the kitchen. "Get the lantern in the barn," she said, "and light this one. I take out the lamp. Then bring the boxes into the hen house. We make it warmer with the lanterns. Bring me at once clean straw." She looked at him an instant, then she shook her head. "No," she said, "I will get it. All my wishes cannot make you move faster."

Like a great tattered banner she carried above her head a pitch-fork full of straw. Strands of it had fallen on her hair and shoulders and the air was sweet with its fragrance. Adroitly she arranged her burden. Waldemar, holding the flickering lantern, watched her. Suddenly she stopped.

"It is so rough," she said, "like sticks. Wait—" and she pushed by him. In an instant she returned with a great pillow stuffed with goose feathers.

"See," she said as she ripped open the end. "See, I told you it might snow to-day." At once the air was filled with a smoothering whiteness. "Have a care for the lanterns," she commanded.

Then, after the storm had abated, he brought her the crates and one by one she lifted out the tiny, yellow chickens. "Oh, they are cold," she said, "and this one. I tink his leg must be broke. Waldemar, cup your hands so, like this." He did as she ordered. "Take this now into the house, and this one. Put them close by the stove in the fruit basket. No," she said, "I will do it. Your hands are too heavy."

For an hour she worked with the intenseness of a surgeon performing a long operation. It was past nine when the last tiny, fluttering occupant had been given food and water and stowed away in the downy whiteness. Finally Vanda straightened her tired back. "It is necessary you stay here and watch the lanterns. I am afraid someting might happen. Soon it will be warm enough." He followed her with his eyes into the darkness. "I must go back to the sick ones." In the kitchen she bent over the fruit basket anxiously. One tiny ball she lifted up to her cheek. "I did not find you soon enough, eh?" she whispered.

For a long moment she crouched there, then she stood up slowly. Outside in the darkness he was waiting for her, waiting. She looked dully around the room, at the stove and the bed and the chairs, at the cheap colored picture, at the crucifix. Then she took down her shawl from the hinge of the door where it hung.

It had stopped raining but fast sailing, white rimmed storm clouds raced after the moon, captured it and raced on. Her head bare Vanda ran across the grass of the pasture to the main road. The lights of an automobile streamed to meet her, turning into patches of silver the pools of water in the road. She was out of breath when she arrived and her skirt and arms were spattered with mud.

"Vanda!" He was at her side in an instant. "Sweetheart." A moment she lay in his arms. He did not kiss her. It was enough that they had found each other again. Overhead drove the storm clouds, like great, strange birds, and the moments passed.

Finally she loosened his arms around her and they faced each other. At last he looked at her, incredibly. "Vanda—" he caught both her wrists with his hands, "Vanda, Vanda——"

Finally she nodded. "It is true. I am not

coming." Her face was white but her eyes were calm. "I love you. You know. But you do not need me." She lifted her shoulders in a quaint little appeal for silence. "I have learned this tonight, but it has always been true, I tink. To some women it is more to give than to have give to. Do you understand? You I love but he I can help. See now?" Again there was a moment of silence. "I cannot talk fine enough maybe to tell you."

"Vanda." He could only repeat her name. He wanted her—more than anything else in the world and he was used to taking what he wanted. But now he stood before her baffled, powerless. "Vanda, honey—" He was frantic with longing, with apprehension. "Can't you see what it is you are doing? It's not only me you send away but you too. It is the magic of life you snuff out like a candle." He was standing close to her but he did not touch her. Between them stood already a barrier more real than a wall of stone. Between them stood the barrier of a greater need.

Again she shook her head. "No, I am sure, sure." Her eyes never wavered. "And I go now."

Though he held her again in his arms and felt the sobbing of her breath against his throat he knew she had said good-bye, that they had lost each other.

"Vanda, Vanda, little one," he repeated. Her arms held him with a strength he had never suspected, the strength of a frantic longing. He knew he would never feel them again around him, never touch her hair with his lips, never even see her.

Finally she broke away and he stood without moving. For a brief path the lights of his automobile followed her but she knew his eyes kept on staring long after she had disappeared into the blackness.

In the kitchen again she washed the mud from her arms and changed her dress. She seemed to move very slowly. "I am tired," she thought. "It is late."

Then she went out to the hen house. Waldemar stood waiting outside the door. "It is hot in there now, like the hell," he explained.

Again she inspected her charges. "Good," she said finally, "bring the lamps."

She followed him back to the kitchen. He seemed incredibly big in the darkness, walking between the two glowing lanterns. In the kitchen he turned down the wicks, snuffed out the flame with

his fingers and made fast the door. As he passed
the stove he stopped and looked down at the peach
basket. Vanda stood silent in the middle of the
room and her eyes watched him strangely.

Finally he turned around. "It is damn lucky for
them," he pointed with his great hand, "you are
here." Then he came a step nearer and in his eyes
was the same look she had seen that first night at
the lunch counter when she had bandaged his hand.
"Vanda—" She wondered suddenly if animals, if
trees and grass tried to speak, if everything in life
struggled to call out—and found no words with
which to call. "Vanda," he repeated, "it is me who
is damn lucky too."

He sat down by the table and began tugging off
the great boots, stiff and crackled with many wet-
tings. Without moving she watched him. His
face grew red with effort. At last, with a wrench,
he tore loose the soggy lacing. He looked up at
her suddenly chagrined and embarrassed, the
boot discarded on the floor, his hands between his
knees. "I ban great clumsy Swede," he said.

At once there was a curious ache in her throat
and it was difficult to swallow. Slowly she came
over to him. She pushed the tousled hair back
from his forehead, finally she drew his head against

her side. Her face was old, at once, and in her eyes was the look of those first pioneers, left behind on the plains, when the rest of the band travelled westward. She, too, saw the last fleck of the sun on the white roofed wagons as the trail curved beyond the horizon.

Then she looked down at the man beside her and she smiled. "Perhaps it is lucky for you," she said, "you 'ban' big clumsy Swede."

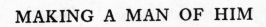

MAKING A MAN OF HIM

MAKING A MAN OF HIM

THE Eureka Lunch Room was the only eating place in Black Hawk that was open after eight o'clock. The Eureka operated on no regular schedule. If the weather was blizzardy, it closed early. If it was Saturday night in spring, after the loggers were back and when the roads were good enough for the farmers to come to town, it stayed open until ten o'clock. Fritz Weber's old woman did the cooking, Fritz, toothpick in mouth, took in the money and in times of stress lent a heavy assistance to the two waitresses who were Annie Larson and Aida Sparks.

Annie Larson was the daughter of old Swen Larson, one of the richest and tightest fisted farmers in all northern Minnesota. Working out was Annie's only method of getting into town. For two years she had stayed at the Bakers', earned two dollars and fifty cents a week and gone to

273

school. Now she was independent. There was no staying in at nights any longer to look after the Baker kids, there was no keeping an eye on Caspar when she wanted to read a novel. There too was no stuffy Mrs. Baker to say that Eddie Skenk was not a nice boy and that she couldn't go to the band concert with him.

True, the work at the Eureka Lunch Room was just as hard and the pay was no better but it was a heady tonic to be your own boss. Annie's vitality was elemental. Each night she slept, the window tightly closed, with a soundness nothing could disturb. It took Mrs. Weber five minutes to get her waked up at six o'clock every morning.

"Like as not she'd sleep right through the trump of doom," old Fritz observed tartly, "and there'd be one hash slinger less in paradise."

Life in Black Hawk to Annie was no end entertaining. There was so much going on, there were so many folks on the street, so many lights from the store windows. It was fun, too, joshing the men who came to the lunch room, saying to them "go chase yourself," and "like it or lump it," and "put that in your pipe and smoke it."

Of course they joshed her back and sometimes a man would give her a sack of candy or pinch her

arm slyly as she brought him a plate of beans.
Annie would blush with pleasure on all such occasions and say "oh, go on," or "now you quit."
This represented repartee in Black Hawk, Minnesota. Crude and banal as it was, it contained the
eternal feminine archness, the world old beckoning
of the pursued to the pursuer. Annie was intox-
icated with excitement. Black Hawk was to her a
city of enchantment, a never ending carnival.

Annie Larson had been born and brought up in
a mud thatched cabin on the prairie where there
had been no nearest neighbors. Small wonder that
to Annie Larson Black Hawk was New York,
Paris and Vienna.

Aida Sparks was different. No one knew much
about Aida. She was older than Annie and not so
strong and there were lines around her mouth and
eyes one does not see in a country girl. Aida said
she had come north from Mankato. Perhaps she
had, but Mankato had been but one of a long list
of places where the name of Aida Sparks had cast
forth a doubtful glimmer and flickered out. Aida
was thirty, maybe thirty-five, and she had burned
her candle senselessly and magnificently. But Aida
Sparks at thirty had more past than most women
have at eighty. At thirty-five she was facing

nothing with seven dollars in cash, with a gentleman's platinum watch hidden deep in her bureau drawer, and with a sense of the beauty and bitterness of all existence.

Over the counter where Fritz Weber made change and kept the chewing plug and the two boxes of five cent cigars, Aida had tacked a picture. It had been cut from a magazine with a two ply color press and it represented New York in the twilight of a soft winter evening. Like lavender castles of paste-board the great buildings came out of the dusk. Blurred and yellow gleamed the thousand lights of the city. The pavements were lavender white from the snow fall, the tops of cabs were white and thin lines of white outlined the cornices of buildings. It was a moment of unbelievable beauty and softness, a moment exquisite, mysterious and yet glamorously New York.

Cheap and torn reproduction that it was, it was enough to break the heart of a New Yorker half dead of loneliness already. It was the first thing Larry Mitchell raised his eyes to as he sat down at the counter of the Eureka Lunch Room and ordered an omelette and coffee.

Aida Sparks looked at him a moment with graveness, then she smiled slowly and kindly. "Dearie," she said, "omelettes don't grow west of the Mississippi. But you can have 'em sunnyside up."

Larry Mitchell's eyes focussed almost with interest. "All right," he said, "sunnyside. Sunnyside." His thin lips drew into a line of mockery.

The woman behind the counter looked at him shrewdly again and she hesitated a moment as though about to speak. Then she went out to the kitchen and ordered the two eggs fried after the Pollyanna designation.

Meanwhile Larry Mitchell was alone in the lunch room and his eyes went back to the torn print on the wall. He did not move, it seemed as though he hardly breathed but he drank in every detail of that picture as the eyes of a returning peasant soldier search down the road for the first sign of his village.

It was a young face, not very strong perhaps, but likeable and intelligent. Aida knew that in spite of the weakness there showed breeding. He was no travelling salesman come up from the twin cities with a line of goods he would display next day in the long bleak show room of the Black Hawk Commercial House.

There was something about the way his jacket fitted his shoulders that made Aida homesick.

There was something too in the way his eyes had hung on the shabby picture that made something rise in her throat. He was like no one she had seen in Black Hawk, in Mankato, in Minneapolis. He was one of her own, she knew it, neither very wise nor very strong, but with a capacity for joy that few can even dream of and with an equal gift for suffering.

Aida put the food before him gently. She had warmed the plate and polished it to a shine with a napkin. She was careful the coffee did not spill from the heavy white walled cup into the saucer. Generally she didn't care. The men she served mostly poured it into their saucers anyway. She even stole one of the linen napkins from the old woman's black walnut side-board and gave it to him. The young man accepted her service without either question or comment. Once he caught her eye and he smiled, not because he wanted to smile but because it seemed the only decent thing to do.

Aida busied herself about the counter, lining up mustard jars and catsup bottles, filling the empty salt cellars, wiping off the top of the sugar bowl with the same soiled napkin. Then she reset the counter, placing at irregular intervals along the dingy wooden slab a meagre assortment of knicked china and plated silver.

"All set for to-morrow morning?" he asked at last.

Aida smiled. "I reckon you're our last customer this evening." She stopped a moment and looked down at him. "I can't say the night life of Black Hawk is anything to write home about."

They both smiled and then their eyes ran away from each other. Neither one wanted to invade the privacy of the other or have his own invaded. Yet each one knew he was bound to the other by a tie of mutual longing, of mutual loneliness. Larry Mitchell made the meal last as long as he could with any reason, then he looked up again at the woman before him.

"Where shall I stay all night?" He pointed to the little pile of smart and shabby luggage. "You see, I just got in on the train from Huntley."

Aida considered a moment. "Oh, the Commercial House, I guess. They're all bad enough, both of them." Then after a moment, "You're not going to be here long?"

He shook his head. "No. I'm going up to Albia, just north of here I believe." He waited a moment and his face tried to take on an expression of amused and cynical indifference, but the attempt did not work. "I've had a farm—wished on me. There seemed to be no alternative but—farming, if I cared to eat."

Aida looked at him a long moment in amazement. Black Hawk was a Paris in comparison with Albia, and the country north of Albia was as remote as the plains of Tibet, as the wastes of Patagonia.

There is a type of man who can live upon that country, break it, plant it, make it fertile. But the boy before her was not like one of these. They would do something awful to him, those flat, unfertile acres with their never ending ridge of gray hill against the never ending gray of sky. Yes, they would do something awful to him, his nerves were too near the surface. He would see that land in all its starkness and solitude. The pioneer type doesn't see things except as, "this piece will be good for potatoes. There is sand in it," or "next spring, when the frost is out, we will root up the pine stumps on Section Four."

Larry Mitchell gathered up the pieces of luggage, put his cap on and walked to the doorway. Then at once he stopped and looked back at the woman at the counter. "I wonder," he said. She could see he was embarrassed, that what he had to say was not easy. "I wonder if you would let me have that —" his eyes went back to the torn piece of paper on the wall. "I—come from that place," he said finally. "That's—home."

Aida Sparks took a step toward him, then she stopped. Suddenly he stood before her quite as dim as the lines of that phantom city. She mustn't cry, she was an idiot. Crying would only hurt him. She would give him the scrap of paper, she would give him anything he wanted if it were in her power. She wanted now to put her arms around him, to tell him he mustn't go out into that wildness. It would destroy him, kill him, or perhaps it would only make him mad, for it did that to some men. He was so young to her, as he stood there, so weak, so unknowing. Of course he could have that picture. She started to take out the pins that held it, then she stopped.

"No," she said, "you mustn't take it—out there with you. It's like taking the picture of your sweetheart and knowing all the time it's no use to go on hoping. Don't you see, you mustn't take it up to Albia with you? Just leave it here. It will be—waiting for you."

Larry Mitchell bit his lip and squared his shoulders. "Perhaps you're right. I'll leave it." He stopped a moment. "Perhaps it means something to you too."

Aida Sparks smiled again, a little wearily. "There was a time when I couldn't look at it either, but I can now. I've got by that." This time she smiled with a swagger and she too squared her shoulders. "When you get to be my age you toughen. As for me, I've got an epidermis like an elephant."

Larry Mitchell looked at her and smiled. "You're a—bird," he said. "The dear God should have made more like you. I shouldn't be here now if He had." He stopped a moment, then he blundered out of the doorway. "Good night," he said—and he was gone.

Aida looked a long time at the door that had closed behind him. She did not move. It was as though she had been enchanted. Then she sighed and took the dishes out to the kitchen, covered the fire and went upstairs to her room. It was cold up there. Annie was still out. There was something going on at the Commercial House. Annie had been in a flutter of anticipation all day. Aida remembered the first ball she had gone to. It had been at Rector's, the old Rector's in the days long before prohibition.

After she had turned out the light she slipped her hand under the pile of things in the drawer of her bureau and her fingers touched the beautiful watch of platinum and the slender chain. He had been like that boy this evening, gay and slender and not very strong. He hadn't been very square either —but he had loved her, she had really touched him. It has been very beautiful, surely, and a very long time ago.

Aida saw Larry Mitchell twice in the course of the next six months. Once he came into Black Hawk to enquire about the price of a harrow but when he found out how much it cost he shrugged his shoulders with amusement and walked out of the store.

"Queer chap," Si March observed to Dan Gills. "Don't seem like the sort that would fit into this country."

Dan Gills made no comment but he had watched the young fellow with all the shrewdness of a country doctor. He had noticed that the boy did not seem to know what the price of the harrow should be within many dollars. He was green, all right, and this wasn't the sort of country that was kind to greenhorns.

Dan Gills watched him stroll down the street, hesitate a moment before the Eureka Lunch Room, then go in. There was another queer one in there, he thought. They were a little alike, except that life had done everything to the girl it was going to.

There were only two people in the lunch room when Larry Mitchell entered. Aida looked up with indifference at the opening door, then her eyes took on more interest than they had shown for weeks. He glanced at her casually and nodded.

"How d'you do?" He came toward her slowly and she saw that already there was the purposeless slough of indirection in his walk.

She smiled at him kindly. "Well, how's everything by you?" she demanded.

"All right." His eyes had again slipped away from hers and he sat down at the counter. "Ham and eggs," he said, "please, and coffee."

She brought him his order and stood looking down at him. She was curious and this reticence alarmed her. "Well, it's spring to-day."

"Isn't it." Still he did not look at her.

"It must be almost beautiful now in the country," she offered.

This time he looked at her strangely. "Is it? I hadn't noticed."

Aida Sparks' shrewd eyes narrowed. He was thinner than when she saw him before and he looked someway vaguely unkempt though his face was shaved and his suit was the same well fitting city one. Aida laughed softly. "You're just like all farmers, never know whether it's hot or cold, spring or fall. About as much eye for the beauties of nature as a ground hog. All you know about is crops."

This time he looked at her as a sick man might look at his nurse. "Well, that's something to think about, isn't it? That's better than —vacuum."

She wanted to say something to him, to make him be candid with her, but the moment passed and in an instant she saw he was getting up from the counter. She leaned toward him, anxious and awkward. "You're sure everything's all right then?" she demanded.

"Couldn't be better—" Again he did not look at her and she noticed his eyes slid around to the little torn print above the counter, hastily, just to assure himself it was there. At the door he turned back and she knew his smile was in apology for his rudeness.

"So long," he said. "They're selling lilacs back home to-day on the street corners."

Again she looked a long time at the door that

had closed out both his figure and the pale distant sunshine of April.

"Who's the guy?" Annie asked.

Aida Sparks shook her head. "I don't know."

"City chap." Then after a moment. "He don't look awful healthy to me, kinda puny."

Aida Sparks made no comment. "How far is Albia from here?" she asked finally.

" 'Bout thirty miles. Why?"

"Oh, nothing." And when Aida spoke that way it was impossible to make her answer a word more fully.

The second time he came to town was August. It was hot that year and reddish dust lay over everything. The grass for pasturing had dried up early. The wheat looked sere and rusty. Already the leaves of the beech and willow were brown with the premature autumn that drought brings. At midday the land was as forlorn as a treeless desert, but with evening a crimson sun dropped back of the hills and a saffron moon hung long, fantastically magnified by the dusty atmosphere.

It was a gloomy season for farmers, and, heaven knew, their margin of gain was small enough even in good times. They were a silent lot at best the Danes and Swedes that had homesteaded that region. When they came to town they drank quietly and such quantities of gin as only those northern races are capable of and then they drove back to their lonely farms, sitting as stiff on the box of their wagons as so many wooden soldiers.

Larry Mitchell came into town on Saturday and wandered about like a man shorn of every purpose. It seemed he had nothing to buy and no cattle or grain to have weighed and shipped. Long moments he stood silent in front of store windows, his eyes making inventory of the medley of objects displayed for sale, lanterns, nails, saws, candles, bolts of gingham, shoes, bonnets. Whenever he suspected any one was looking at him he would saunter on, embarrassed but with a fine pretense of preoccupation.

At supper time he walked in the direction of the lunch room. Two or three times he strolled up and down in front of its rain streaked windows. Suddenly he leaned over and picked up something small from the sidewalk. Then he put the tiny something in his pocket and pushed open the door to the lunch room. He ordered a stew and coffee but Annie noticed he ate almost nothing and he drank his coffee black. She was curious about him. His color was gray, his cheeks were hollow and around his mouth and eyes had gathered the infinitesimal lines that come to a face that has suddenly become thin. He paid no attention to Annie and Annie was used to being noticed. Finally she leaned over the counter toward him. "Dance?" she said.

He looked up at her startled. He had not been aware of her presence. "Why, yes," he said, "anyway I used to."

Annie smiled upon him expansively. "Big shindig goin' on to-night at the Commercial House. For the church," she said. "Better come."

Again he looked at her as though he were trying to focus his attention. "Thank you. I'll come, if I can."

"All work, you know," she giggled. This was the high point of Annie's repartee.

Aida saw him as he was starting toward the door. She had been busy in the kitchen. Without unloading the order of eggs and coffee and pie she was bringing to a customer she put down the tray, so quickly that the coffee slopped over into the saucer, and, darting around the end of the counter, she intercepted his path.

"Hello," she said. She was embarrassed and a little out of breath with excitement and hurry.

His haggard eyes rested on her face. "How do you do?" He was frigidly polite.

"Going?" She blushed at the inanity of her question. Why couldn't she be casual? What had become of the old aplomb that had carried off so many situations in the past?

"Yes," he said.

"He's going to the dance," Annie Larson sang out from the counter.

Aida looked up at him sharply. "Oh—" Well, why not? Then, after a moment. "Is everything all right on the farm?" She did not mean to pry, she did not want to wound him or make him think she doubted his ability. "With the drought and all, you know, everybody's gotten sort of edgy."

He looked at her sharply. "Everything's fine," he said. "Thank you." Then he lifted his cap, bowed politely and was gone.

It was Aida's night to stay in at the counter. Everybody else was going to the dance. She watched Annie go, her cheeks scarlet, her pompadour an architectural triumph. Annie wore a new waist of lavender silk with a pink ribbon twisted around her neck and fastened in front with a pin of gold plated wire that read "Baby." Aida looked at the waist and Annie grinned with satisfaction.

"Hope I don't sweat it out," she said. But Aida knew she didn't really care. She was too full of joy of anticipation to let even such a calamity as this would be overshadow her spirits.

"Have a good time," she said.

"Sure," said Annie. From the door she looked back, a little guilty. "Sorry you ain't comin'. But then, you don't like to dance much, anyhow."

Aida smiled. "I'm not so young as I used to be." Then to herself she added mockingly, "not by a couple of centuries."

Larry Mitchell had of course no intention of going to the shindig but he drifted down the street with the others. It was one of those summer nights when the spluttering glow of the gas light, hung at the street intersections, is pale in comparison with the moonlight. The shadows of beech and poplar fell black across the roadway. Everywhere was the sound of voices and excited laughter.

Finally came the twang of the fiddle being tuned and the barbaric, oriental wheeze of the accordion. Larry Mitchell strolled down to the Commercial House and looked in at the open window. The dance was in the dining room where the tables and chairs had been pushed back against the walls. This room had always seemed to him particularly ugly.

The wall paper, soiled and torn lose from the moulding, had the same primitive colors and pseudo oriental design as the ingrain carpet in the parlor. The woodwork had been painted a dirty plum color. From the ceiling hung three kerosene lamps which could be raised and lowered over a wheel, like buckets in a well.

Larry Mitchell stared in at the window until some one saw him and called out. "Pay your twenty-five cents and come in yourself. This ain't no the-a-ter."

Startled at having been made, even for a second, a figure of notice, the young man stepped away from the window and back into the shadow. Another dance was begun and finished and still he stood there. He was faint with weariness, sick with loneliness. His head ached and there were queer tremors that went up and down his spine. It seemed at once he could not stand there another moment. It also seemed as though he could not move. He wondered if perhaps this might not be the beginning of madness.

Another dance was begun and like a man in a trance he came forward, but this time he sought out another window. It was the one nearest the door into the dining room and just below it stood the table where the gate keeper sat to collect the tickets and make the change. Sam Barlow, the treasurer, had deserted his post and was busy adjusting a smoking lamp. The crowd continued to dance, jeering at him good naturedly and making sport of his clumsy efforts to readjust the wick and burnish off the blackened chimney.

"Reckon this old hotel ain't had one of them lamps cleaned up since Buchanan was president," opined Si Larkins.

Everybody's eyes were on Sam Barlow. Nobody noticed the table by the door on which the change money stood. It was no trick at all to put in one's hand through the open window. He would not even have to stand on tip-toe and lean over to accomplish it. All one had to do was to move his arm up and inward—and then out again. It was all so simple, so childish.

"Hey, boys, haul her up there," Si Larkin shouted again when the chimney had been replaced, "all together now, pull."

There were great guffaws of laughter at this sally. Sam Barlow pulled the lamp again into place. "Anybody'd think I'd grown a third arm, or somethin'—all this commotion."

Aida Sparks, coming down the main street after

the last customer had been fed at the lunch room, stumbled sharply against a young man at the drug store corner. Each had been walking head down, at a rapid pace, each was absorbed with his thoughts.

"Gosh—" said Aida as she started back. Then she saw who it was she had charged into. "You ——"

He looked at her a moment in amazement. "I don't know whether it is or not." There was no expression on his face but his eyes were strange.

"Larry—" She came up close to him again and she lifted her hand to his cheek. "Larry," she said, "you're hot. You've got a fever."

A second he crushed her hand against his face, moving it slowly across his eyes, his lips. It seemed as though it must hold some sort of magic.

"Larry," she whispered.

Suddenly he threw back his head and straightened up. "Don't let me make a fool of myself. I've decided to do something. I've—made—up—my mind."

He turned away from her but this time she caught him in her arms. "Larry, tell me," she pleaded. "Tell me. God knows I'm no angel. It's only—mortal to blunder—and be forgiven. It's only human. Larry——"

He wrenched himself away from her embrace though her thin arms held him with a strength he would never have suspected. "Let me go," he cried. "I'm a fool. I'm a fool. I'm no use fussing over. I tell you it's no use. I'm sunk."

In a panic of strength he broke away from her and started on a run across the street to the court house square where the farm wagons all were tied. At once she heard the sound of a horse jerked sharply out of a drowse and struck into a gallop. After a while she could hear only faintly the sound of hoofs and finally not at all. He was sick, she thought, maybe very sick. Then at last she looked down at her arms. Strange, she had felt something hard against them, something thick and hard. It had been in the pocket of his jacket and it was of a shape she could not identify.

That night Annie told her how the money out of the box had been stolen. Annie was at once outraged and delighted. It was awful, of course, to take the guild's money, the money with which they were going to buy a picture of George and Martha Washington for the church parlor, but it had made the evening much more exciting.

Aida waited until Annie had turned from her and was busy brushing the ratting out of her pompadour. "Have they any idea who took it?"

Annie shook her head vigorously. "Nope. Some tramp probably. Stuck his hand in through the window. Sam Barlow says he'll get him, sure's shootin'. Sam's as mad, like an otter." Her cheeks still glowed with the excitement of reminiscence. Then she yawned and blew out the light. Aida heard her charge into bed and yawn again. "Say, your friend from the city never showed up at all," she added. "Though somebody saw him for a minute lookin' in the window. He's a funny one." She yawned again. "A—funny—one." Then there was silence and the regular healthy rise and fall of healthy breathing.

For a long time Aida lay and stared up into the blackness. Black Hawk was surely noted not for its astuteness. Annie Larson suspected nothing, of that she was certain. But surely, among the rest, there must be one who could put two and two together. Yes, there must surely be one.

It was dawn before Aida Sparks finally went to sleep, but it was not a sleep of refreshment. It was light and troubled. Aida Sparks had made up her mind what to do.

The next day was Sunday and Aida's day off. Once every two weeks the girls had a whole day free. Annie sometimes went home, if the roads were good. She went home, not so much from a sense of duty as for the joy of release which came each time upon her return.

Aida never did much with her Sundays. She rested, she read a story in one of the cheap magazines left in the lunch room by a traveling salesman. She could never get quite rested enough, someway. It was a losing game she was playing with fatigue. Indeed, it was a losing game she was playing all around. As she glanced in the mirror now it was difficult to remember how she had looked when she wore the soft thick white fur collar drawn with luxurious cosiness close about her throat. Her face above it had been lovely and as pink as a rose-bud and the delicate blue of the plume on her hat had traced out the blue in her eyes. Her frock, then, had come from Paris and so had the hat and the coat and the feather boa and the gloves.

The room in which she had lived was hardly comparable with her costumes but there were chintz overdrapes at the windows and the bureau of imitation mahogany had been cluttered with a magnificent though tarnished collection of silver picture frames.

There had followed a succession of other rooms without any gay chintz curtains and when the number of frames on the bureau had dwindled at last to one. These places had been lighted mostly by a single gas jet and they had coarse lace curtains at the windows and a powder of dust rose with each foot-step upon the worn carpet. And finally there had come the room that she shared with Annie over Fritz Weber's café. In all there was not more than twelve years between the room with the chintz and this one. Well, this was the sort of thing that happened to you if you weren't either intelligent or lucky. But it had been beautiful, some of it, worth almost the contrast of the present.

This Sunday morning Aida did not leave the house until eleven. No one in the lunch room saw her go and no one in the village. It was the hour when every one was either in the kitchen or at service. Aida walked briskly until she came to the Lutheran Church. Tied to the fence rail at the side stood the shabby row of farm wagons. Aida's eyes found Olaf Swenson's with its team of bays, the feet of which had pawed hollows of restlessness into the sun baked earth. There was no one at all on the road. Cautiously Aida walked to the wagon and looked around.

Through the open windows of the church she could hear the preacher thunder forth the end of the sermon. Then he read the number of a hymn, "one hundred fifty-six, page ninety-three, 'Crown Him with many crowns.'" Then came the first explosive bellow of the organ. "Hymn one hundred and fifty-six, page ninety-three, 'Crown Him',", the pastor shouted. "First, second and last verse."

Aida smiled. There was something amusing in the pompous minuteness of his orders. He got three hundred dollars a year and his house. He could not be said to be a person of much importance, but to-day was his day of authority. He commanded his congregations to sing that hymn as a Prussian lieutenant commands his battalion. He even made an arbitrary selection of verses and in this too his flock must follow him. It was a moment truly not without drama.

Aida knew this was the last hymn. In another five minutes the doors would open and the congregation swarm out. She must act now. Quickly she climbed over the back wheel of the wagon and lay down flat upon the straw in the box behind the back seat. The chances were more than even no one would see her. Olaf Swenson was a slow going, dull old fellow, of peasant stolidness and a little deaf. Aida felt him get into the wagon, she heard him cluck and grunt to his horses and finally back them clumsily into the road. If she could get out of the village she was safe. It was uncomfortable down there in the straw, she was jolted and joggled and fairly suffocated with dust. Finally she screwed around and looked at the back of her unwitting host. He was turned straight ahead, his body settled down into the slump that means hours of endurance. At last Aida sat up. The seat still half protected her but she could look about. The sun blazed down upon the country with the cheerless bleakness of noonday. There were no shadows anywhere, nothing to soften the dreary stretch of scorched pasture lifting at last into sand colored hills against the sky.

"Gosh, but it's ugly," she thought. A timber hawk winged a clumsy flight above them, black against the brilliance of the sunshine and out of the empty sky itself, rasping and insistent, its cawing seemed to come.

Aida did not know how far she had to go, only that it was a long way. Well, she was lucky to be able to ride even part of the road. Olaf Swenson was, unwittingly, a gracious person. From Crazy John's corner she knew she would have to walk, for Crazy John, as the countryside called the hermit-like Russian, lived at the parting of the road. The Swenson team would cross the tracks, cross the bridge and turn just before you went up the hill. Olaf Swenson would walk his team across the bridge, a farmer, even though drunk, always does that. Aida would clamber out of the wagon there. It wouldn't be difficult and the chances were Olaf would never notice. The rest of the way she would have to walk, up over the hill and westward. She had never been this far before but she would not be lost. There was only one direction in which she could go.

Somewhere, along that road, lay the acres Larry Mitchell was supposed to have broken. Somewhere, squat as a prairie-dog mound, would stand the shack in which Larry Mitchell cooked his food and lit his pipes and escaped each night in slumber from the misery of each day. Somewhere she was bound to find him. Somehow she was bound to save him. This was the most difficult thing she had ever attempted and yet she knew, some way, she would not blunder. Aida Sparks had at that moment the convictions of an artist who knows there is but one way in which his work can be done and that he will do it that way.

Low as an adobe hut against the desert stood the tar papered walls of Larry Mitchell's hovel. It was a hundred yards from the road, perhaps, at the end of a trampled path worn into the weeds of the meadow. The door was open but the windows closed. They had been closed probably, she thought, since the winter. They had stuck in their crudely built casements and the boy had not known how to fix them. No, Larry Mitchell was not the sort to be clever at makeshifts.

On either side of the hut stretched the pasture, dry now and blotched with tufted grass and the thick leaves of burdock. Not one foot of earth had been rolled back into a furrow. It was the same land over which the buffalo had nosed and the Indians padded. It had never been broken, sending up from its blackness the spectre of fever that stalks by the pioneer. Back of the shack lay a square of weed choked garden. In it were withered cabbage plants and above the weeds reached the feathered tops of onions. No chickens scratched along the path or clustered expectantly around the doorway. There was no sound in the hovel or without but the long sigh of wind in the grasses and the distant scream of the timber hawk.

Aida walked up the path to the doorway. It was a second before her eyes adjusted to the darkness of the room. The floor was of boards laid on the earth of the meadow. The mud huts of Dakota were perhaps only less primitive. In one corner stood a chair and a table, in another a cook stove, rusty and with one leg broken, in another, underneath a tumbled heap of bedding, was a bed. Aida took a step into the room. She could see now everything, the rotting floor, the walls through which zigzagged streaks of light where the tar paper had been ripped in a tempest, the collection of broken china on the table, the unblackened stove, the face that lay on the uncovered pillow, the eyes closed and the two red spots on the cheeks.

He had not heard her come and he seemed not to hear her now, even when she came close and looked down onto him. A long moment she stood there. Then from the table she selected a crock and went back of the house to the well on the edge of the garden. The water was cold that came up from its depths. It was a good well and this was not a bad quarter section. Olaf Swenson, or a man like Annie's father, could make it pay back in abundance. They would put cattle on it and till it and there would be horses and pigs and chickens. Aida Sparks was no appraiser of real estate but she knew this was good farming country, better than most.

Back in the hovel again she poured out a cup full of water and carried it to the bedside.

"Larry—" He looked at her a moment curiously, frightened. She slipped her arm under the pillow. Then she held the cup to his lips and he drank from it and she lowered his head again gently. A long moment she sat there in silence, then she drew her arm back to her side. The head on the pillow turned faintly.

"Don't go."

She made a quick gesture to the hand that had moved out toward her and took it in both of hers.

"It won't be far." She smiled as one does toward a child—as one does toward a lover, for there is little difference in the quality of the affection. "It won't be for long or very far," she repeated. "I—just thought I might cook you up something."

The face on the pillow smiled grimly. "You won't find it's any Ritz Carlton here." He struggled up suddenly from the bed, swayed an instant and dropped back again.

"Larry——"

His eyes were black and strange and his body swayed like one drunk with fatigue.

In an instant she was beside him and her arms went around his shoulders. "Larry——"

"I'm all right. Just a little shaky." Again he made an effort to rise, to break away from her and again he sank back, exhausted, helpless. Suddenly she felt his shoulders tremble with sobbing. "Go away," he said. "Why did you come anyway? Can't you see I don't want you? Can't you see I can't bear it to be hunted down and found out? Why couldn't you let me alone—the way the others did? The way she did——"

"Larry—" Again her arms tightened around him and she pressed his head against her shoulder. Gently her fingers smoothed down his hair and touched his cheek. "Oh, my dear, my dear," she whispered.

A long moment they clung there in silence.

"It's no use," he said. "I'm beaten."

"You're starving."

Suddenly he looked up and his eyes took in every detail of the hovel. "They sent me out here 'to make a man of me'," he mimicked. "They bought me a ticket and gave me ten dollars. Ten

dollars. They owned this land, somebody discovered, and they thought it was a good place to
park me. Inconspicuous, as far away from New
York as Taihiti—and not so pleasant." He stopped
a moment. His anger had drained all his energy.
"That's it," he went on. "They couldn't stand my
being happy. They can't get happiness. They
wanted me to grow up—cagey—like all the rest
of them." Again he stopped. "I was never any
worse than Uncle Eustis only I wasn't so inconspicuous about it. I never had any talent for keeping things hushed up."

"I know," she said.

"Well, the last thing got into the papers." His
voice was thin with sarcasm. "That was the worst
crime of all. It didn't matter that I loved her, that
she was as pretty as a peach blossom. She was
the loveliest person in the world, I can't think of
her even now without the feeling I had when I
first saw Romney's 'Duchess', you know the one
with the tiny pom and the castle behind her."

Aida didn't know but she nodded.

"Well, they hushed things up—after it was too
late, and they paid her off." He waited a moment.
"She was an actress." Again he waited a moment.
"They sent me here—" he laughed suddenly and

there was a sound of madness in it—"to make a man of me."

Again Aida's arms held him against her and for a second time she felt something hard and lumpy in the sagging pocket of his jacket.

"Larry—" she stopped and her hand searched inside the pocket.

"Yes," he said, "it's a pistol. I bought it last night of—a fellow. I bought it with the money I stole through the window."

She did not take it from him. Instead she sat down on the bed beside him. For a long time they sat there in silence. Then his head dropped against her shoulder and she knew that he slept. Cautious as a mother she slid away from him, smoothed out his pillow and covered him gently with a blanket. It was five miles to Crazy John's place but she must go there for food and come back. It didn't matter what Crazy John thought, she reasoned. He must give her something to eat and let her take it away with her. She wasn't afraid of him. To-night she wasn't afraid of anything.

Crazy John did not even ask her any questions. Without a word he gave her bread and butter and a cheese and a flask of warm milk. "You are keeping a tryst," he told her, "with a past that is over."

She looked up at him startled and waited a moment. Crazy John of course was crazy, but his words were true. "Yes," she repeated slowly, "with a past that is over."

It was twilight when she came back, the eerie half light of a prairie evening. The wind blew her skirts around her as she raced along the roadway. Thin and gray and fast sailing against the horizon the wind clouds skudded westward. Sky and earth and air were all one color and she one color with it, she was part of its grayness, its swiftness, its mysterious drama.

"It's beautiful here to-night," she thought. "No matter where you go you can't get away from beauty. But, Lord, what a lot I've had to go through with to be able to recognize it."

Back in the cottage she built up the fire and warmed part of the milk in a sauce pan. On a shelf she had found a candle which she lighted and held above the face of the sleeping boy. Cautiously she touched his forehead with her fingers. "It's not fever," she decided. "It's only hunger and heartbreak." Thank God it wasn't fever. If it were she couldn't carry out the plan she had settled on.

This was a healthful sleep, she knew. She hated

to disturb him until it should be time. Twice she looked at the beautiful platinum watch she had brought out in her silly plated-silver hand bag. Finally she shook him gently and raised the cup of warm milk to his lips. He drank it gulpingly, and then another one. Again Aida held him firm with her arm around his body.

"Listen," she said finally, "you're going away from here. You're going back east where you and I both come from. Back home. It's August in New York. The evenings are long and warm and blue. There are white moths in the park and the moon glints along the pavement and turns the buildings to marble." She stopped a moment and her eyes stared out through the open door across the prairie. "You're going back to-night. In two days you will be there, you will smell the wind that comes off the harbor and see the gray wings of gulls." Again she stopped for a moment. "I don't care what you've done—I don't care much what you do. But I can't see you suffer. You get me? You're one of those that have got to be happy. It isn't safe for them not to be. See? You've got a talent for happiness—but you've got a genius for suffering."

He did not speak but his eyes had never left her face.

"To-night," she said, "at eight o'clock the flier comes through Albia. It slows down at the bridge by Crazy John's. I know it, they're making some repairs there. You can get aboard and to-morrow you can get a train for Duluth. Then you're started. All the rest will be easy."

A long moment he watched her in silence. "You're crazy."

"Yes, I am. But I know what I'm doing. And now it's time we were starting."

She helped him get up, put on his other coat and make himself presentable. Almost like some one hypnotized he followed her. Then she made a packet of the bread and cheese and ordered him to drink the rest of the milk. From the crock she emptied water on the fire, blew out the candle and closed the door behind them. In the moonlight they followed the road toward the bridge where the flier slowed down. Her will alone seemed to carry him. He did not even stumble. At the bridge they stopped, the train was not in sight yet but any moment spears of light might spring down the rails toward them.

"Listen," she said, "this is your ticket." She pressed into his hand a piece of paper and something thin and hard and shiny. "Five dollars," she said, "and—this watch. You can raise enough on it in Duluth for a ticket east—and then some. When you get to New York it's up to you. I can't help you. But you've got a chance there."

A long time he looked down at her in the moonlight. She was almost pretty then, all the hard lines were gone and the weariness. She looked some way like that other one that had been paid off and hushed up, the one who had gotten him into the papers. "Why are you doing this for me?" His eyes drove her eyes for an answer.

"It's silly," she said. "For a memory." Still her eyes did not waver. "He was like you," she went on, "and I got him into the papers. Well, his family bundled him away too. They sent him to sea and the night he left he gave me this." Her finger touched the watch he was holding. "It was all that he had. You see, I hadn't been paid off— and he loved me. Well, I've kept it till now but to-night I'm returning it. See? To him, through you."

Down the rails shot the first gleaming spears from the engine and the thunder of wheels sounded like a battery of cannon.

They gripped each other's hands. "It's all even

now," she said, "or as even as things come in this world."

"Aida——"

The train was almost upon them. In another instant he would be swinging aboard. He would be leaving her.

"Aida," he repeated, "I'm not worth it."

"Yes, you are," she said, "anyway, I don't care. Now, kiss me."

And then he was gone.

A long time Aida Sparks stood by the track where the train had pounded eastward. She was alone and a long ways from home. She was bankrupt, but she was at peace. Some way she would have to restore the money that Larry had stolen. Somehow she would have to invent a plausible story. But all that did not matter now.

Crazy John had been right. It was a tryst she was keeping that evening, a tryst with the past. He would be happy, that boy she had rescued. He would fit some day into a niche where his talents would serve him and his fellows. But it was some one else Aida Sparks had sent back this night. She had sent back the boy who had kissed her good-bye on a hot night in August before his boat sailed for Rio. He had worn a sailor's cap and middy. He was shipped as a common seaman on a dirty frigate for Rio and his eyes had looked like the boy's she had sent back to life this evening.

"Yes, I did it for you," she whispered. "It was crazy but I did it for you."

NO MESSAGE

NO MESSAGE

FATHER FONDA looked now into the eyes of his congregation. "And any man who carries in his heart anger toward his neighbor sins only in a less degree than as though he should lift his axe and strike his neighbor dead."

It was the Sunday before the men went up into the woods for the logging season. Two weeks before there had been a snow flurry, white dust that had sifted down between the needles of the spruces, that lay along the street of the village in straggling scallops, like the line of highest tide. Three days before it had snowed in earnest, and the ground was covered even where the timber stood thick. To the south of the village, where the land had been cleared, stretched an undulating blanket of white. It would lie there too until March, maybe April, for spring in Minnesota comes slowly and unwillingly.

By Tuesday the men would be off, gone until the

thaws of spring should open up the rivers and bring the aisle of logs down to the mills at Black Forks or St. Pierre or Haut Mont. The Sunday before they left there was always a special mass in Petit Pré, just as in seaport towns in New England they hold special services for the fishing fleets that go up into the fog islands of the north.

Father Fonda had been fifteen years in Petit Pré. It had been only a tiny meadow when he came, a clearing on the bank of the river where the first French settlers had made their farms. In fifteen years the land to the south had been stripped clean of forest, and the Swedes had come in and the Norwegians, the way blueberry and aspen thicket rush in, in the wake of a fire.

Since the days when Petit Pré was a little pasture, the North Star Lumber Company had bought up all the land to the north and west. Now the young men of Petit Pré, and a dozen other outfitting villages, worked for wages where before they had gone as adventurers. There was greater peril in the old days, perhaps, when there were no bunk houses, the walls of which are now snugly ceiled in with tar paper, no well stocked larders, when there was no great reserve of tools, if the steel of a man's axe went bad.

But life today was no less bitter. The cold still wreaked its toll in bleeding chilblains. There was the same desperate loneliness. Father Fonda knew that life was fairly primitive among his people, that a man was boss, as a rule, because he had quicker fists than the next man. He knew there was gambling and fighting up in the woods, and an orgy of carousing when the release of spring came finally and the pay cheque could be cashed in the first saloon in St. Pierre or Black Forks. It was the last mass these men would hear until the fields to the south were again brown with ploughing and lupin lined the roadways. What he told them this day about the sins of anger and the blessings of forbearance would have to stay with them through the long months of winter, through the short, mad days when there would be money and drink enough for all.

It was a cheap little building in which he preached. In the winter the snow drove in through the casements and the hinges chink until the floor looked powdered with dust. At the altar his hands were so numb he could scarcely lift the sacred vessels of the mass, and his breath rose as white as the fumes from the censer. Father Fonda might have had a parish in Duluth or even in Montreal, but he understood these people on the edge of the Northern forests. Even the tawdry chapel with its hideous plaster saints did not offend him. Father Fonda had made a brilliant record at St. Xavier's back in Brittany. He might have gone to Paris or Nancy and taught in the university. Instead he was content to preach to Jacques Merceau and to Pierre Geraldy and to Rudi Hansl, who had come clear from the Black Forest in Germany.

Now Father Fonda came a step nearer his congregation and lifted in blessing the slender hands from which the vestments fell revealingly away. The people bowed their heads while he called down upon them the peace that passeth understanding, the peace that the world can neither give nor take away.

Rudi Hansl's hands were folded heavily together and his head, with its shock of thick blond hair, was bowed, but there was no peace in his heart. Across the narrow aisle knelt Patrick Connor. Rudi closed his eyes in a childlike hope that he might so keep Patrick Connor's image out of his mind. It was not safe for him to hate any one as he hated the man who sat across that unpainted, narrow aisle.

Patrick was younger than he—by ten years perhaps, gray eyed and slender hipped and charming.

He was a devil of a fellow, quick as a cat in his movements, reckless, and at the same time bewilderingly gentle. His body gave complete response to every mood. He could swing an axe as well as Rudi Hansl; he could dance better than any man in the village; he could lift a child with the gentleness of a mother.

Though Patrick Connor was only twenty-five, there were already around his mouth lines not without significance. He had come, he said, to Petit Pré from the Soo, and the Soo was a long way off. No one knew anything about his past, but the lines were frankly etched by liquor and by passion. Physically his excesses had taken toll as yet neither of his strength nor of his energy. He would go much further up than he was now before he should come down. Already he was next to Rudi in the gang. He would probably be Rudi's successor. He might even go one day to Winnipeg where the company's Headquarters were. But Rudi did not fear him in the woods. Up there he still was boss. It was when he thought of Berta that his heart seemed for a moment first to stop beating and then to pound in his breast, like the heart of a partridge caught in a snare.

The priest had told him he could not hate his

neighbor, that it was a sin for which God would
not forgive him, and Rudi had the peasant's fear
and the peasant's humility. He must try not to
hate Patrick Connor; he must try not to think of
what he had seen the afternoon before. It would
drive him mad, if he could not forget it when he
was 'way up there in the timber with the sight of
Patrick all day in his eyes. Now he shut his eyes
tight and drew his heavy brows together in an
agony of concentration. The skin of his forehead
was coarse and stiff. He could not even frown
without an effort of will. Patrick Connor's face
was a mirror of every thought and mood, as re-
sponsive as quicksilver and as unstable.

Why did he have to see the tableau he had come
upon yesterday? Why couldn't he have gone up
to the woods again, as he had gone now for thir-
teen years, with peace in his heart? Each year he
had saved his pay cheque and with it he had bought
more acres to the south of the village. Some day
he would quit being a logger, he would build a nice
farmhouse and red barns and hay ricks. There
was a spring on his land. That was where he
should have his dairy. There his cheeses and his
butter pats would stay cool, as they had back in the
old country. He would have a garden and flower

beds, with rocks painted white and shells along the garden paths. He would make it very fine indeed. No woman would be ashamed of it.

Always in the picture somewhere was Berta, with her blue eyes and her grave brow and her gentle hands. Berta Larson was one of the Swedes that had moved into the clearing. The land was still jagged with stumps and most of it only thin grazing country, but acre by acre these people had wrenched out the stumps and ploughed under the soil. It was a labor full of agony and heartbreak, but these people knew how to endure it. Berta Larson knew as well as that great Viking, Peter, her father. Until the winter Peter Larson had had the lung fever, he had been a fellow straight out of a Norse legend.

Since her mother's death Berta had been mother as well as sister to little Olaf and Sina and Anna. It seemed to Rudi that he had always loved Berta, first as a little girl of seven, because she was gay and because her eyes were the color of lupin. He loved the quietness with which she had accepted the labor that her mother had been forced to give up. Berta now made the three children's clothes, as well as doing the scrubbing and baking and cheese making and taking a hand in the harvest herself when the hay was cocked and loaded and brought into the barn. Rudi had seen her once at work in the haymow, distributing and arranging the dusty, fragrant mass as rapidly as the men in the carts could pitch it up to her. Her arms were bare above her elbows, the neck of her blouse turned in, her body warm and sweet with labor.

Berta Larson had never had any playtime until Patrick Connor came. Rudi had wanted to give her presents, to make her laugh, to make her eyes sparkle, but all he had ever done was to add slowly year by year to the land that adjoined her father's. Some day all that land would be hers and she should have the best dairy in all Minnesota. Of course he had never spoken to her yet. He had still not enough to offer. It had not been easy indeed to keep silent, but all the time the thought of Berta had been to him like the promise of spring when the winter has been long.

It had never occurred to him everything would not work out all right, if he could only wait long enough. Even after Patrick Connor came, Rudi still believed that his longing for her would be strong enough to claim her, no matter how flashing the smile of his rival. He had believed this until yesterday.

Yesterday he had come upon them unexpectedly.

It was in the spruce grove on the way from the village. Rudi had left the path to follow a fox's trail in the soft snow. He had no notion of hunting down the fox, but it was early yet and Peter had told him at the farm house that Berta had not yet come back from the village. Then, at once, he heard voices and from behind a thicket of hazel and cedar he could see them. Berta had on her plaid skirt and the little poke bonnet with the feather. Her cheeks were as pink as coral and the blue of her eyes was like the sky of June.

They were walking very slowly, she and Patrick, walking as though they begrudged every step that led them out of the furtive paradise of spruce grove into the open. Finally they stopped, and neither one could have said that they were not walking. Rudi Hansl thought they surely must see his breath or hear the beating of his heart, but they saw and heard nothing.

"Berta," Patrick said, "are you sorry I'm goin'?"

Berta made no answer, but she turned her face away and Rudi could see it.

"Berta"—he had stepped around before her now, but her body still strained away from his entreaties. "Berta," he pleaded, "can't you give a fellow an answer?"

"Sure, I'm sorry." She giggled, embarrassed at her seriousness.

"Listen to me." He put his finger under her chin and lifted her face to his. "Listen to me," he blustered, "I'm goin' to be boss of that gang this year yet. I know it."

Berta did not draw away from his hand and her eyes never left his face.

"Rudi Hansl's too slow an old coach for me." He laughed good-humoredly. "But I'm not goin' to stop with him, or with bein' boss of a lumber gang. I'm goin' to be rich some day and build a big house in Duluth and have a billiard table in it and a bowling alley—and a sewing machine and a parlor."

She laughed at his extravagance, but with the sweetness of one who believes.

Patrick Connor squared his shoulders. "Laugh all you want," he boasted, "but you'll believe it when I come back for you with my team of bays and with rubber tires on the buggy."

A long moment they stared at each other, then he took a step toward her. "Berta—" At once their arms were around each other, and he kissed her gently, fiercely. He kissed her as a man does whose lips have already the wisdom of many kisses.

"You won't be forgettin'," he said at last, "while I'm up there choppin' down a palace for you? You won't now?"

Berta Larson's eyes glowed like the sky of June. It was a long moment before she answered. "And me you will not forget either?" Her words were grave and slowly spoken.

He laughed at her solemnness. "And what do you take me for?" he blustered. "Would I be after forgettin' the prettiest one in all Minnesota?" He held her away from him an instant. "You'd be elegant in a dress of green satin. And you'll get it too, and a parlor with a sofa and a sewing machine and a statue of the Virgin with a blue robe."

"I'm a Lutheran," she protested.

Patrick Connor laughed. "You're whatever I make you." And he kissed her.

Then they walked on at last from the grove, his arm around her waist and her body soft against his side.

Rudi Hansl did not move until they had gone. So that was what Patrick Connor planned to do? First he would take Rudi Hansl's job away from him, Rudi who had been boss for ten years now. Then he would take the woman Rudi loved, whom he had loved ever since—so many years. Patrick

Connor had known her less than two months, and yet his lips had touched hers, his eyes had conjured up the sky of June in hers, her body had leaned toward his, drawn there by the only magic there is in the world.

This was the man Rudi was going up into the woods with. This was the man whose face he would have to see day after day through the long white months of loneliness, this fellow with a girl in every port, with his thin lips and his gay eyes and the lines etched deep around his mouth. This was the fellow who could call into her eyes the gladness of springtime and could make her mouth wear that soft look that belongs only to women who love.

And this was the man the priest said Rudi Hansl could not hate. Seven long months in the timber with him and not hate him! The dear God must be, after all, no fool. Father Fonda with his pale face and his long white hands might not understand, but the dear God would. He would have to. There were beads of sweat on Rudi Hansl's brow as he prayed for he knew not what. Would it not be enough, if he could keep his hands off Patrick Connor? The dear God must have a little sense about a man's feelings.

After service Rudi Hansl left the church, head

down. He did not want to see Patrick Connor, at least not with the priest and all the saints there watching. Afterwards, up there in the timber, who could tell?

The gang of which Rudi Hansl was boss were no green hands at the timber game. French Canadians, most of them, the sons and grandsons of the men who had followed the St. Lawrence westward, clearing out the virgin forest to plant their tiny farms. These men knew trees as a boy in a fishing village knows winds and ships. They had well-nigh been born with an axe in their hands, and they knew how to handle it as an artist knows how to handle the bow of his violin. There was never a waste motion; their blows fell with a rapid and exquisite accuracy, and their muscles had the quick responsiveness of an animal's.

Rudi Hansl was no longer either as young or as agile as the men he bossed. But Rudi was a tradition in the North Star Lumber Company. He was slow in his mind and in his speech, but he was honest. Strangely enough he managed the young Kanucks better than one of their own countrymen could. They were children, easily swayed, and, like children, they could adapt themselves easily to a routine. Rudi was nothing but a habit. Patrick

Connor was the only man who would stand out against him.

Patrick Connor was ambitious and able, quite as able as he had boasted of being to Berta. Like as not he would be the next boss of the gang, and, if he were boss, without doubt the company would send him up into the North as a cruiser. Already he had begun giving orders, and the men accepted his leadership with a curious acquiescence. He was shrewder than they and more daring and always good natured. There was little withstanding the flash of his white teeth and the swing of his shoulders. He knew less about timber than they did, but he knew more about people.

A month passed—six weeks—and nothing had happened. Rudi Hansl never spoke to Patrick Connor except when he had to, and so far Patrick had never openly defied him. Perhaps, after all, the dear God had a watchful eye on them—and then came the day when the temptation fell.

As they had started out that morning from the cook house Patrick Connor had struck up a song. It was not a very decent song, but he had sung it with a gaiety that was irresistible.

"Once again," cried Jacques Merceau. "Name of a name, but you carry a tune."

Patrick Connor laughed. "All right," he said. "Gather around and I'll sing you another."

The gang closed in, jostling each other like school boys on a frolic. They had work to do, but what did that matter? Patrick Connor's song was already in their blood.

In the center of the group stood their leader, his legs far apart, his body defiantly graceful, his breath rising white in the bitter air. The evil one surely was in Patrick Connor this morning.

"There once was a Dutchman, and he lived all alone,
    And he worked at the lumber trade.
His feet were big and his hands were too,
    But his heart it was little and 'fraid.
Well, he loved a girl and her eyes were blue
    And her hair was the color of wheat. . . ."

There was a stir in the circle of grinning listeners. Patrick Connor stopped suddenly, and his lips stretched into a smile of pleased defiance. "Don't care for music, eh?" He did not move, but the smile on his face was as sharp a challenge as though he had struck Rudi Hansl.

The group opened slowly and let Rudi in. "Pick up that axe,"—he pointed—"and go to work."

Patrick Connor drew down his mouth in a gro-

tesque imitation of Rudi's "—and go to work,"
he mimicked.

There was a shout of delight from the group of
watchers. Again they closed in like a pack of dogs.
They were not mean fellows by nature, but they
were outrageously human. The time had come
when some one had defied their boss. Well, there
would have to be a settlement, one or the other of
them would have to win. The odds were fairly
even, and nobody cared much which man came
through. But the thing must be settled now.

Rudi Hansl stood stock still. He was numb with
anger. He was not afraid of this man with his
white teeth and his jeering smile. At that moment
Rudi Hansl knew no fear. The pack of faces,
stern with excitement, did not exist for him. He
scarcely saw the face of the man before him. His
whole body had become one concentrated emotion,
one throb of hate.

"Come on," Patrick Connor challenged.

It was the great moment of Rudi Hansl's life.
If he won here he would be master for all the
future.

"Come on," Patrick Connor repeated.

Rudi hesitated a moment, then he lunged forward and the thing that happened then was one of

those things that change the whole course of a man's life, one of those hideous trifles that make a man believe the hand of fate is against him—that, out of all his fellows, he alone has been chosen for misery and ridicule. Rudi Hansl came a step forward, then he stumbled and fell, flat on his face.

An instant the group stood there, awe-struck. The thing was amazing, incredible. Then the situation became clear to them. It was Patrick Connor's axe over which Rudi Hansl had fallen, the axe he had ordered Patrick Connor to pick up.

A moment Patrick Connor hesitated, then he drew himself up like a sovereign. "Pick up that axe," he commanded, "and go to work."

The pack of watchers stood silent; then they let out a roar. In that instant Rudi Hansl lost his leadership, just as surely as though he had been struck dead. He could never come back. Well, the king was dead. Long live the king!

Without waiting an instant for his power to dissipate Patrick Connor snapped out his orders. "Work north from the blazed pine," he commanded, "every man jack of you. It's a record fell we're going to make to-day—and all the days. I'm the boss here now, and it's me you're obeying. Now track."

Slowly Rudi Hansl got up and slapped the snow from his jacket and knees. A moment the two men stared at each other.

"Well, I reckon it's you that will be goin' back now to the settlements." Patrick Connor's voice held the same mockery as his face. "Am I right?"

Rudi Hansl nodded.

Again there was silence. Finally Patrick Connor took a step nearer the man before him. "Could I be askin' you to do me a favor?" he said.

Rudi Hansl made no answer.

Again Patrick Connor laughed. "Would you perhaps be tellin' the 'girl with the eyes of blue' "— he stopped a moment—"that I'll be comin' back for her some day? It may not be this spring—or next. But I promised her a dress of green satin and a sewing machine and a parlor." Again he stopped and his eyes never wavered. "You'll be tellin' her that when you see her," he ordered.

Then he turned on his heel and left; and Rudi Hansl stood there alone, in the midst of the trampled ring of snow.

It was February when Rudi Hansl got back to the village, and three days after Peter Larson had died. Rudi heard about it at the store where he went to buy supplies to take out to the little shack on his land. He was going to live there and be a farmer, he told Olaf Tegner, the store keeper; he was through with the timber.

"Blamed queer about Hansl," Olaf had remarked to his cronies. "Reckon he must have frosted his feet."

All the way out to his farm Rudi had thought about Berta. So Peter Larson had died and Berta was all alone—alone with the three children. He remembered her as he had seen her in the fields with her arms bare to the elbow and the pink health of her throat. He remembered her when her mother had died, and she had had to step into her mother's place. Berta's face had matured then. She had become a woman grown at sixteen. And now Peter Larson was dead. There had been little enough youth in Berta Larson's life. Now her last chance for freedom was gone. He remembered her face when Patrick Connor had kissed her, Patrick Connor who was coming back to her some day with a dress of green satin to give her.

Across the fields of snow he could see the lights from the Larson kitchen. She was in there with the children, he thought. She was cooking the supper. He could see her now, her face pink with the heat, her eyes grave and her strong, white hands.

The next day he tramped across country to call on her.

She was surprised to see him, and he saw the quick color mount under her skin. "You——"

A long moment they faced each other in the doorway. "I have come back," he said finally. "My acres lie next to yours. I will help you."

He came into the kitchen and she closed the door behind him. He said nothing of Peter Larson or of her sorrow. His acres lay next to hers. He would help her. That was all.

It was twilight in the kitchen, and she lighted the kerosene lamp on the table. Without a word he got up and went out to return with an armful of wood for the woodbox. He would have to chop up some small pieces to-morrow, he thought; the kindling was almost gone. Through the hinge's chink in the kitchen door he noticed the wind rattled and a thin dart of snow stretched across the floor.

"A strip of leather," he pointed, "will fix that, tacked along the edge."

A long moment she looked at him. The children sat at the kitchen table, before them their yellow bowls of mush and milk. They were noisy and busy, their heads bent forward in the eagerness of eating. Rudi's hand was on the latch of the door.

"You are very good to me," she said slowly, "very good."

A dull flush stained the bronze of his cheeks. "I am not good at all." Then after a moment. "To-morrow I come back."

In the open doorway she watched him as he stamped down the steps. When he turned around she still stood there. "Rudi"—he could see that she wanted to say something; her whole body was tense with the urge of her question, "did the others go on up into the North—just the same? I—mean without you?"

He nodded.

"And you?"

"I got frost bite." He stopped a moment. "The left foot. No good any longer for going."

"Oh"—she too waited a moment—"I am sorry." The wind jerked her skirts around her. It was bitter cold; still she did not go in. "And Rudi—Patrick Connor,"—her voice was like a whisper one hears in the dark—"is there any word from him?"

Rudi Hansl did not answer for a moment.

"Rudi?"

Even in the darkness he could feel her eyes upon his face.

"Is there any word from him then?" she repeated.

Rudi Hansl's eyes fell to the ground. "No word," he said. "He left the gang at Calgie. I ain't seen him."

"Oh"—it was almost a sob, like a child that has been struck and is too hurt to cry out. There was a moment of silence. "He never sent back any message then?" she asked at last.

"No message."

Next morning Rudi Hansl came again. He chopped the wood and tacked on the leather strip. He fixed the flue in the stove. He shoveled wide a path to the barn and cleaned out the stalls and mended the leak in the roof of the cattle shed. Rudi was clever with tools, like his German forebears. He was ingenious and thrifty. Winter is the time when all the odd jobs on a farm are tended to, the machinery is tinkered, repairs are made in the interior of the house and barns. It is tedious work, most of it, but Rudi Hansl possessed the dogged patience that belongs to peasant people.

Long hours he sat in Berta's kitchen by the stove mending harness, his hands moving slowly, almost clumsily, but always with effectiveness. He put up neat shelves above the stove and sink and covered them with newspaper, the edge of which hung down an inch and was cut in a fantastic design of figures linked together hand and foot. He made also a board on which the dishes should drain, and one day he gave Berta a half dozen spoons, as smoothly polished as metal and bearing on the handle a rude spray of oak leaves.

They were alone in the kitchen when he gave them to her. For a long moment she looked at the spoons in her hand and then slowly at the man beside her.

"Rudi," she said, "do you never do anything for your little place, then?"

He looked away from the graveness of her eyes. "Enough," he said, "but I work very fast. For me there is little pleasure in it."

February passed. Finally March came and the first warm rain. All night one could hear the melting snow as it felt its way off in gurgling rivulets. Next morning the land was black with wet earth and heavy with the first warm smell of spring. In three weeks, in two weeks the panic of planting would set in, for summer in the northland comes in a leap, and man and beast labor under a tropical sun until the treacherous frost cuts short the harvest.

One evening on his way up to the house from the milking Rudi found Berta standing on the doorstep. "Look," she said, "the swallows have come back to-day to the eaves. They did not forget."

He put down the pail of milk, and his eyes followed her gesture. "Berta——"

He repeated her name a second time but she did not seem to hear him. "Strange," she said at last, "that there is more loyalty in those dumb things than in the higher creatures that God made."

"Berta"—this time it was no more than a whisper—"you must not say that."

Slowly she looked down at the man beside her. "I did not mean you, Rudi." She smiled as she would at a child whose feelings she had unintentionally wounded. "Rudi, you are good, too good. You are perhaps the best man in the world."

"Berta"—he caught at her skirt as though to hold her—"you must not say that. I am wicked. But I love you."

"Oh——"

He bent his head and his great hands hung at his sides. "I had not meant to tell you that way." Again he stopped. "Berta"—he looked up at her finally—"to-morrow it will be spring. You know how it is then, a man is too busy to think of anything but plowing and seeds and animals. This is a big farm your father left. Berta——"

She held up her hand to stop him. "Wait," she said, "give me a short time to think. There are so many things I must think of." She beat her hands together in an agony of mental conflict, but no sound came.

"The children——" his voice again was almost a whisper.

"Don't," she said, "don't. Let me think by myself." Then after a moment she spoke again, and it was as though she stood there alone. "You would be good to the children." Then suddenly she turned toward him. "Oh Rudi, is it any use waiting for spring—you know, for the spring in one's heart?"

He took both her hands and gropingly pressed them against his cheeks, against his lips. "I don't know; I don't know," he whispered. "I only know that I love you."

For a long time they stood there in silence. She did not come closer to him with her body, but she did not draw her hands away. "Give me a little time yet to think," she pleaded. "I will let you know by the next new moon. By April."

"By April——"

He trudged off alone across the fields in the twilight. "By April," he repeated. But he knew in his heart she would take him.

At the end of the month they were married, and Rudi Hansl brought his cedar box over from the little shack that stood upon his acres. In the box were the tools with which he had carved Berta's spoons.

He took them out gently and slid his heavy thumb along the blade of the knife. "Next winter," he said, "I will make you many fine things, more spoons and napkin rings for you and for the children and a bowl for nuts." He stopped a moment, shyly. "You will like that?"

She nodded, as she would to a child. "That will be very fine."

Lingeringly he put them back in the chest. "Now all that I can do for you is plowing and planting and taking care of your cattle."

She smiled at this belittling of his services. "That is not so little, is it then?"

"Berta"—suddenly he reached out toward her and bent his head upon her breast—"Berta, Berta."

She patted his head and his shoulders and her fingers found their way through his tousled hair. "There," she said, "there. You will do everything very fine, I am sure."

Every one in Petit Pré thought that Berta had done a very sensible thing. Rudi Hansl was a thrifty fellow who saved his money, and he would be a good farmer—much better than that Patrick Connor fellow. He was a fly-by-night. Rudi Hansl was one you could count on.

One by one the young men from the logging camps straggled back to the village, and the story they told was a strange one—how Patrick Connor had ousted the boss without even raising his hand against him. Very strange. Of course, by this time, the story had grown distorted and no two loggers told it the same way.

"Funny doings," said old Sandy Martin at the post office. "We will never know the straight of it, what with Patrick Connor gone up to Canada and Rudi Hansl not being the sort of man you would care to question."

Rudi Hansl had been right in his prediction about Patrick's future. He had gone up north for the summer with the surveying party. He was now the pet of the office. Patrick Connor would never drift back to the village like the Merceau boys or the Geraldys. At least that was what Rudi Hansl kept telling himself over and over.

Berta never mentioned his name, but she asked

who had come from the camps, whether Jacques was back yet or Pierre. Rudi answered her questions, but he could never quite look in her eyes when he did it. Her face was so eager then, so expectant, like one who listens in the night for the step of a loved one. He wondered if after a while her face would not look that way, if after a while she would no longer strain to hear, if after a while she would forget. Meanwhile, there was so much to do; they must work so hard, both of them. There could be little time at the end of the day, he thought, to call back one's dreams.

Berta was never sad, he thought, but she was quiet, too quiet, and there was no longer in her eyes the look of June sky. He remembered how she had laughed with Patrick Connor and how happy her eyes were. What strange gift was it one man had to do that to a woman, while another man got from her only the knowledge that the eyes of her mind were not seeing him at all?

Perhaps she was too tired to be happy, for everything that spring had gone badly. The rains came early and lasted late. They made a slough of the pasture; they unearthed the seeds of the garden. The cornfield behind the swamp had to be twice replanted. Berta had had to help, for the fair days were rare and maliciously brief. Rudi was peasant and old world enough not to have any false chivalry about the doing of a man's work by a woman. Berta was as strong as a man—almost, and she was willing to help. But he did not like to see her shoulders grow heavy with labor, or her step sedate, or the straight line come between the straight brows.

June was fair and July.

"It will all go better now," he said.

They were coming back together from the wheat field. Berta made no answer. His eyes hung upon her like a shepherd dog's.

"It will all go better now," he repeated.

She lifted her shoulders skeptically, and her eyes swept the horizon where the sun still hung, beautiful and hot as brass. "It is too damn dry," she said finally. "It is weather like this that the rust comes."

"Berta!"

She turned toward him sharply, angry at the protest in his voice. "Well, it is true, is it not?" Then at once the rebellion went out of her body. "Forgive me. I had no right to speak like that. But, sometimes, it seems—" she stopped again.

"Yes?" he said.

She looked at him, and again he had the sensation that her eyes did not see him. "It seems as though one of us were being punished for something. As though one of us had done a crime, and this was a penance."

"Berta"—a cold fear lodged around his heart—"you at least have done nothing. You are a saint."

"Saint!" she laughed harshly. "I'm a Lutheran." Then after a moment, "The saints in your church must have queer things in their hearts. I'm afraid." Again she stopped. She was like a child that is frightened of its own maturity. "I'm afraid of the things that come into my mind—terrible things that I want. Oh," she covered her face with her hands, "I am wicked, wicked."

He looked at her in silence, but he did not touch her. It was not of him she was thinking; he knew that. It was some one else whose arms she wanted around her, whose arms she imagined around her, whose lips she imagined against hers. All at once he knew how matters stood between them. She had married him because some one must plant her fields and help her take care of the children. She had married him because it was the only way out. She did not dare wait any longer for Patrick, and Rudi had said that there was no message.

"Berta"—he touched her sleeve and she lifted her eyes to his. "Do not think any more about me. I will help you. I will get in your harvest. I will live in my shack, and you are not to think anything about me." He stopped suddenly, words were such blundering things. "You are not to worry about me one moment. Just let me work for you."

She looked at him unbelievingly, pondering. What strange thing had he said? She wondered if she could have understood him. "It is you," she said finally, "who is the saint."

Berta had been right about the dry weather. All day a low sun hung over the fields, drawing the sap up out of the wheat, and the leaves of corn flapped as sere and ragged as at the time of the harvest. Along the roadways stood brittle stalks of milkweed and goldenrod, powdered with the white dust of a parched land. There was little to harvest that autumn. In September, just after the frost, the rains fell, wantonly, dismally. But one day of them in time and the crops would have been saved. There was surely a queer twist in the world. Could Berta have been right and this all was a punishment? Rudi remembered what Father Fonda had said about the hand of God being raised against any one who had hate in his heart? But why, then, was not the hand of God against Patrick Connor? Was there, perhaps, no justice?

It would soon be snowfall again, and the men would be leaving for the camps. Just a year ago he had been boss—just a year. Well, he could get a job in Duluth with the Canadian North West Company. He could hire young Nils Olsen to come over every day and do the heavy chores for Berta. In winter she could make shift of managing herself, and Rudi's pay up North would help out. It was the sensible thing to do, and the new company wouldn't know anything about Patrick Connor and the scene that had taken place last winter up in the Calumet. Berta would let him go, he was sure of that, and Nils was a good worker.

In November he told her he was going to sign up. A long moment she looked at him gravely.

"You will be gone a long time," she said, "and the life up there is hard. You have no duty to do this for me."

Rudi Hansl tried to be merry about it. "I should not be comfortable," he said, "without a few frost bites and chilblains to scratch at."

The last of November he left, and from Duluth he wrote Berta a letter. He was assistant boss this time, but the gang was a large one and the pay was good. It was a stupid letter, he thought, not even a page in length. He wished as he wrote it in the company office, bent over the rough deal table, he might tell her all that was in his heart. But he could not put it into words, even to himself, much less put it down on a piece of paper with a hand that held the slow pen so meanly. Well, he would have a long time to think up in the forests. By spring surely there would be some way out.

And spring came at last, cold and grudging, as the springs of the North always come. On his way to the village Rudi noticed that there still lay banks of glacier snow in the shadow of the ridges, though crocus blossomed along the roadways.

In the village all the townsfolk greeted him. "What kind of a year had it been? Did he like the Canadian folks? How much timber had they cut?"

He answered their questions idly. He had answered the same ones every year for ten years. Then Sandy Martin told him a piece of news.

"Patrick Connor is coming back to Petit Pré." Rudi knew the man had no intention of being unkind. "It's the old cut over land they're to make a survey of—think maybe there's iron under it—

or gold or diamonds." He laughed uproariously. "Connor's quite a fellow now. Olaf Tegner saw him up in Winnipeg, and he was drivin' a buggy that had rubber tires. Who'd a thought it now?"

Rudi Hansl walked alone out to the farm. The months up in the timber had not helped him much. He wasn't quick at thinking. Sometimes the longer one thought, the less clear the whole thing became. He wasn't even trying to think now. He knew someway that when he saw Berta he would know. Stumbling, head down, he trudged on. The road was heavy from the spring thaw, and his great boots slipped in the clay mud. At last the lights from the kitchen window shone over the meadow. He was almost there.

Heavily he stamped up the steps to the kitchen, and he threw open the door.

"Rudi," Berta straightened her back from the stove where she was stirring the porridge.

The children were glad to see him and clambered about him, begging for the trinkets he had promised them from Duluth. He had a tinsel star and a monkey that climbed, part way at least, up a string, and a toy piano.

It was a merry supper that evening, and a long time before Berta could get the children off to bed and quieted down for the night. At last they sat alone in the kitchen, Berta in a rocker brought up to the stove and Rudi on the edge of the wood box.

His body was bent forward, and his great hands hung idle between his knees. "Berta," he did not look at her, "they tell me in Petit Pré that Connor is coming back. He has made fine with the company, they say. He is rich." He stopped, but she made no comment. "It was he took my job last year up in the Calumet. When I left there he gave me a message." Again he stopped, but she still sat there as dumb as an image. "I told you he gave me no message. Well, I lied. He said he was coming back for you. He said he was bringing you a dress of green satin. I loved you so much I did not tell you. I wanted you. I suppose it was a sin, but"—this time his eyes held her fast—"I know I would do it the same way again."

Still she did not move, but her eyes no longer seemed to see Rudi Hansl. She was not thinking of him. She looked at him indeed, as though he no longer sat there, as though he did not exist. Then slowly the lines of her mouth relaxed, the color crept into her cheeks and her eyes were the blue of the sky of June. She was happy—and only the sound of another man's name had brought back the youth to her heart.

Rudi Hansl looked away finally from her face. There was no need now for her to speak. "I thought it was only fair that you should know," he said.

It was not until Patrick Connor had been back a whole week that Berta saw him. He had been busy supervising the surveying. All that country had been blazed and recorded in the casual manner of pioneer people. What difference one way or the other did a hundred feet—or a thousand feet— make? All the timber in the world stretched black to the Northwest, and it was any man's with the strength and wish to cut it. Now there was a madman's dream that under the worthless stumps on the cut over land lay the wealth of an empire. A hundred feet mattered—so did one foot.

It was twilight, and Berta was driving back from the village, the collection of Saturday packages wrapped in coarse brown paper on the driver's seat beside her. This was the day all the countryside went to Petit Pré, the day all the lonely ones from the far lying farms exchanged their bits of gossip about crops, about weather, about their neighbors. Berta did not linger to talk, and yet she was leisurely about her purchases. This was the village in which he was. Bleak and ugly, with its rotted corduroy road and its one block of wooden shacks, it was, just the same, a city of enchantment.

On the road toward home she saw a man on horseback. He was still far away, but she knew that it was he. He was coming toward her. In a moment they would be face to face. Berta made no cheap gesture to assure herself that her hair was smooth and her bonnet neat. Loose in her lap her hands still held the reins. She looked as calm as an old woman telling over her beads, but in her throat she could feel the fierce beating of her heart.

He was coming as slowly as she, for the going was heavy, his head bent forward with weariness, his eyes vacant with the stare that is turned inward. Then, with an oath, he drew to the side to let the team pass and his eyes lifted to the woman's beside him. A moment he stared; then a slow look of recognition vanquished the scowl.

"Berta?" he said. Yes, by George, that was her name! "Berta," he repeated, delighted with his excellent memory, "by all the saints."

Their horses had stopped; and her eyes rested full on his face, but her lips did not move.

"Berta"—adroitly he maneuvered his horse so that he came close to her and his hand rested on the box of the wagon. He was aware now of the nearness of a woman who pleased him, and his presence held again all the effrontery of his old charm. He leaned toward her very gently. "Aren't you glad, then, to see me?"

Still she did not speak.

"Berta"—there was now in his appeal a shade of irritation; he wasn't used to having things go so slowly—"have you been forgetting then that we once walked this road together, that I kissed you here?" He smiled again with charming wickedness. "And if I haven't forgotten, it seems to me you kissed me here."

Berta Hansl shook her head slowly. "I have not forgotten."

"The devil you haven't!" He laughed unpleasantly. "That was a long time ago." He leaned close to her again with all the old grace of assurance. "Come on, let's give ourselves something a bit newer to remember." His face was almost touching hers now, and there was something in his eyes that turned her body into marble. "Berta, kiss me."

Berta Hansl did not move.

A second he waited. Then he drew her to him savagely and pressed his mouth against hers. She could hear his rough breathing and feel his body grow to steel. "There," he said, finally releasing her, "that's how it's done."

For a long moment Berta Hansl looked at him. His face was still tense, and his eyes were defiant. This, then, was the man whose name had been to her like the sun upon the willows. Something in her eyes made him feel uncomfortable. He wished she would say something.

Finally her lips moved. "I must be going. It is late and the children are waiting—and Rudi."

"Rudi!" His amazement was patent.

"Yes"; her eyes met his gravely; "we were married the spring he came back from the Calumet."

A long moment he stared at her shrewdly. So she had married the Dutchman? It was humiliating to have to yield anything to that fellow. Patrick Connor laughed again unpleasantly. "Well, I'm sorry I wasn't here to dance at your wedding, though I can't say much for your taste. You're the prettiest girl in the backwoods; only you're too damn solemn." Again he leaned toward her appealingly. "You won't call it quits then and say you're glad I've come back?"

Again there was a moment of silence. "Yes," she said finally, "I'm glad you have come back."

This time too he found it was not easy to look into her eyes. It seemed almost for a moment as though she did not see him, and that is not pleasant for any man to endure.

Then she slapped the reins sharply and the horses stumbled into a walk.

Patrick Connor stretched around in his saddle, and his eyes followed her into the twilight. "Well, I'll be damned," he said slowly. Then he clucked to his horse and started on toward the village. In another week, thank the Lord, he could get back to Duluth. There was something in Duluth to do evenings.

But Berta Hansl did not go home, as she had said. Instead she drove through the timber lot to the field where Rudi's shack stood on the edge of his land. There was a light from the window and she hitched her team to a sapling beside the door. At the door she knocked; then she entered slowly.

Rudi looked up, startled, from his chair by the table. "I was just having a little snack." He grinned foolishly. "Won't you have some?"

She came forward and sat down on the chair

facing his. He knew that she had not heard him. "Rudi," she said, "I've seen him."

The man sitting opposite her made no answer.

"Rudi——"

He looked at her. "Well?"

"He'd—forgotten."

Rudi Hansl shuffled his feet awkwardly. "Maybe—you startled him; you surprised him; he didn't know what he was saying."

A moment she looked at him in amazement. Then she smiled. "Yes, he did. He knew everything he was doing. Rudi"—she got up and came to him slowly, "you're not trying to take up for him, are you?"

Slowly he raised his face to hers, but he did not stand. "I'm not trying to take up for him. Only —it don't seem natural."

"What?"

"That any man could forget you."

Berta smiled wisely. "That's just because you —like me." Her hand rested on his shoulder for a moment, then her fingers wound their way into his hair. Slowly her eyes took in the clean disorder of the cottage, the uncurtained windows, the empty shelves, the little pile of shavings by the stove. Finally her eyes focussed, and it became hard at once to swallow.

"Rudi," she said, "you have been carving some more spoons." She pointed.

He moved uneasily. "I like something to do in the evenings." He stopped a moment. "I thought I might sell them maybe."

She smiled again, and in her eyes was gentleness. "Maybe you might—sell them to me," she said.

"Berta!" At once his arms groped their way around her and drew her to him.

Like a child she knelt down on the floor beside him, and for the first time her body leaned against his trustfully.

A long time they stayed there in silence. Finally he spoke her name.

She lifted her face to his. "Rudi!"

A moment he waited.

"You remember that day when you told me there was no message?" She looked at him, and never before had she seemed so beautiful, so beloved.

His arms dropped away from her, but he could say nothing to her. He knew only that he cared enough now to let her go, if she wanted to.

"Rudi."

"Yes."

Timidly, very gently her arms felt their way around him and held him fast. "It was the truth that you told me. There *was* no message. And I know now that I am glad."

"Berta, oh Berta!"

When she lifted her face, he saw that her eyes were happy and as blue as the sky of June.